A DARK PSYCHIC STAIN LEFT ON A DEVASTATED CITY

"There are monsters among us. There have always been monsters among us."

THE OMINOSITY

In the aftermath of a catastrophic New Year's Eve explosion in the heart of the city, Miki Preston embarks upon a treacherous odyssey into the devastated area known as the Quarantine Zone in search of her famous photojournalist sister, Jennifer, who has mysteriously disappeared.

With only the help of a disgraced former homicide detective, a cagey teenage street dodger, and a set of provocative photographs her sister left behind, Miki will come face to face with the manifestations of malevolent psychic energy called *Paramentals*—and the sinister conspiracy that created them.

RESIDUE

RESIDUE

PARAMENTALS RISING

JOHN HARRISON

WFP
WORDFIRE PRESS

RESIDUE

Copyright © 2024 John Harrison

EBook ISBN: 978-1-68057-735-8
Trade Paperback ISBN: 978-1-68057-736-5
Dust Jacket Hardcover ISBN: 978-1-68057-737-2
Library of Congress Control Number: 2024944773
Cover design by Miblart.com
Kevin J. Anderson, Art Director
Vellum layout by CJ Anaya
Published by
WordFire Press, LLC
PO Box 1840
Monument CO 80132
Kevin J. Anderson & Rebecca Moesta, Publishers
WordFire Press eBook Edition 2024
WordFire Press Trade Paperback Edition 2024
WordFire Press Dust Jacket Hardcover Edition 2024

Printed in the USA
Join our WordFire Press Readers Group for
sneak previews, updates, new projects, and giveaways.
Sign up at wordfirepress.com

For Leslie, my consigliere in all things.

PART I

It had been eight weeks since her last drink, but she couldn't resist any longer. She had come straight here after she left the office, grabbed the first available stool, and ordered a double Johnny Red neat. The very thought of it made her salivate. The first sip had gone down like hot honey, and a moment later she felt that desperately longed for click at the back of her brainstem. The lock on her mood gave way to a welcome wave of calm, embracing her, warm and lovely, like sinking into a pool of peace where nothing frightened her. Especially not the recent bugbears of her troubled mind.

She instinctively clutched at her two-thousand-dollar Prada Vitello Daino Hobo making sure it was still secure between her feet. If anyone at work found out what she'd hidden there, she'd be fired. But that wouldn't be the worst of it. If certain other people knew, she might not make it through the night. She gunned the rest of the double Scotch and ordered another. Then another. It took that many to submerge her fear, her shame, her anger.

Tomorrow everything would be better. Tomorrow, when the secrets hidden in the arcane prose of purloined legal documents, title transfers, and escrow filings tucked inside her bag would become known. Tomorrow, when the city's nightmare would start to end. She hoped.

Three men at the other end of the bar were eyeing her. Checking for "availability" signals no doubt. She glanced up at herself in the mirror behind the bar. Nice hair. Damn good body, nicely wrapped in beige Armani, turquoise blue Hermes silk gracefully draped across her shoulders. Not a bad presentation. Except for the fatigue tugging at her expression and the slightly wild glare in her eyes. If her harried expression and indifferent posture didn't warn the men off, the multiple drinks she was downing would surely send them packing. Who'd want to pick up a sloppy bitch with a bad attitude? By the time the bartender cut her off, she was the only one left in the place.

Except for the gaunt silhouette sitting alone at a table at the far end of the room. She caught sight of it in the mirror's reflection after the bartender turned back to his sink, but when she blinked away the blur of too many drinks, it was gone. Maybe it had never been there. She asked for a nightcap. The bartender refused. He suggested she Uber it home. She declined. Thanked him anyway with a healthy tip and stumbled out the door.

Outside, the neighborhood was empty and quiet. It was late and most people were sensible enough to be in bed by now. She was really drunk and knew it. Maybe she should have called for a car, but the subway wasn't far. The walk would clear her head a bit.

In the near distance, the abandoned buildings of the Quarantine Zone leeched darkness and dread like a contagion. A surge of nausea swept over her. The goddamn QZ. Everything wrong with her life had its source there.

She stopped at a red light and sensed that specter from the bar was suddenly right behind her. She could feel it vibrating. Her adrenaline quickly ignited the alcohol's sugar in her blood, shortening her breath, jacking up her heartbeat. The thing moved closer and whispered into her ear, muttering its dark chorus of dissonant gibberish. Something awful about its atonal drone.

Something feral and grotesque. And maddeningly beautiful. She wouldn't turn to look at it. She knew if she did, she'd lose her mind.

The light changed. She stepped off the curb.

The subway station was empty when she came down the stairs to the platform. She drifted up to the edge and let a gush of wind from the tunnel buffet her face and tangle her hair. She slid her feet across the yellow warning line, pushing the toes of her precious Jimmy Choos over the platform's edge. Leaning forward, she could see the Diamond symbol of the approaching train. An Express. Not stopping. For anything. Or anyone.

It would be so easy. So quick.

She lurched back just as the train roared through the station.

She knew the specter had followed her down here. She could see it suspended in the reflection of the cars' dark windows racing past, lurking right behind her, quivering like some sped-up movie. She only caught a glimpse of its face as it came for her. Its eyes bottomless sockets of inky mist. Its skin pale and diaphanous. Its mouth a huge lipless cave entrance coated with swarms of something slithering around the edges. And the sound that came out of that hole, a freakish shriek, made her instantly insane.

She lurched toward the tracks and the speeding train, hoping for oblivion. But it was too late. The specter was on her. The Prada Hobo went flying, scattering its papers to the tunnel wind like fleeing bats.

There was no one around to witness what happened next.

There are places everywhere in this city where hostility gathers.
A toxic fog of malice and wickedness. It coagulates and festers.

And where it does, nasty things happen.
Nasty things without reason, without explanation.
Vile and squalid things to frighten the most hardened skeptic.

I should know. I used to be one of them...

THE OMINOSITY

$$1$$

It stinks down here.

Anyone reading through Miki Preston's journal of drawings and prose would come to the same conclusion. Each page divided into panels like a graphic novel or some methodically illustrated diary. Each panel a minimalist but provocative scene accompanied by cryptic, evocative text. A young woman's odyssey through the labyrinthian bowels of this city. Images so vivid that multiple connotations of the word "stinks" immediately come to mind.

*"There are places everywhere in
this city where hostility gathers."*

She is meticulously copying the text of Ominosity's latest blog into the margins of her newest chiaroscuro sketch. A subway car interior.

Then, as if to endorse Ominosity's turgid sentiments, she adds ...

*"I can't sleep. So I ride the
underground. Sometimes all night.
The speed calms me down. The noise*

makes me relax. But I can't ignore
the fact that it's the City's
intestines down here. It's where
everything gets digested. Some of
it gets barfed back out. But most
of it stays down here and rots."

Thin, delicate calligraphy every bit as gossamer as the sketches of what she sees.

Miki leans her head against the hard plastic seat of the train car. Closes her eyes. A mistake, she knows, but she can't help it. She hasn't slept in almost two days. Within seconds the monotonous roar of the subway has lulled her senses. The notebook falls into her lap and she drifts into that half sleep of free association often more frightening than any REM nightmares.

It stinks down here.

She's jerked back to consciousness by a sudden stop. The train's lights flicker and go out, bathing her and the few other nervous passengers in a sickly green spectrum of emergency LEDs. Just like the interior of the MRI machine she was forced to endure a couple of years ago by her father.

"Everyone please remain in your seat," a monotone voice crackles on the PA system. Sounds pre-recorded. It isn't. "We're experiencing a minor power outage. We will resume speed momentarily. Please do not leave your seat!" This last command is not reassuring. It is unmistakably alarmed.

The journey does not resume momentarily. Miki feels anxiety rising among her fellow passengers. As if sensing it too, the intercom crackles again.

"For your own safety and that of others, do not leave your seat! We have entered the Quarantine Zone. No one can disembark at this time!"

Several seats away a young woman in Michael Kors groans.

"We will resume speed momentarily," the disembodied PA responds.

The Quarantine Zone. The quarantine. Quarantine. So far, no contamination has been monitored underground, but trains are still not allowed to stop. They speed through as fast as possible. No wonder everyone is jumpy. A young man wearing earbuds turns his iPhone up so loud Miki can hear the thrash metal beats twenty feet away. Must be trying to drown out his anxiety.

Through the windows Miki can barely make out the gray abandoned station in which they're stopped. The vacated kiosks and deserted benches, the trash cans left unemptied, the pages of forgotten newspapers drifting like tetherless kites. A place out of time. An archaeological curiosity for some future explorers. If there are any future explorers.

She's about to resume scribbling in her sketchbook when she sees it. The figure. The shape. Vaporous. Insubstantial. Vaguely humanoid. Hovering by the barricaded stairs to the street. Is it really there, or is it a trick of light? Or of mind? It doesn't appear to obey the laws of gravity. It floats. Sometimes upside down. Then it stops. Turns. There's a face. An approximation of a face. Unrecognizable because its features are continuously vacillating, like a reflection in a pool of oily water. A mouth, if that's what it is, opens there. The orifice grows larger and larger until there's no more visage, just mouth. Suddenly it propels itself toward the car. And the mouth shrieks. Or maybe that's just the wail of steel wheels on subway tracks.

Because the train is lurching forward. Zero to sixty in a few seconds. Miki is thrown back in her seat. If anyone else saw that specter on the station platform, they don't let on. Michael Kors woman has bowed her head, arms wrapped tightly around her chest as if trying to keep her insides from spilling out. Earbud Boy is pumping his head violently back and forth to his music. Only the wino at the far end of the car has his rheumy eyes open. One of them winks conspiratorially at Miki. She looks away so as not to encourage further interaction.

There is no notification from the PA system why the train stopped. It's as if it never happened. And Miki tries to convince herself once again that what she saw didn't either. Just a vivid hallucination triggered by tension and exhaustion.

"Chambers Street," the PA system squawks a few minutes later.

Miki stuffs her sketchbook diary deep into a scuffed leather shoulder bag and hangs one-armed by the door until the train comes to a complete stop. She is out of the car before the doors fully open, hurrying eyes-down toward the exit, mentally composing the next entry she'll make in her diary.

"I ride the subway because a lot
of answers can be found down here.
You just have to be willing to get
dirty. Real dirty. But mostly I
ride because it's the last place
anyone saw my sister."

THE WALL STREET JOURNAL.

THE CATASTROPHE'S LINGERING EFFECTS
The Tragedy Still Haunts Us

The New Year's Eve Catastrophe, as it's come to be known, was once thought to be a freak bio-industrial accident that rendered a wide swath of the urban landscape uninhabitable. Authorities finally admitted that a forgotten cold-war chemical weapons storage facility abandoned ten stories below the blast site was breached by the explosion. But if you believe the conspiracy theorists, and they are legion in this city, the blast New Year's Eve was instead a military security scheme gone awry, a sinister out-of-control corporate experiment, or some insane terrorist attack so horrible no one has ever been willing to claim credit. For some, it was the visitation of the Lord's wrath on this Gomorrah of self-indulgence and greed. For others, it was the inevitable result of our slavish, overconfident reliance on technology. What everyone can agree on, however, is that it destroyed the psychic balance of the city as swiftly as it rendered a large portion of the urban landscape uninhabitable. People who lived and worked in the area have been forced to evacuate. "Potential spread of contamination," the official reason given. Families have lost homes, businessmen their livelihoods, children their neighborhoods. The rest of us have lost whatever fragile sense of peace and order that had previously existed. A several-square-mile district of homes and businesses remains quarantined six months later, off-limits to everyone except the HazMat teams roaming the abandoned streets like alien ghosts, or the highly armed security contractors patrolling the perimeter to keep everyone out. And still, no one can tell us exactly what caused the explosion. No one can tell us who might have been responsible. And no one can tell us when the quarantine will be lifted. To this day, the Quarantine Zone remains an open, raw wound on the city's soul. An incurable injury to its fragile spirit.

2

Levi Mathis is sitting at his usual spot at the end of McBride's mahogany bar. As far from the door and street as possible. He likes it here. His "living room," he calls it. The sawdust on the floor, the cloudy mirror behind the bar with McBride's name elegantly etched into the glass, the cracked leather stools, the four-item menu. Meatloaf, hamburger, fried fish sandwich, grilled cheese. No substitutions. What more could a guy need? The regulars know each other by sight and occasional nod, but they rarely converse beyond monosyllabic salutations when someone comes or goes. Mathis likes that, too.

Best of all, no cops. No colleagues from the precinct hanging out to wash down the day's shift, entertaining each other with gallows humor about vics and perps. The "brotherhood bonding" thing. Mathis needs none of that. He's the lone wolf, and he intends to keep it that way. For his own protection.

Sammy, the bartender, brings him the usual. A double Laphroaig sixteen-year-old, neat, and a glass of club soda on ice. Mathis lays a twenty on the bar and reaches for the soda.

"If you're not going to drink it," Sammy says, eyeing the warm glass of Scotland's finest amber, "why don't you let me pour you the cheap stuff."

"Wouldn't be the same, would it?"

Sammy moves off without comment. Another reason why Mathis likes this place. The taciturn barkeep.

A news anchor on TV is interviewing a panel of so-called experts about the continuing rash of spontaneous violence that's plaguing the city since the Catastrophe on New Year's Eve. Seemingly unprovoked murders, baffling nervous breakdowns and impulsive suicides, mysterious accidents and fires. Incidents for which there are no apparent motives. And now there are reports of people seeing strange phantoms in the vicinity of these incidents. A kind of collective hysteria, one expert opines. An instinctive retreat to the fantastic in order to explain the inexplicable.

"Some sort of 'weird-vibe' flu going around," Sammy opines as he wipes the bar.

On TV, another "expert" suggests maybe there's something in the water. That might explain the hallucinations people are having. And she's not kidding. Someone else sarcastically notes that that sounds like something the anonymous provocateur Ominosity would say in his blog. An argument erupts about why everyone assumes Ominosity is a man. Why not a woman?

Mathis stares at his Scotch. Maybe he *should* start drinking again.

"I figured you'd be here." It's Miki. Standing hands on hips behind him. He never saw her come in. "Even though it's not even five yet." Taking the stool next to him without invitation.

"It's five somewhere," he says, hoisting his club soda. "Want something? You're old enough, right?"

Sammy arrives.

"What he's having. Minus the booze," she says without looking at him. "On his tab." Mathis just smiles and shakes his head. "Look, I'm gonna try to be polite," she says after Sam moves off.

"Don't hurt yourself," Mathis chuckles.

"You were supposed to be a good detective ..."

"*Am* a good detective," Mathis corrects her. "Present tense. I'm just not undercover any longer, that's all."

"So what the hell, Mathis!? What are you doing sitting here like s ... s ... some pathetic l ... l ... loser, staring at an expensive glass of Scotch you'll never drink." Her stutter-trigger is surging forward. This goddamn Tourette's tic every time she's frustrated. The plague she's had to endure since she was a child. The cerebral malfunction that turned her into a guinea pig for her brilliant father's curiosity. "You were one of the last people seen with Jennifer. You knew her. She m ... m ... mu ..." She pauses to get control. "She must have ... trusted you." Stutter dodged.

Mathis almost reaches for the Scotch.

"I've told you, your sister made a lot of noise, pissed off a lot of people," he said in almost a whisper, "and she went places she shouldn't have."

"Are you going to help me find her or not?"

Mathis finally turns to her. "Lemme ask you something," he says. "What kind of neighborhood you grow up in?"

Miki slaps the bar disgustedly and turns away. "Why do I even b ... b ... bother?" It's not really a question.

"Wait, don't tell me. Neuroscientist father, corporate lawyer mother, successful sister. I suppose I only have to guess."

"You d ... d ... don't know anything about me."

"Don't I? I was supposed to be a good detective, remember?"

"Until you got yourself arrested for murder."

Mathis holds her unblinking stare. Something about it he really likes. But it's time for some tough love.

"You think living with Mommy and Daddy, the obedient child, the one who stayed behind, the one who didn't rebel ... you think that'll balance the scales? Maybe ease that nagging fear you have of not measuring up?"

"Whoa ... hitting below the belt, Mathis."

"Speaking of below the belt, that tattoo down there, that supposed impress anyone? Make you a hard case like your sister?"

Miki instinctively pulls her shirt down to hide Bonaparte, the beautifully detailed great horned owl she tattooed on herself just above the panty line.

"By the way," Mathis continues. "What about boyfriends, lovers? Ever had one? A real one? One who broke your heart? One who made you take a hard look at the world? I'm guessing no, but then again I'm just a 'pathetic loser staring at an expensive glass of Scotch,' right?"

She's clearly stung. Mathis can tell. It's the way she's gripping the edge of her stool, the slight squint in her eyes as she tries to block her tear ducts. He knows she'll never admit it, and suddenly, for some inexplicable reason, he feels bad. But he won't admit that either. He turns away to hide it from her.

"I suppose there was a point to that rant," she finally says.

"This city is under siege, in case you hadn't noticed. It's no place for someone like you. You're not hard enough. Go home."

"Wow. I've overestimated you, Mathis." She can feel her stutter-trigger being numbed into submission by an ice-cold fury. "All this time I thought maybe you were a beaten dog, licking your wounds. Turns out you're just a lonely coward." She gets off her stool and heads for the door without a word. Just as Sam arrives with her soda.

"You're still paying for it," he tells Mathis as he watches Miki storm out the door.

McBride's is feeling claustrophobic all of a sudden. Mathis was being cruel. He meant to be. The only way he could think to bring her to her senses, get her to abandon this futile, potentially dangerous odyssey she's embarked upon. But she was right. It was cowardly. And now he's pissed at himself. After all, she isn't maddeningly boring like his colleagues, definitely not laughably dim like most of the morons he's busted. They deserve his acid attitude. But why the girl? She's more interesting than any of them.

He tosses some money on the bar and hurries out the door. No sign of her, though. He convinces himself that he's not worried about her and turns east toward the river. It only takes him a few minutes of brisk walk to arrive at St. Eustace. Why do they have to hold these goddamn meetings in a church?

He hurries around to the back of the building and the door to the basement. Not even maintenance men have to go in this way. Apparently the upstanding parishioners of St. Eustace prefer to ignore the existence of the Washouts' Self-improvement Club down below.

Everyone acknowledges Mathis with slight nods and barely perceptible smiles when he comes in, obviously late, and joins one of his infrequent Narcotics Anonymous meetings.

No one there notices the several oscillating skeletal grimaces hovering in the shadows at the back of the room.

The Quarantine Zone is a savage scar on the city's psyche ...
as corrosive and dangerous as any of the toxins that were
supposedly released that terrible New Year's Eve...

... and as long as we don't know what really happened ... as
long as we're not told who was responsible ... this tragedy
will continue to poison us ...

THE OMINOSITY

3

Dawn is seeping into these skyscraper canyons with long fingers of sunlight chasing away shadows as Miki comes down Eighth Street to her sister's apartment. She's been wandering all night, hoping to catch a glimpse of her night-owl sister. Instead, she's been haunted by the feedback loop of Mathis's admonitions. *"Obedient child. The one who stayed behind."* He's right, of course. Jennifer always was the bold one, the one striking out on her own. But why did she let him get to her? Why did she have to start stuttering again? It's taken her years to get that damn tic under control, despite all the helpful "therapy" her parents forced on her.

What the hell am I doing here? she can't help thinking. It's a feeling only exacerbated by the sight of that strange graffiti popping up everywhere around the city. This one, a block-letter graphic sprayed across the beams of an elevated subway platform, looms over the boulevard like an omen.

OMINOSITY KNOWS

They're everywhere these days, these salutes to the cyber oracle who has been using the website theominosity.com to hint at dark mysteries behind the Catastrophe and the quarantine that followed. Speaking of which ...

There's a Quarantine Zone checkpoint up ahead. Razor wire and cement barricades sealing off a no-man's-land of operations tents and military security, leading to a fifty-foot-high scaffolding wall of curtain-like sheets topped by blinding light fixtures that obstruct a view of what's beyond, but suggesting that whatever it is can't be good. No one going in. No one coming out ... except for the full-suited HazMat teams lugging high-tech environmental monitoring gear. In the distance, she can see the QZ skyline of empty buildings shrouded in plastic. A landscape of evacuated streets. A sterile, lifeless void in the middle of the city. Still. Eerily quiet.

A convoy of military vehicles suddenly rumbles through the gates into the QZ. Patrolling for evacuation refuseniks, vandals, or looters. That's the official line anyway, but there have also been press reports, instantly denied and heavily censored, of bodies still being brought out. Even after Public Safety spokesmen have assured everyone that the evacuation was effective and complete. *"There are no more victims or survivors of the Catastrophe,"* the official line goes, repeated ad infinitum in press conferences, TV appearances, radio talk shows. Miki still vividly remembers watching TV with her parents as Jennifer's boyfriend, Jonas Flack, spokesman for the Public Affairs Office, stood right there, at the gates of this checkpoint, flanked by his boss, Angela Rossi, and a phalanx of intimidating military officers and Emergency Services officials, trying to reassure the press and public.

"The focus of our efforts now is to make the area safe for people to return," Jonas had said. *"Unfortunately, Emergency Services are still reporting toxic contamination as far away as a quarter mile from the blast site. Until they can assure this office there is no more contamination, the quarantine must remain in effect."*

That was weeks ago.

Miki continues down the street only so far as the small encampment of protestors the authorities have allowed to remain here. Evidence of the deadly riot a week ago is still everywhere to be seen. Broken bottles, bricks and broken furniture, torn homemade signs demanding everything from the resignation of city officials to the end of the quarantine to the immediate capture and prosecution of whoever set off the bomb that caused this dislocation.

Miki is paralyzed by the despair hovering over the area.

One of the bitter-enders emerges from his cardboard shack to shamelessly relieve himself on the perimeter fence. "Makes you wonder, don't it?" he chuckles when he sees Miki there.

"Wonder what?" Miki asks averting her eyes for the sake of his privacy.

"The birds. They fly around it." He nods to a flock in the sky. "They fly around it, never over it. Ever notice that?"

Miki stares up at the birds abruptly veering off in separate clusters to avoid flying into QZ airspace, as if some invisible wedge had been driven suddenly into their midst.

A scalding white light shoots down over them. The beam of one of those insect-like drones buzzing the QZ vicinity, supposedly surveilling for "malcontents and other bad actors." One can't get within a few blocks of the QZ perimeter without falling under their gaze. The thing hovers annoyingly just inside the perimeter fence, only restrained there by judicial injunction. Otherwise, Miki is certain, these robotic spies would be loosed upon the entire city.

"Move on there!" a flak-jacketed soldier shouts, rushing to the fence, his MK40 ominously aimed in Miki's general direction.

"Just takin' a piss here, boss. Just takin' a piss," the bitter-ender says, waving his junk so the soldier can see.

"Move it!" the soldier insists.

Miki hurries back up the street, but not before catching a glimpse of Mr. Bitter-end offering a middle finger salute to that drone.

She turns into the Korean deli at the corner by Jennifer's apartment for some microwave ramen and a can of Hire's Root Beer. The extent of her diet, these days.

"You need meat, girl. Noodle not enough," Mrs. Oh chastises from behind the counter while she opens up the store.

"I don't eat meat, Mrs. Oh, you know that." Miki laughs.

"You say, but I don't like. You no eat right. Not healthy. Young woman as you need meat." Unequivocal.

"Let me have a half-pound of those cashews, then. Plenty of protein there." An inadequate surrender to Mrs. Oh's mothering, but the old woman nods and changes the subject.

"Any luck?" she asks, struggling with the letter *L*.

"Not yet."

"She all right. Your sister, she strong. Smart and strong. You see."

"Thanks Mrs. Oh. I need to believe that."

Miki sits alone at the granite-top center island in Jennifer's sleek, spare kitchen, eating her breakfast of ramen, cashews, and root beer. A pigeon watches from the ledge outside the window, coveting one of those nuts. In the near distance Miki can see rooftops of the Quarantine Zone.

The knock on the door startles the pigeon. It leaps off the ledge into space. Miki can hear Mrs. Deluca's wheeze beyond the door.

"Miki, darling ..."

When Miki opens the door, the old woman is standing in the hallway holding a small box carelessly wrapped in what appears to be torn pieces of a brown grocery bag.

"Someone left this outside your door. I was just coming back from church."

There's no name on the box. No address.

"Did you see who it was?"

"One of those messenger boys, I believe. Although he seemed a little young for that. Couldn't have been more than twelve. He wouldn't stop when I asked him what he was doing."

"Come on in, Mrs. D," Miki says, taking the little box. The woman shuffles into the apartment dragging her oxygen tank cart behind her. "Want some tea?"

In the kitchen, Mrs. Deluca settles into a chair at the center island but ignores Miki puttering back and forth between sink and counter. She's more concerned with the remains of the girl's so-called breakfast.

"What are we going to do with you?" she sighs.

"What?" Miki mumbles.

"Out all night. Sleeping most of the day. And then this." Twirling a cold noodle on a spoon while furtively shoving a handful of cashew halves into a torn bathrobe pocket. "I swear I'm coming back here this afternoon with a quart of pasta fagioli and some ricotta calzones. Gonna sit right here until you eat every bite."

Miki smiles affectionately at Mrs. Deluca. What is it with these older women wanting to mother her? They're sweet and funny, and she's genuinely touched by their concern, but it's becoming a bit suffocating. Is it some kind of pheromone she's secreting that begs this compassion? If so, why doesn't it work on her own mother?

Stuff that thought. Mrs. Deluca is crying.

"Mrs. D, what's wrong, what's the matter?"

"Hand me a tissue, darling, will you?"

"Out of tissues. Paper towel do?"

Mrs. Deluca sighs again. "What are we going to do with you?"

"C'mon tell me, Mrs. D, what's up? Are you sick?" Miki asks tearing off a sheet of Bounty and handing it to her.

"Sick at heart. I got another one of those notices in my mailbox."

"Oh no."

"Oh yes. You'll find one for you, too. Says those developers won their appeal. They can relocate the few of us left and convert the building."

Miki holds Mrs. Deluca's hands as the old woman makes a valiant effort to stifle her emotions. There isn't much to say. Mrs. Deluca is one of a handful of holdouts fighting the developers who bought this building. Right after the Catastrophe. Since it was within blocks of the Quarantine Zone, properties like this have become the real estate equivalent of those proverbial Arizona beachfronts that will be available after a "big one" drops California into the sea. They'll be worth millions if converted into condominiums. Assuming the quarantine is lifted, of course. Most of the tenants have taken extremely generous offers to move out. Not Mrs. Deluca.

"This is the only place I've ever lived," she weeps. "My parents raised me here. My Henry moved in after we got married. He died in my bed." She hits the table with her fist spilling some of her tea. "And that's the only way I'm leaving here. In a box!"

"Don't say that, Mrs. D. They can't just kick you out."

Mrs. Deluca manages a weak smile. "They can do anything they damn well please." The certainty of that remark precludes any encouragement Miki was going to offer.

"Your sister was so good to me. She used to take me for walks in the park. Did I tell you that?"

The non sequitur surprises Miki. "Yes. You fed pigeons. She took pictures."

"She told me all about you two. You were inseparable. Mischief makers."

"Maybe we should stop now." Miki laughs.

"I love the story about the time she pummeled some boy into a quivering pulp because he wouldn't stop bullying you. I loved that one."

Miki smiles, indulging her. She's heard all this before. Mrs. Deluca isn't senile. She's just lonely. But one can listen to stories about oneself only so long before fact becomes fiction and you can't tell them apart.

"She was always standing up for me. Mostly because of my imp ... imp ... pediment."

"She was ... what, only twelve?"

"Ten. The boys were older. They were making fun of me. Pushing me around. So she b ... b ... beat the c ... c ... crap out of their leader. The others ran home to Mommy."

"She told me the boy ended up with a punctured eardrum and a permanent scar from his hairline to his chin."

"Made him slightly better looking," Miki says sardonically.

They sit there in silence. Outside, sirens wail up and down the avenues. Mrs. Deluca grips her teacup harder. Miki notices.

"It's become a city of monsters, darling." Another non sequitur. "More and more of them every day. You must be careful, Miki."

Miki fingers her notebook on the counter, thinking of that strange *thing* she saw in the underground earlier.

"I can take care of myself, Mrs. D."

"I know you don't believe me, darling. You think I'm just a senile old lady ..."

"I don't think that at all ..."

"... conjuring up boogeymen around every corner. But they're out there. I've seen them!"

"I'm careful. Really, I am."

"You're just a girl ..."

"Twenty-three, Mrs. D."

"Like I said. Just a girl. Too young for a terrible place like this."

Or too soft, according to that cop, Mathis, Miki thinks.

"I have to know what's happened to Jennifer."

Mrs. Deluca nods sadly and finishes her tea. "She thought she was invulnerable, too."

Mrs. Deluca shuffles with her oxygen tank down the hall unaware that she's dropping the occasional cashew from the hole in her bathrobe.

"Don't give up, Mrs. D." Miki calls after her. "Remember, possession is nine-tenths of the law." She means it to be encouraging, but it sounds hollow even to her. Mrs. Deluca manages a small wave, but her body is deflating right before Miki's eyes as she slips into her apartment and closes the door behind her.

The rust-colored stain above Jennifer's bed is disturbing. Every time Miki lies down she can't help wondering about it. Is it a leak from one of the apartments upstairs? She's thought about moving the bed in case the plaster gives way and comes crashing down, but some perverse defiance always prevents her. It looks more like a scorch than something sodden anyway. So how did it get up there?

The little box Mrs. Deluca brought her lies at the foot of the bed demanding attention. She finally relents and picks up scissors she brought from the kitchen and slices through the yellowed Scotch tape on the box's seam.

A roll of 35mm negative and a red flash drive tumble out.

At Jennifer's workstation, Miki boots up the system and inserts the flash drive. A moment later, images begin to tile the screen.

No message, no text. Just photos. Cab drivers, businessmen, tourists, the homeless, the wealthy, the poor, bankers in bespoke suits, bicycle messengers in formfitting nylon, ladies doing lunch, kids playing in parks, addicts, cops. Exquisitely composed shots.

Each one a story. Superficially, an objective, unsentimental commentary on urban life. But if one looks closely enough, there is a genuine humanity and compassion in each of the faces Jennifer has chosen. In those magnificent, haunted stares.

Miki scrolls page after page of these portraits, admiring her sister's pictorial essay of the city. But then she stops abruptly. At the bottom of the screen, there's another folder.

Labeled: *"In Case Something Happens To Me."*

Miki hesitates to click on it, as she's if afraid something toxic might leech out.

"So what happened to turn you into such a wuss?" she murmurs to herself.

Deep breath.

Click.

More photos. But not portraits like the others on this drive. These are more like frame grabs from a movie. Frozen moments of the city's kinetic energy. A businessman yelling at someone on his cellphone while commandeering a cab from some startled tourists who thought it was theirs. A young couple and their inconsolable infant on the stoop of an uptown tenement, trying to stay cool in the oppressive summer heat, the young woman already exhausted by her life, the young man obviously bitter about his. A middle-aged man lying in a crosswalk while a bicycle messenger stands over him, probably having knocked him down, other pedestrians barely glancing at them as they hurry by. A woman standing alone on the walkway of the bridge over the river, staring down at the water. An old man holding an even older toy poodle, looking anxiously out the third-story window of his elegant East Side apartment. A pretty girl standing in the middle of an avenue in a pouring rain ignoring the yelling and honking of traffic trying to avoid hitting her.

There is no denying the stark, aggressive beauty of these photos, and Miki is reminded of what an artist her sister was. *Is!* But why were they kept separate from the others. What's so special about them that they've been segregated in a folder labeled cryptically "*In Case Something Happens To Me*"?

Did Jennifer send the flash drive? Is she reaching out somehow with a message about where she is?

JOHN HARRISON

The Times

Art & Design

BY JANET MARGOLIS

We see in color. So why are black and white photographs so compelling? The argument goes that nothing compares to black and white for conveying veracity. It strips away all artifice. The bogus and the contrived cannot be disguised. A photograph is not, after all, a representation of something, like a painting, it is a recording of something. And black and white best records the naked truth. It objectively documents moments of reality. So the argument goes.

Jennifer Preston doesn't buy it. For her there is no such thing as neutral, unbiased documentary. The act of observing a thing changes that thing. The Heisenberg Principal. Intentionally or not, a photographer imposes a point of view on any subject the moment she opens the shutter. She is not simply recording it, she is commenting upon it.

Jennifer Preston prints all her photographs in black and white, but not because it makes shapes and lines and contrasts more prominent, or because its subjects seem authentic and spontaneous and true. She chooses black and white because it drops a veil between the viewer and her subject. You can't look at one of her photos and think it's merely a captured moment of time, a frozen instant of reality. You have to look at the scene not as it is but as you imagine it to be. You are compelled to invest something of yourself in the scene. Because Jennifer Preston isn't showing you the truth, she is forcing you to search for it.

A version of this article appeared in the *Times* print edition on March 21st in the Arts & Leisure Section P. C5.

4

Miki is confused by the *Times* review of her sister's last gallery exhibition. The last time Jennifer was seen in public. It's included as a pdf on that mysteriously delivered flash drive. Jennifer never kept any reviews of her work. In fact, she deliberately avoided reading anything about herself or her work. So why did she keep this one?

No matter how much Miki pores over these photos, she can't figure out what her sister is trying to tell her. It's as if Jennifer's urban photographic odyssey had been suddenly overwhelmed by some new aesthetic, prompted by some revelation she'd had, or by some insight about the subjects she had chosen.

Miki isn't sure what that revelation was but she's certain there must be a common theme her sister was trying to impart.

"What am I missing?" she asks that pigeon who has returned to the windowsill in search of handouts.

And then it hits her. The *Times* review clipping. *"She isn't showing you the truth, she is forcing you to search for it."* These photos aren't an essay on life in the city. They're a map! A chart carefully composed to lead the viewer to some location, or to some conclusion, or both. But where's the map key? Where's the code that will reveal the ciphers camouflaged in the details of the images behind the veil? Only one way to find out. Go to the exact location where the shots were taken. Fortunately, Jennifer has left clues about that. In the photos themselves. Street signs, storefronts, iconic architecture. With a little shoe-leather, Miki knows she can soon stand in the very spot her sister was. And not that long ago.

"Mrs. D," Miki calls out while rapping repeatedly on the old woman's front door. "Mrs. D, it's Miki. I'm going out for a while. You want me to bring you back anything? Stop at the grocery maybe? The drugstore? I'd be happy to. No trouble at all." Miki waits. But her old friend never answers. Miki shakes off horrific images of the poor woman dead or dying, alone in the only apartment she's ever known, no one calling on her, no one to help her if she's suffering.

"Okay, I'll check on you later." *Probably just taking a nap, or watching TV in the bedroom,* Miki thinks as she heads toward the elevators.

The trip downtown is quick and easy. Middle of the day, uncrowded subway, almost running on schedule. No crossing the Quarantine Zone. And yet the tension here is no less palpable than the other night. It's obvious in the faces of her fellow passengers. That middle-distance stare, looking but not seeing, the obvious struggle in each face to maintain calm, to corral fear.

Miki uses the ride to make an entry in her diary. Quick and simple sketches of passengers' expressions, accompanied by a haiku of text in the margins.

"Winter's cold fear rides
The smell still in summer's heat
Contagion of no known virus"

A cute guy with a bicycle gets on at the next stop. His smile is casual, slightly smug when he takes the seat next to her. He could have had the bench opposite, but he chooses to sit with her instead.

She quickly closes her diary because he's trying to get a look at it. She catches sight of his reflection in the window. Yep, he's cute. Looks familiar somehow. But then all guys are starting to look alike these days. It's that underfed, scruffy, "I don't give a shit" pose young men affect. Unkempt, half-shaven, studied indifference. It's their makeup. Hard to tell the corporate striver from the wannabe artist anymore.

"Ever notice how hard it is to make eye contact in this city?" He just blurts it out. Waits to see if she'll answer. She meets his stare, as if to contradict him, but doesn't answer. "It's like everyone's got this cone of silence around them," he continues. "*'Don't invade my space, bra. Not even with a glance.'*" He chuckles in disbelief.

"Guess you have to get used to it," Miki says.

"I'm not from here. Just passing through. And not fast enough. Unless ... you wanna give me your phone number."

"Not a chance," she laughs.

"But you're not like them," he says, looking around the subway car and its withdrawn passengers.

"How do you know?" she asks. She can smell his perspiration now. Not unpleasant. Healthy, in fact.

"I guess I'd like to find out," he says, smiling again.

"I guess you'll have to wait," she says as the train pulls into her stop. She stuffs the diary into her shoulder bag and gets up. But he doesn't move to let her pass.

"You don't know what you're missing," he says. His scent has now soured.

"Well, we all have our regrets." She holds his stare. If he doesn't move soon, she'll miss her stop.

He finally relents and she slips past him to the car doors. She steps out to the platform just in time. The doors slam closed behind her.

"Train departing," the station PA system barks. "Step away from the train."

Miki turns back. Bicycle Boy is staring out the window at her, but he's not smiling now. The lights inside the car strobe as the train starts up. Suddenly, there is someone sitting next to him. This new companion turns to look out, too. Winter's cold fear slithers up Miki's spine. The face is vague, almost transparent, just like the figure she saw the other night. A rictus grin pulls back against sharp teeth. Maybe it's just a reflection, a trick of the flashing. Miki whips around. No one behind her. She turns back. Bicycle Boy is alone, laughing to himself as the train disappears into the tunnel.

Something is worming through Miki's mind. Something relentless. She opens one of the photos she downloaded to her iPhone from Jennifer's portfolio, and now she realizes why Bike Boy was so familiar. He's the guy standing over the middle-aged man lying in a crosswalk. Miki didn't notice it before, but there's that same detached, slightly condescending smile on Bike Boy's face.

When Miki gets to Fulton and Broadway, she opens her iPhone to another of Jennifer's photos. The one of the businessman stealing a cab from a couple of appalled tourists. Miki tries to orient herself by going corner to corner until she's satisfied she's at the exact spot where her sister must have taken the shot. She looks back and forth between the picture and the reality. Nothing has changed since the photo was taken. The same buildings border the intersection, an almost identical flow of pedestrians streams up and down the avenues. Why here? Why that particular moment? What was Jennifer really looking at?

"Lucian Price, I'll be damned." The voice is right behind her. Miki is so startled she almost steps off the curb into traffic.

"Whoa, there little lady." A WWE wannabe grabs an arm to steady her. He must be six foot fifteen, built like a Hummer. Blue blazer, gray slacks, a walkie-talkie on his belt, and a bulge under the jacket that suggests a gun. The patch on the jacket says Blackburn Security Services. "Used to work in my building," he says, pointing to tower behind him. "Forty-Fourth floor. You know him?" He's staring at the photo on her iPhone.

"It's just a picture my sister took," she volunteers. She wants him to tell her more. "Never met the guy."

"You're lucky."

"Why's that?"

"Guy was a scumbag. Ran a Ponzi scheme to launder millions for some Russian mobsters over in Brighton Beach. Ended up ripping off lots of honest people, too, before the Feds caught on. Your sister took that, huh? Working for the Feds? Surveillance?" He sounds excited at the prospect. Maybe an opportunity here.

"No way," Miki answers quickly. "Just taking photos, you know. Street scenes. A photo essay."

His expression falls. "Well, she caught a celebrity with that one."

The traffic light changes.

"Lunch break. Be cool, little sister," the man says, trotting into the street.

"He still around? In jail, maybe?" Miki calls after the man. He's piqued her curiosity. Did Jennifer mean to take a picture of this felon? Did she know him? Maybe Miki can talk to him and find out.

No such luck. The security guard laughs and points to the ground. Then he takes a finger and slides it across his throat. The classic sign. Six feet down. And very dead.

The rest of the day goes like this.

Uptown at the brownstone where Jennifer photographed the young couple and their baby, no one wants to talk about them. The photo makes people nervous. A few cross themselves, or they back away flashing the Corna sign to ward off evil. The exception is a hyperactive twelve-year-old who confuses his salacious remarks about Miki's breasts with bad boy charm.

"Bet those get 'em chasing after you like pit bulls in heat, huh?" he says, eyeing her chest while holding out a hand for the five bucks he extorted from her in exchange for information.

"Your big brother teach you that? Or you just quoting from some movie you're not old enough to see?" Miki yawns.

"Hey, I get around. Wanna try me?"

"I don't tutor preschoolers."

The kid laughs and snatches the five from Miki's hand.

"Those were the Morenos. Lived downstairs. The guy, Benny, fuckin' hard case. Always unemployed. He went crazy one night. Strangled his kid and threw Gloria out the window."

The images flashing through Miki's mind make her shudder involuntarily.

"What h ... h ... happened to him? To Benny?" Miki asks.

"Cops shot him, yo! You didn't hear about it? Man, it was big news." When Miki shakes her head, the kid whistles nervously. "Wow. Where you been? They shoot him like twenty times and he still don't go down? Damn."

"You wouldn't happen to remember a pretty girl taking pictures around here, would you?" Miki asks. "Little older than me. Fancy camera. She took this one of the Morenos." But before the kid can answer, someone yells down from a window above.

"Frankie!" The boy stiffens. "Frankie Brown, you get away from that skank. Get your ass inside right now!"

"My ma," Frankie smirks sheepishly. "Nice, huh?"

"What I told you, boy!" the voice upstairs shrieks. "You get that stupid butt of yours in the door right now or I'm sendin' Ray down!"

"Better get going," Miki says. "Ray doesn't sound too cool."

"No worries. He's just a dog on a leash."

"Well, thanks for the four one one."

"Anytime, sugar. You know where to find me," Frankie says with a lewd wink as he scurries up the stairs to his building.

Dusk is creeping up on the city when Miki finally decides to pack it in for the day. She doesn't feel any closer to finding her sister than when she started. But now her mind is reeling with visions of slick businessmen with their throats slit, women being catapulted out apartment windows, and all the terrible things she's been able to find out about some of the other people in Jennifer's photographs.

The last person she spoke to recognized the old man Jennifer photographed in the window of his East Side apartment. The woman worked as a housekeeper in a building across the street, and Miki was lucky to catch her leaving for the day. Police think the old man started the fire in his apartment on purpose, she said. He just stood in the window holding his little dog until the flames and smoke ate them up.

That was it for Miki. She couldn't take anymore.

As usual she has retreated to the subway, to ride without destination, to take solace in her diary, sketching the scenes, trying to make sense of them.

"All these horrible things happen
to people in Jennifer's
photography. People remember them.
But no one remembers Jennifer."

After a couple of hours, Miki decides to go home. Rush hour crowds shove and push.

It stinks down here.

By the time she comes out of the Canal Street station, it's already dark. She hurries past Oh's Deli. She can't take Mrs. Oh's maternal badgering at the moment. All she wants is a cup of scalding coffee, a piece of burnt toast, and a warm, mindless bath.

She hears the scream as she starts to cross the street toward Jennifer's building, but she can't tell where it's coming from.

Until the body smashes into the roof of the Chevy Malibu parked outside her front door.

5

*"I can calculate the motion of
heavenly bodies, but not the
madness of people."*

Isaac Newton, the first person to explain the laws of gravity, said that. He would have some *'splainin to do* if he were here to see this.

The body hurtles down the side of the building with unnatural speed. The noise the body makes when it crashes into the Chevy is so loud and awful it makes every other sound in the area stop. Except for the insane howl of the car's alarm, the perpetual din of the city suddenly evaporates into shocked silence.

For a few seconds pedestrians don't realize what's happened. A few seconds longer for any of them to approach the car. Some people start running the other way as if fearing a follow-up explosion of some kind. Too much twenty-four-hour news fraying people's nerves.

Miki is one of the first to get to the Chevy. She is propelled by a different kind of fear, the fear that she knows exactly what has happened.

The body is almost indistinguishable from the twisted metal and shattered glass surrounding it. Arms and legs protrude at unnatural angles as if they were not part of the same anatomy. There's not much blood except for a steadily growing puddle underneath the broken steering column.

People are shouting and screaming. A cacophony of horror, astonishment, and futile cries for help. Mobile phones are coming out, most to take pictures, not call 911. Texts are flying into cyberspace as fast as tremulous fingers can type.

Miki takes one look in the car, then backs away like a confused zombie. Expression blank. Eyes vacant. The torn pieces of fabric hanging from the jagged remains of the car's roof simply confirms Miki's fears. She'd recognize Mrs. Deluca's tattered bathrobe in a Black Friday shopping mob at Macy's.

A man next to her suddenly shouts incoherently then starts to gag. Miki looks over to see what's freaked him out. Mrs. Deluca's severed head is in the street by the right front tire. Like one of those blocks they put in front of a parked airplane. How the hell did it get there? Miki is too staggered to be sick. The image is so absurd she knows right then and there that she will have to draw it in her diary. She looks up the side of the building to trace the course of Mrs. Deluca's mad dive, and when her eyes land on the open window of the old woman's living room, curtains fluttering, trying to escape into the wind, she thinks she sees someone there. Or is that just a reflection in the window glass from the shiny building across the street, an adrenaline illusion incited by light and shadow?

Suddenly it's not there anymore.

The noise of the city is cranking back up. Sirens are approaching. Miki wants to feel guilty that she didn't insist Mrs. Deluca open the door earlier, but she's in shock. She can't feel anything.

A police car squeals to a stop beside the crushed Chevy. Then another. And another. Uniforms are quickly in the street, pushing lookie-loos back, barking questions about what happened, calling for assistance into walkie-talkie microphones perched on their shoulders. Miki quickly slips away and into the building to avoid getting caught up in the chaos. She wants to know if there really was someone upstairs in Mrs. Deluca's apartment.

To her surprise, she finds the apartment front door unlocked. Did Mrs. Deluca unlock it? Did she try to answer Miki's knocks too late? Or did she let someone in, someone who was leering out of the window a few moments ago?

"Hello?" Miki calls out. "Hello? Anyone here? The police will be coming up any minute now." If someone is here, maybe that will prompt them to show themselves. Miki hasn't thought about what she'll do then, but no one appears.

Miki moves quietly from room to room, taking in the museum of Mrs. Deluca's life. The decor looks unchanged from the Eisenhower era. The air is stale, except for a faint electrical smell lingering somewhere. There's no sign of a struggle. Nothing out of place. In fact, it doesn't look like anything has been moved in years. This is a home of unvarying routine.

Mrs. Deluca's oxygen tanks are propped up by the open window in the living room. The tubing and cannula are neatly coiled around the regulator valve. Everything set to be packed up and shipped back to Home Medical Supplies, Inc. Client has no more need of them. Miki sneaks a quick peek down to the street. Police officers are staring back up at her. They point and signal to their colleagues. This place will be swarming with them any minute now. Miki wants to have one last look around before the yellow crime tape goes up and the barrage of questions begins. The kitchen is as clean as a showroom model. Not even a used tissue in the garbage can. Just a single cup of tea, still steaming, sitting on the table next to the letter from the building Super telling Mrs. D she would have to move out. The woman couldn't even summon enough hope to take a sip.

In the bedroom, emotion finally sneaks up on Miki. She grabs the doorframe for balance. It's the perfect symmetry of this room that causes her to feel faint. Bed carefully made, hospital corners tucked tight, throw pillows pleasingly placed, furniture dusted, perfumes and toiletries ritualistically aligned on the dresser in front of a single photograph in an ornate frame: Mrs. D and her Henry. Younger, newly married, happy. Everything perfectly neat and tidy.

Like so many suicides, she didn't want to leave a mess.

There's no note, though. At least none that Miki can find in her cursory tour of the room. She wants to weep for the old woman who was kind to her, the woman who loved her sister, the lonely woman who was finally defeated by the struggle of living.

That's when she notices the stain.

It's on the wall above the bed's headboard. A rust-colored scorch, just like the one in her sister's apartment. What the hell? She reaches out tentatively to touch it.

Behind her someone is breathing heavily. Raspy shallow breaths. Almost like Mrs. Deluca herself. There's a face in the vanity mirror. Shimmering unnaturally in the doorway, a strange mewling sound hissing out of the hole where a mouth would be. Miki whips around but no one is there. She can still hear it but doesn't know where it's coming from, if it's near or far. It sounds like it's being projected from a stereo or TV somewhere. She races into the hallway and thinks she sees a shadow disappearing around the corner up ahead.

"Step away from the door," a man's voice demands.

The police. They've finally arrived. Two of them are coming into the hall behind her. The first one a seen-it-all short-timer, the other younger, a rookie perhaps, trying to look tough because he's clearly unsure of himself.

"Who are you?" the older one says.

"Miki Preston. Mrs. Deluca's neighbor," Miki answers calmly.

"What the hell you doin' in here?" the younger cop says, trying to sound intimidating. "This is a crime scene. You can't be touchin' nothin'."

The older cop glances at his young doppelganger with weary expression.

"I thought I saw someone in here," Miki says. "She's my friend."

"Not anymore," the young cop says, attempting a gallows humor attitude. Miki hates him.

"Let's go," the older cop says, gesturing for Miki to follow.

"Go where?" she asks petulantly.

"Listen, young lady, a woman just fell or jumped out a twelfth-floor window. You're standing not ten feet from where that happened. I think you can appreciate we need to ask you some questions."

They take her to the kitchen and make her sit at the table in front of Mrs. Deluca's tea while older cop searches for the phantom Miki insists she saw. Younger Cop waits by the door to prevent any attempt at escape. Ludicrous.

Older Cop can't find anyone else in the apartment. He confers with colleagues who are now securing the scene. No one comes to talk to Miki. No one tells her anything. When she asks how long she's going to have to sit here, she's simply told to be quiet and wait. This goes on for the better part of an hour.

Through the doorway, she can see plainclothes and CSIs traipsing through the apartment like scavengers. All of a sudden there's an argument in the other room. It starts as a murmur, but Miki can hear the anger in it rising. Then someone is telling someone else to *"get the fuck outta the way."* She can see a couple of the plainclothes turning from what they were doing and moving towards the front door, which she can't see. The yelling stops, and the argument settles into a dark muttering. Then it, too, stops.

A moment later, Mathis appears in the kitchen doorway.

"C'mon!" he orders her. He needs to get her out of there before the Special Crimes Task Force boys get here and she's caught in their net.

———

The two of them only get a few feet inside the hallway of

Jennifer's apartment when Mathis grabs her arm and turns her around.

"What they hell were you thinking?"

"Oh, I dunno. I just saw a f ... f ... friend of mine take a header into a p ... p ... parked car. Maybe I'm in shock."

"They could book you for interfering with a crime scene."

"Right. Hardened criminal that I am. Maybe they think I p ... p ... pushed her."

"Don't be a smart-ass."

"What the hell you doing here?" she demands, trying to be as contentious as he.

"I hear the call about the swan dive out a window of this building. I know you live here. I'm thinking, Christ Jesus, I hope it's not that silly Preston kid."

"Like I'm the suicidal type. You know me so well."

"Hey, all I know, maybe it was your sister."

"What!?"

"Maybe she showed up. Maybe whatever unhinged her doors and sent her scurrying into who-knows-where-ville is still working its black magic."

"Who said she's unhinged?"

Mathis wants to tell her about the last conversation he had with Jennifer Preston. But he holds back.

"No one vanishes into thin air without telling Mom, Dad, Sis, the boss, BFFs, whoever, unless they got something to hide, or something they can't deal with. Either way, it's not exactly healthy behavior."

"Maybe she didn't choose to disappear. Maybe someone or something decided for her."

"So you keep saying."

Miki is struggling with her stutter-tic trigger. If she keeps this conversation going, she knows she'll say or do something that will cross the line. A blurto. She can feel the "urge on the verge," as her father inconsiderately says. Like a pot about to boil, like a watch spring wound too tight. Once critical mass is reached, too late. It will come rushing out of her like a cola belch, or an allergy sneeze. Unstoppable.

She needs to change the subject.

"Let me show you something," she says and leads him to Jennifer's bedroom. She can tell he's suspicious. Maybe she's got something nasty in mind. Probably wouldn't be the first time, she surmises. She had friends in high school who had no problem offering sexual favors to cops to get out of trouble, especially if the cop was cute. Like Mathis.

"Someone left this at my front door couple days ago." She shows him the flash drive.

"What's on it?" he asks.

"Photos."

"Of what?"

She boots up her laptop. A moment later, pictures from that folder marked *In Case Something Happens To Me* appear.

"There's a message here somewhere. I haven't been able to figure it out, but I know that something bad has happened to all the people in these pictures. I've checked them out. I think Jennifer saw something, or found out something, and whatever it was frightened her. These photos must be really important. Otherwise she wouldn't have hidden them away. She didn't leave them with her gallery. Didn't give them to her agent. She left them with someone to give to me." She points to the words on the file folder: *In Case Something Happens To Me.* "What does it mean? What's she trying to say? What does she want me to see?"

Mathis doesn't answer. He's not looking at the computer screen anymore. He's staring at that odd stain above the bed.

"Yeah, and that's another thing," she says. "There's a mark just like it in Mrs. Deluca's apartment."

Mathis takes a step back. At first Miki thinks it's so he can get a better look. Then she realizes that's not it at all. The color has drained from his face. His eyes are wide and unblinking.

He's completely unnerved.

He's seen this before.

43

2   THE EXAMINER Wednesday, January 30

OBITUARIES

Louise Ellen King, 14. Shepherd's Bay, Passed away after injuries sustained during the terrible events of New Year's Eve. Beloved daughter of Joanne King. Also survived by her father, Detective Levi Mathis, Metropolitan PD. Services to be private. Family requests memorial contributions be made in Louise's name to VictimsofCatastropheFund.com

6

Mathis reaches down to clear dead pine needles away from the impatiens Joanne planted in front of the headstone. Why does she insist on doing this? They'll just wilt and die, and Louise's grave will be more depressing than ever.

That stain in Jennifer Preston's apartment has him spooked. Big time.

When Joanne opens the front door of her tiny two-bedroom house across the river and sees Mathis standing there, she doesn't say a thing. She's too surprised to do anything but glare. They haven't spoken since the funeral, and to be honest, she's grateful.

Those first weeks after the Catastrophe, when Louise didn't come home, when they hadn't yet found her body, she and Mathis had become characters in some awful tragic melodrama. The two of them trying to be there for each other but sharing nothing except panic and grief, making clumsy, futile attempts to pretend true affection where none had existed. Ever.

The day of Louise's funeral was the final straw. They'd had an awful scene right outside the church. In front of the priest.

Mathis showed up late bleary-eyed from the pills he constantly popped and the alcohol he used to wash them down.

"I hate you," was all she could think of to say when he finally arrived.

"I hate myself," was all he could come up with in response.

Joanne pummeled him with ever-weakening blows until she slowly collapsed and almost dropped the brass urn with Louise's ashes. Mathis just stood there and took it, but when he tried to help her up, she just shook him off and stormed away.

"Can I come in?" he asks. The friendliest tone he can manage.

She backs away and lets him.

"I've got to be at work in an hour, so I gotta get going," she responds impatiently.

She's lost even more weight, he thinks. Her once-gorgeous womanly figure is gone. She's a twig. And he can smell alcohol on her breath. She never used to drink, but now, even this early, she's started. *She's sinking,* Mathis thinks to himself, *and there's nothing I can do to save her.*

"Can I go into her bedroom?" Mathis sees her tense up. "It'll just take a moment."

"Why?" Joanne is struggling not to cry. Still too angry to ever allow him to see her vulnerability.

"Something occurred to me, that's all." He says it as gently as possible. He doesn't want to come off like the grieving father who won't let go, or worse, an indifferent cop just doing an impersonal job.

"Like what?"

"Probably nothing. It'll just take a second."

She's used to his evasions. Even when they were dating all those years ago, he kept everything close to the vest. No wonder he turned out to be good at undercover work. She didn't even know he'd lied about his age and enlisted in the Marines until the day before he was shipping out. That was the moment she knew their relationship was never destined to last. Trapping him with the obligations of fatherhood wouldn't change a thing. She decided then and there not to tell him she was pregnant.

"Make it quick," she says.

Mathis heads off down the hall. He can't help but notice how neat and clean the house always is. A slight scent of lemon lingers as he crosses the threshold into Louise's small room, former room, and Mathis is suddenly nauseous. For some ridiculous reason it reminds him of the smell in the morgue the day he had to identify her body.

"You've taken the pictures down," he says.

"Decided to paint the room," Joanne answers coolly.

Mathis is disappointed. Louise is slowly being erased. The furniture is the same. The bookshelf is still teeming with her personality. The dresser is still organized with her intimacies. But soon, he knows, Joanne will neatnik these away, too. Item by item, the moments of his daughter's life will become stored away forever, just like her body has been for the past six months.

"You covered it up," he says, standing by the bed.

"Covered what up?" she says, irritated.

"The stain. The one on the wall here."

"I painted the room, Levi." Duh. "You came over here to see if I'd left a stain on the wall!?"

"You ever wonder how it got there?"

"Jesus, Mathis, who cares?"

"Was it always there? Do you remember?" He's straining to reign in his impatience.

"I can't remember even seeing a damn stain until I started painting the room." Which Mathis knows is probably true. Joanne was catatonic for weeks after Louise died. She wouldn't come near this room. And even if she had, her state of mind would not have been what one would call clear and sharp-eyed. "Maybe she painted something there when she was a kid," Joanne continues. "Tried to hide it. She had so many pictures and posters and calendars tacked up everywhere, maybe they left behind a smudge or something. I don't know. What's this have to do with anything?"

"Never mind."

"What is it with you, Levi? You think the reason for our daughter's death can be discovered in some fucking stain on the wall? This some sick reflex action you can't control, some knee-jerk cop behavior you're addicted to?"

"Good one, Jo."

"Can't you just leave it alone?"

"Can you? What was she doin' over there, Jo? Why wasn't she home with you?" He can't help himself. The alcohol scent of her body odor doesn't make him sympathetic, it pisses him off. At himself. For being tempted.

"Here we go again," she says, deflating right before his eyes.

"She was only fourteen for Christ's sake. It was three in the goddamn morning."

Joanne straightens up. Wounded and cornered. Dangerous. "It was New Year's Eve. She was looking for you! Again. If you hadn't been passed out ..." Her voice drops to a whisper and she doesn't finish the thought. Doesn't need to.

So there it is. His fault, her fault. The exchange of gunshots. Each one a direct hit. The death of their child the weapon of choice. The one thing they shared, the only thing they shared, the memory of their daughter, now mutated into an ugly toxic wedge, inextricably jammed between them, keeping them apart yet paradoxically fusing each to the other in perpetuity, leeching its poison drip by drip, contaminating any compassion or empathy that might have enabled them to comfort one another. The loss of Louise. So sudden, so senseless as to be incomprehensible, a forever-curse on any sliver of peace they might have hoped to expect. Fuck all the psychobabble about learning to live with the pain. That's nothing but a manipulative ruse, offered like a sedative to calm someone in danger of making a scene.

"I just wanted to see her room again," he says

It's at moments like this Mathis wishes Louise had never

found him. That he'd never discovered that he had a daughter. He wishes he'd never had any idea whether she lived ... or died. He thinks he hates Joanne for having her in the first place, then for allowing her to find out about him. But he knows he really just hates himself for feeling that way.

He's going to need a meeting at Narcotics Anonymous tonight for sure.

7

In her journal, Miki extends the swirls of the elaborate question marks next to the sketch she's just drawn to make sure they stand out. The image captures Mrs. D's suicide moment as she imagines it happened. But it isn't the detail of the drawing that's compelling. Miki's sketches are never detailed. It's the feeling this one conveys, the kinetic energy of the scene that won't allow you to look away. The apartment building is just a suggestion in the background, a gray impressionistic pile. The street is a nebulous smudge, its greedy lookie-loos mere silhouettes staring up a woman's body floating on her back, bathrobe fluttering at her sides, legs spread, arms reaching skyward as if to the angels, just inches from fatal impact with the car beneath. Almost elegiac. Not the gruesome scene Miki came upon after hearing the crash.

Miki's eyes finally settle on the insert frame she sequestered in the lower right corner of the panel. Mrs. Deluca's head in the gutter. As close to a photograph as Miki could make it from memory. The expression haunts Miki. Fear? Astonishment? Certainly not resignation or despair.

Emotion finally overwhelms her. She shoves her sketchbook aside afraid the flood of tears will stain the drawing and smear it. But she's happy to be crying at last. All day she's been gripped by the constipation of her grief. Just lying there inside her gut like an indigestible piece of sausage. It was starting to make her sick. This is exactly what she needed. A wet, messy purge.

She cries herself into a state of semiconsciousness while looking up at that odd stain above her sister's bed. The sound of the same strange breathing she heard in Mrs. D's apartment starts to seep out of it, and that hideous face she saw in the subway suddenly oozes out of the scorch, grinning maniacally, dripping like warm molasses toward her. Miki is paralyzed. She wants to roll off the bed, but she can't. The gelatinous face gets closer and closer, its moray mouth widening, baring concentric rings of greasy needle-teeth, attaching itself to Miki's face like some inescapable French kiss, draining her.

The chirp of her mobile yanks her out of the trance. The face from the ceiling vanishes. Just a hallucination. She hopes. The iPhone chirping is annoying. But it could be Mathis with some news. It isn't. It's her father. Texting her. *"So much more efficient,"* he used to say. Less prone to emotional entanglement is what he really meant.

"Any sign of your sister?" the message asks.

"I'm fine, thanks for asking," Miki mumbles to herself. "Not yet," she keys in return.

"Taking your meds?"

"Jennifer first, my meds next. Story of my life," Miki sighs.

"Of course," she lies. "Ooops, battery dying. Gotta run. Hot date." That'll provoke him. She clicks off before her father can swallow his surprise and answer.

The grim gray of evening has subdued the apartment. She must have fallen asleep for a couple of hours. Her mouth is a desert, and her head is pounding. She can barely rouse herself to get a glass of water. But the shadows make her nervous. Long abstract shapes are thrown across the floor and cupboards by the buildings in the Quarantine Zone as the sun retreats behind them. They sway and slide as if they were sentient every time a breeze pushes against the window glass refracting the light.

She has to get out of here.

It's a fair walk to Tenth and Twenty-Fourth, but Miki decides it's preferable to sitting in the stifling subway during rush hour. Even if it is raining. The downpour has thinned out pedestrian traffic nicely, so instead of having to forge rivers of eyes-averted, destination-obsessed zombies, she simply has to dodge the occasional spikes of umbrella ribs. Pity the poor fool who is standing in the middle of the street trying to flag a taxi on an evening like this.

By the time Miki reaches the minimalist galleries of Armstrong-Diehl, she's a wet cat. Furtive, jumpy, skeletal. Most people dripping like this would be too embarrassed to venture in among the perfectly coiffed Upper East Side clientele braving the wilderness of Soho, sipping Chardonnay and munching dim sum and fois gras, courtesy of some au courant event caterer. But she repels any snobbish glances with direct what-are-you-gawking-at eye contact as she helps herself to ample food and drink along the way toward Evangeline Diehl, grande doyen of the Armstrong-Diehl Gallery and acknowledged supreme arbiter of all things photochemical.

"Oh my God, look at you," Evangeline laughs as Miki approaches. "A wretch come to life from one of your sister's photographs." The guests surrounding her laugh, too, but they don't know why.

"I need to show you something."

"Of course, darling, of course."

She leads Miki towards the back of the gallery, defying

Bloomberg's nanny campaign by lighting another Gauloise Blonde on the way. It's her hardwired sense of independence, having had to learn self-reliance and resourcefulness as a child. Six years old, rescued from Treblinka before the Nazis could gas everyone as the Allies closed in, she was "resettled" in a displaced persons camp, which turned out to be only marginally better. Seven years later she was still there, until she ran away and made her way back to war-ravaged Berlin in search of her parents only to learn they had been starved to death at Bergen-Belsen. Alone and penniless, Evangeline scrounged her way to Paris where she became a model and muse for struggling artists infatuated with her stunning good looks and bitter intelligence. Soon after being introduced to the French diplomat Bernard D'Estaing, Evangeline became his lover and travelled with him to Vietnam where he was negotiating an end to French colonialism until he was assassinated by Vietminh agents. Legend has it she became a spy for the CIA there, which she will neither confirm nor deny. No one knows how she ended up in New York in the '60s, but she quickly fell in with the city's avant-garde, particularly Andy Warhol's Factory.

For the past quarter century she has reigned over the New York art scene, suffering the pretensions of clients from all over the world with grace and humor so she can redistribute extravagant sums of their wealth to artists she is fanatic to support. Like Jennifer Preston. Minus the hefty commission off the top, bien sur. At six foot three, she towers over Miki and just about everyone else here. One can spot her gloriously wild white mane from any spot in the room. And her anorexic frame makes her lope across the gallery seem otherworldly. Even at eighty-six, Evangeline Diehl can make young men weak at the knees.

"I'm sorry for intruding," Miki says as Evangeline slides closed the door of her glass-walled office.

"I hope this means we've heard from our dearest Jennifer?"

"Not directly."

Evangeline chews on her cigarette holder pondering the ambiguity. "Well, that is distressing."

Miki can't tell if the sentiment is compassionate or mercenary.

"This was delivered to my door," she says, holding out Jennifer's flash drive. "Her photos are on it. I think it's a message."

Evangeline eyes the flash drive covetously. "Maybe some new essay she's preparing," she says, taking the flash drive and shoving it into the USB port of her workstation.

"Open that file," Miki says, pointing to the folder labeled *In Case Something Happens To Me.*

Evangeline puffs on her Gauloise as the photos scroll down the screen.

"She must have been in a hurry with these, your sister. The compositions are intriguing, but there's something unfortunate about them."

"Unfortunate?"

"The detail in the backgrounds, it's evasive. Not like Jennifer."

"Maybe she was trying to hide some flaw," Miki suggests.

"Peut-être. Adams used to do it all the time. He'd manipulate exposures over different parts of the frame to draw the eye away or toward something. But these, ooh la la ..."

"What was she working on, Evangeline? What was her next show about?"

It takes a moment for Evangeline to answer.

"I'm not sure exactly. '*Mine the penumbra of the city*' was the way she put it. She kept saying there was something dark out there, haunting us, since the Catastrophe. She wanted to capture it, to prove its existence. I could never tell if she meant it metaphorically, or if she really believed some curse had been visited upon us. Your sister was a bit of a poet, you know."

"You don't sound like you were enthusiastic about the project."

"We don't need fairy tales and myths to explain the evil abroad in the land, darling. All we have to do is look in the mirror."

"But why would she label that folder *In Case Something Happens To Me*? Was she in danger?"

Evangeline lights another cigarette. "Left at your door, you say?" Evangeline says, avoiding the question.

"A messenger. A kid. My neighbor saw him leave it, but he wouldn't tell her where or who it came from."

The cigarette smoke is starting to overwhelm the office. Miki's not sure how much longer she can take it.

"Perhaps," Evangeline finally says, "perhaps she's asking you to start over. If she's not able to, that is."

Not exactly what Miki wants to hear. Evangeline extracts the flash drive. Hands it back to Miki.

"Your sister always wanted to make the darkness visible, darling. It's what artists like her do. But one has to be careful. Darkness can rub off on you."

THE  OMINOSITY

I thought I knew this city. It's people.
But now...
I feel like there's something settling over us.
Something dark and menacing.
Ever since New Year's.
Ever since the Quarantine.
I see it everywhere.
This barely contained rage.
This seething despair.

That's why I'm writing this blog.
Nothing is the same anymore.
We haven't always been like this.
Have we?

THE OMINOSITY

8

Jennifer's dark room is not much more than a converted utility closet off the front hallway. Just enough room for a table of developer baths, accessories, and an enlarger, crisscrossed by a clothesline for prints to hang dry. Her boxy Mamiya 645 camera sits in a corner, a wide-angle view of the room, the fat round lens silently staring at Miki like some CCTV snoop as she hovers over the fixing trays watching a new eight-by-ten come to life.

She has spent the night in here, making prints from the negatives she found in her sister's just-in-case box, trying to remember everything Jennifer taught her when they were teenagers. No dodging, no flashing, just exposure of the raw negative, but enlarged over the areas of the flaws.

"Perhaps she wanted someone to start over," Evangeline said.

Miki's lost all track of time. For all she knows, it could be dawn already. She was just about to give up when she discovered it. In the photo of that couple uptown, sitting with their infant on the stoop of their tenement brownstone. A small almost imperceptible smudge over a window in the upper corner of the frame. A chemical stain? A nick in the physical negative itself? Miki compared the contact sheet she'd made from that roll of 35mm against the image on the flash drive. Sure enough, Jennifer had "dodged" that area in the digital version. A subtle but effective camouflage. Miki picked up Jennifer's small magnifying loupe and checked other frames. In each one, a similar flaw. Were they just some coincidental defect, maybe some flaw in the lens, or a manufacturing malfunction that corrupted the entire film roll? Or would they turn out to be a kind of repetitive motif Jennifer wanted someone to find and deconstruct? She had an impish sense of humor, that girl, and Miki has considered the possibility tonight's speculative investigation might end with nothing but the pyrrhic discovery of a punchline to one of her sister's mischievous jokes.

Only one way to find out.

The print is starting to emerge in one of the baths. This is the part Miki always loved whenever big sister would allow her to help. Miki didn't really want to learn photography, she just wanted to hang out with Jennifer, to diagnose why she had such quiet confidence, why she was so self-directed, qualities Miki found severely lacking in her own personality. She never did fully figure it out, but standing there silently, feeling her pulse start to race as splotches of dark and light competed for space on the submerged sheet of photo paper, she came to understand Jennifer's passion. This was magic. This was conjuring. A reality revealing itself moment-by-moment right before your eyes. You might be thrilled, Jennifer had said, you might be disappointed, but you would always be surprised. No matter what you thought you'd seen looking through the viewfinder, it was sure to turn out differently in the processing, changed by light, chemicals, and time. A birthing process.

The form of the brownstone is becoming clearer now, the detail much sharper than in the Jennifer's digital version. And when the young couple fade in, Miki is surprised that their expressions are flat and inscrutable. Not nearly so emotionally distinct as in the digital. It's because Jennifer deliberately muted the background exposure in order to highlight the contrast around their faces, to draw your eye immediately to their demeanor and the pain and anxiety there. She had exposed for them, not the background. Miki's exposure here has been more neutral and even. And the result is that the smudge in the window behind them is now more distinct. But it's not a smudge. It's not a nick in the neg, or a flaw in the lens.

It appears to be a face! Suspended in the glass of the window. Faint and featureless, as if hovering behind a curtain sheer, or befogged by smoke. Maybe the glass was dirty or steamed. A reflection, maybe? Improbable given the angle of the shot and Jennifer's distance from the building. Where would the person have been standing?

A spasm of nausea churns in Miki's gut. Something about this face glaring down at the couple reminds her of that hallucination in the subway station the other night. The one in the Quarantine Zone. And the one next to smarmy Bike Boy who wanted to pick her up.

It's that same maniacal grin.

She hasn't had a shower in a couple of days and is feeling pretty rank. The chemical smells trailing her out of the darkroom only enhance the sensation. She yanks off her frayed jeans and black tank top and kicks them into a pile with other dirty laundry which has been ignored for over a week and has congealed into an amorphous monochrome collage of stiff smelly fabric. Down to her underpants, Miki pauses in front of the bathroom mirror while the water heats up. She must be losing weight. Again. The muscles of her arms and thighs are too stringy. Her ribs are too conspicuous. Mrs. Oh down at the deli is going to have a lot to say about this. At least her small melon breasts are still supple.

Bonaparte, the beautifully detailed great horned owl she tattooed on herself just above the panty line, stares up at her with those binocular eyes and slightly challenging gaze that Miki modeled after her own default expression. It took her several painstaking days to ink him on the flat rigid surface of her abdomen because it was her first attempt at body art and she had no idea how to correct mistakes, and because, frankly, it hurt like hell. But after that first searing stroke, there was no turning back. It was a silly thing to do, Miki knows, but it made her feel rebellious. Made her feel bold and independent. Like her sister.

In the shower, she stares up at the showerhead, water beating down on her like a steaming Venusian rain. When her skin has finally cooked to a rare-steak pink, she reaches for the shampoo and uses more than she needs for her short hair above and below. Purple streams from the faded dye with which she streaked her pubis two weeks ago in a fit of pique after an argument on the phone with her mother trickle between her legs to the drain.

"Feel better?" she says to Bonaparte while toweling off.

No answer. But the glistening moisture on her stomach down makes facets of the bird's feathers seem almost three-dimensional, as if Bonaparte was breathing.

She feels revived and clearheaded, a feeling she knows will only last a few minutes. She quickly settles in at the kitchen counter with a twelve-ounce Rockstar Punched to study the rest of the eight-by-tens she made from Jennifer's negatives. These now-dry exposures have been cropped, refocused, and enlarged to highlight the areas her sister purposely masked in the digital versions. Miki scours the one of the brownstone couple with Jennifer's loupe. Her eyes are burning and watery from too little sleep, but she's hoping the Rockstar will juice her long enough to determine if her sister's photographic camouflage was a deliberate act of concealment or simply an attempt to rescue an "unfortunate" roll of film, as Evangeline Diehl characterized it.

At first, Miki is afraid Evangeline's assessment will turn out to be correct. Despite the grin, the face in the window seems too nebulous to be anything but a simple distraction. Someone innocently passing by in the apartment upstairs. A trick of light, an accident of angle or reflection. But when she picks up the enlargement of Bicycle Boy standing over the man he probably ran down, Miki recognizes a similar figure in the background that wasn't in Jennifer's digital. An anomaly across the street, just like the face in the tenement window. Another figure, slightly out of focus from the rest of the scene, as if superimposed into the crowd instead of really there, staring at the scene in the intersection while everyone else is looking elsewhere. She drops that print and retrieves the one of the money-laundering Lucian Price stealing a taxi from a couple of appalled tourists. Sure enough, another aberration leaps out at her, something she never saw on her sister's flash drive. A spectral figure, slightly blurry as if vibrating too fast for Jennifer's shutter speed, standing right behind Price as he shoves the tourists away. Finally she picks up the new print of the old man holding his little dog staring out the window of his apartment. Miki had noticed a slight smear in the neg just behind the man's head which she enlarged refocused. In the reprint that smear has turned out to be some elongated wraith, hovering near the ceiling, glaring down at the old man with an expression Edvard Munch could appreciate.

Miki leans back from the counter. A strange disquiet sweeps over her. At first she tries to convince herself that the anomalous figures in these photos must have been intentional double exposures, that they represent some new style Jennifer was experimenting with, but she instinctively knows that can't be the case. Jennifer was no fantasist, no surrealist. If she manipulated her photographs it was only to highlight something authentic she wanted you to see, never to invent one that didn't exist. She must have meant for someone to engage in the kind of forensics Miki has to uncover these unusual phantoms.

Did Jennifer send the flash drive? Is she reaching out somehow with the possibility that these things, whatever they are, could be real and present? The thought makes Miki's mind ache.

That's when her mobile goes off. She recognizes the number. Baako Kenyata. From the city's paramedic services.

This can't be good.

ATLANTIC
MONTHLY

SEPTEMBER 1930

Chronicles of America
by
Meade Kensington-White

It is an over-crowded, raucous mega-metropolis, this city, with widely varying neighborhoods of extreme wealth, desperate poverty and everything in between. Some areas are vibrant, others utterly forgettable. A mélange of races and ethnicities coexist here, more out of symbiotic necessity than any genuine commonality. Sleek limousines share streets with weary pedestrians. The well-dressed live only a few blocks from the threadbare. It is a perpetual motion machine, this city, propelled by the constant friction of ambition and indifference, extreme success and dismal failure, constantly accelerating, but always on the verge of flying apart. It is not difficult to imagine that from its combustible fuel of relentless social competition, inescapable clamor and restless transience, monsters will emerge.

9

When Mathis comes up the steps from the basement of St. Eustace, he is surprised to see Miki across the street. Good thing tonight's NA meeting was calm and undramatic. Usually he comes away from these pity parties more depressed than when he went in. How can anyone listen to the horror stories everyone spills including, truth be told, his own sorry self, and still believe the human race possesses even the dimmest spark of nobility? Surprisingly, these wretched tales only drive a few newcomers right back out the door in search of their connections. Most hang in, some for years, like lookie-loos at an accident site, simultaneously repulsed and fascinated by each new testament to degradation. Serves to confirm Mathis's belief that the essence of addiction is really just masochism. The "you-can't-believe-how-low-I-sank" narratives merely stand in as proxies for the real thing. Tonight's session was less tortuous than usual, though, so his misanthropic view of every single person on the planet, man, woman, or child, is slightly subdued, and he's able to stuff his anger away in some small pocket of his psyche for use later.

"What are you doing here?" he asks as she approaches. Comes out a bit harsher than he intended since he already knows the answer.

"Looking for you. Obviously."

"How'd you know where to find me?"

"I can be a detective, too, Mathis."

He's about to tell her in no uncertain terms that now is not a good time to challenge him about her sister's disappearance since he's just finished a gut-wrenching recitation of his failings as a father, but the look on her face makes him hold back.

"You busy?" she asks with a voice that's too small for her.

"What's up?"

"I'd appreciate if you'd come with me." She takes a deep breath to steady herself. "To the m ... m ... morgue."

Baako Kenyata is waiting for Miki when she arrives, and he's surprised to see that she's brought company.

"Baako, this is Detective Levi Mathis," she says on approach.

Baako stiffens. An involuntary reaction inspired by too many nights back home awaiting a midnight knock on the door from the Fanya Fujo Uone, Tanzania's ruthless secret police.

"Off duty, at the moment," Mathis adds, sensing Baako's suspicion. "Just here for moral support."

"Not sure you want to see this one, darlin'," Baako tells Miki.

"I can handle it, Baako," she says.

Baako looks to Mathis to see if he has anything to say, but the detective is inscrutable.

"This one's been out there a while," Baako continues. "Maintenance crew found her stuffed in a culvert on the One Line between Thirty-Fourth and Forty-Second. No idea how she came to be there."

Baako leads them down the stairs into the dismal maze of morgue corridors with their sickening fluorescent light and chemical smells. But Baako Kenyata loves it here. He grew up in the despair of Dar Es Salaam slums listening to the myths and songs about this city. For kids like him it was a mystical beacon of inspiration rivaled only by nearby Mount Kilimanjaro and its witch-doctor legends. As soon as he was able, Baako hopped a Dutch merchant ship and headed west, leaving behind a beloved wife and two small children with only the meager wages from his last week at the clinic where he worked and the cold-comfort promise that he would send for them soon.

That was two years ago.

Wallet-sized snapshots of Alyia, Hamisi, and little Babu pinned to the dashboard of his EMS ambulance are an ever-present reminder of the vow that he fully intends to keep. None of his tedious graveyard shifts as a city paramedic, none of the wretchedness he's witnessed, none of the senseless violence he's had to confront has dampened his enthusiasm for his new home. Though myth has rudely succumbed to reality these past twenty-four months, he's been able to maintain an unshakable faith that this is still the greatest place on Earth. Until recently. Until the so-called Catastrophe on New Year's Eve. Something was unleashed that night, he believes, and it's hard now for Baako to resist the animist superstitions of his homeland.

He turns the corner into a long antiseptic corridor that smells strongly of bleach. When they reach the autopsy rooms, he pauses again, giving Miki a last chance to turn back. She doesn't.

"How did she die?" she asks.

"The doc will have to say. No visible wounds that we could see when we picked her up."

Baako's voice is soft and musical. Every word pronounced carefully and articulately with a hybrid accent that sounds part English aristocrat, part 7-Eleven clerk.

Inside a small observation room that overlooks an even smaller chamber, there's a body on a gurney under a sheet.

"I have to warn you, Miki, you might not recognize her."

"If it's her, I'll know," Miki says confidently but not hopefully. Mathis notices her back stiffening, her hands balling into fists.

Baako presses the button by the window and an overweight orderly finishing a Burger King steps in from the autopsy rooms. Between chews he looks over at Baako for the signal to begin.

"Let's do it, Charles," Baako says into the microphone by the window.

Charles puts his Whopper box on the body's torso then swings the gurney around headfirst toward them. He unceremoniously pulls the sheet off. Miki gasps aloud. The facial features of the corpse are indistinguishable from one another, melted into a waxy lumpy blankness. What once might have been a beautiful woman is now Elephant Man. The rest of her is unscathed. Even her beige Armani jacket is intact. No sign of struggle or violence.

"What happened to her face?" Miki manages to say after catching her breath.

Mathis steps closer to the window. "Looks like she was ... burned."

"There's no evidence of that anywhere else on her body," Baako says. "The blouse, the skirt, they are dirty but not burnt."

Mathis remains at the window, staring hard at the corpse.

"It's not her, Mathis," Miki says. "It's not Jennifer."

"Are you sure?" Baako asks.

"It's the clothes. Too Vogue, too Marie Claire. Jen never wore anything but jeans and a leather jacket. It was a family joke. Getting dressed required too much thought otherwise. I never ever saw her in a skirt, except for her eighth-grade class picture, which she hated."

Miki just stares unblinkingly at the young woman laid out in the next room. There is nothing remotely alive about her. She doesn't look asleep. She doesn't look peaceful. She looks gray and dead.

"It's not her," Miki says again definitively. But she doesn't sound relieved. Just sad.

"Thank you, Charles," Baako says into the microphone. "No ID."

The orderly moves the gurney away from the window, but

before he covers the corpse back up, he does a curious thing. He reaches down and strokes the dead girl's face, tenderly rearranging some errant curls stuck between what's left of the lips. A moment of genuine compassion for a person who doesn't exist anymore by a person who should not be expected to care.

A single tear escapes one of Miki's eyes as she hurries from the room.

<hr>

While Mathis confers with the Assistant Medical Examiner on duty, Miki and Baako retreat outside to share his giant bag of Snyders potato chips. Baako loves these. Lots of grease and salt. The closest thing he's been able to find to the dried sweet potato slices grilled in sunflower oil that street vendors sell in the bazaars of Dar Es Salaam.

"What does your homicide detective say?" Baako asks while shoving another handful of "crisps" as he calls them into his mouth.

"*Former* homicide detective," Miki responds snatching the bag away before the big man eats them all. "He thinks she's probably off on some assignment somewhere and hasn't bothered to tell anyone."

"Could be true, eh?"

"No, Baako. She would never leave for this long without telling me where she was."

They lean against his EMS van and finish their chips in silence.

"Do they ever talk to you, Baako?"

"Who?"

"The dead. The bodies you bring here. When you find them, do they ever try to tell you who they are, what happened to them?"

"And how exactly would they do that, my girl?" Baako chuckles.

"Their expression, their posture. Maybe in their last moments they were thinking of something, feeling something, and they want whoever finds them to know what it was."

"They've got nothing to say, darlin'. Their spirits have long sailed away by the time I get there. Nothing left but their shell." Still clinging to his science, trying to ignore his superstitions.

Miki ponders this, and Baako knows she's imagining her sister on one of his gurneys.

"I hope your detective is right," he says as he pulls her into a quick hug that almost smothers her. He knows she won't mind. He's been her only friend since he found her roaming these lousy hallways a couple of weeks ago pestering attendants for information about any young woman brought in who might be her sister. Everyone ignored her. *Without authorized pass from the Medical Examiner's office, no entry. Period.* No one gave her the time of day. Or night. As far as they were concerned she was just another one of those post-Catastrophe pain-in-the-ass citizens interfering with essential government business. But Baako understood the pain she was feeling. The same pain, no doubt, he had felt on those day-long walks with his father from government building to government building after the rebellion was finally crushed, hoping to find out what had happened to his mother. Authorities treated his father like a child, shuffling him from one so-called human rights charity to another where he'd be greeted with weary smiles and exhausted promises. Even though he was only eight years old, Baako could tell they were just "shining" his father. He could see it in their eyes. They simply assumed his mother had been kidnapped, used up, then killed. The familiar story. Or worse, maybe they figured she'd been one of the rebels and got what she deserved. They weren't really going to do anything to find her. If her body turned up one day, and they could identify her somehow, maybe they would find a way to let his father know. Maybe not. Maybe his mother would simply end up in a common grave and no one would ever know who she was or what really happened to her. So Baako couldn't help reaching out to Miki after the third or fourth time he found her here at the morgue. He bought her coffee, listened to her story. And then he promised, sincerely, that he would personally get in touch with her if any young woman was found that matched her sister's description. Like tonight. Yes, he truly hoped that "former homicide detective" was right about Jennifer, and that she would never turn up here. But if she did, at least Miki would have some idea of what happened. Unlike Baako and his hopeless father.

Mathis shoves his way out the heavy metal door of the building and comes over to them.

"Who was she?" Miki asks.

"Pretty sure it's a young woman named Angela Rossi. Went missing a week ago. Worked in the City's Planning and Development Office."

Baako whistles through his teeth. "Not a job I'd be wanting these days."

"Who would do that to someone?" Miki asks, trying to sound detached, analytical. Not succeeding.

"You'd be surprised," Mathis replies wearily. He neglects to add that he remembers the Hermes scarf Angela Rossi wore the night he saw her meet with Dickie Prince, the loose-cannon leader of the Silver Street thugs. Looked like some kind of payoff going down. He didn't recognize Angela at the time, but she had a wide-eyed, unblinking middle-distance stare that he found unnerving. Like she was looking at some paralyzing horror right in front of her. Mathis was arrested for Dickie's murder before he could put two and two together. But maybe now, the door has opened again. "Want to get some coffee?"

She shakes her head. "But if I don't get something more to eat than these chips, I'm going to faint."

She turns to Baako and hugs him again. "Thanks, Baako."

"Stay strong," the big man whispers as she manages a reassuring smile.

10

I t didn't look natural," Miki says through a mouthful. They're sitting in a deli on the western border of the Quarantine Zone. Miki chose it because it was the first place they came to after leaving the morgue, and because she's been here before and likes their potato pancakes and applesauce.

"What do you mean?"

"Her face. You ever see anything like that before?"

Mathis thinks about it for a moment. "Stuff similar. When I was in Syria hunting ISIS. Guys with faces blown off by snipers, IEDs."

"But not exactly like this, right?" She waits until he finally concedes with a shake of his head. "It's like something latched on to her face and sucked it smooth," she says. "Like a lollipop."

"How come you know so much about clothes?" He's trying to change the subject.

She levels a blank stare. *Seriously?*

"What? You're not exactly a walking fashion statement, you know."

"My mother." And that's all she'll say about that.

Mathis is amused by the way she's still shoveling the food into her mouth. When she realizes it, she's embarrassed. He actually has a nice smile. Gentle, open. But she's pissed at herself for noticing. And for being self-conscious about it. She decides to go on offense.

"Does it help?" she wonders.

"Does what help?"

Again, that blank stare.

"Ah, the meetings," he says as his smile evaporates. "I've got no choice, so I try to make the best of it. And Oxy's not the easiest lover to dump."

He drifts off. To a dark place he's unable to escape and knows he never will.

"That explains the limp," Miki says, referring to his slight left lean when he walks.

"We were backing up an EOD unit in Raqqa. I was Special Forces intelligence. Had sources telling me Johnny Jihad was using the basement of a school as an IED factory. We got all the kids out, but the place was booby-trapped. Fuckers got us with our fingers up our ass. I spent six months recovering at Landstuhl. That's where I got hooked. When I mustered out, I joined the police department. Turns out I was good at undercover, sneaky bastard that I am. They moved me up fast. It was a good veil for my habit. And I was disciplined enough to keep it down-low and manageable."

"Maybe you should consider yourself lucky you didn't graduate to heroin."

"Who says I didn't?"

"Best painkiller ever invented, they say. Especially after losing a daughter."

Mathis holds her stare.

"Sorry. My m ... mouth and my b ... b ... brain just can't seem to get in sync."

"Really? I hadn't noticed." But he's not angry. It was just another one of her blurtos, and he knows her apology is genuine. He lets her off the hook with one of his gentle smiles. "I didn't even know her until I got back from the Middle East. Her mother and I, we weren't what you'd call close. I never told her I was enlisting. She never told me she was pregnant."

"Sounds like the foundation of a lasting relationship."

Mathis concurs with her sarcasm with a half-smile. "I never heard from her after I got deployed. She had Louise on her own. Raised her that way ... until ..."

A vacancy sweeps into his eyes that frightens Miki. A dead, soulless stare. The look of the damned.

"We didn't find her body for several days," he whispers.

"Jesus," she mutters, sorry that she pressed.

"Things went downhill real fast after that. The veil dropped. My using went up."

"And you went after that guy, Dickie Prince."

Mathis's stare narrows. "I had information he was shooting his mouth off about the explosion. He was too stupid to pull something like that off on his own, so I decide to find out who was pulling his strings." Mathis locks eyes with her. "But I didn't kill him."

"Do you know who did?"

"I have my suspicions." He lets that lay there. "Anyway, they never charged me. Evidence was too thin. But the Captain gave me an ultimatum. Regular sessions at St. Eustace or a one-way ticket down Loser Street and all that goes with it."

She can't take her eyes off him now. He's a wounded animal and she can't decide if that makes him vulnerable or dangerous. Why do the dark ones have to be so attractive? She'll want to sketch him sitting here when she gets back to Jennifer's apartment.

She pushes her plate aside to clear space for a couple of her sister's photos which she pulls from her coat pocket and smooths out in front of him. "What do you make of these?"

"From your sister's flash drive."

"But these are reprints I made. Because of those." She points to that vague character she's discovered in the backgrounds. "My sister tried to cover them up, but I don't think it was for artistic reasons."

"They supposed to mean something?"

"They're in every one. At every scene where something terrible happened."

"A regular Weegee, your sister."

"Who?"

"Arthur Fellig. Weegee was his pseudonym. Photojournalist, like her, 'cept in the 1940s. Used to follow the city's emergency services at night to get his shots. Mostly murder and bad death."

"My sister was no ambulance chaser. I think she was trying to leave behind some kind of trail, something she wanted someone to follow. And this ... this ... whoever it is, whatever it is, is in every shot!"

"So?"

"So, I'm saying there's a connection. And Jennifer was on to it."

"A connection to what? Please don't tell me you're joining the choir about some evil Svengali wandering the city like a phantom, making people do horrible things."

She almost tells him about her own encounters on the street, in the subway, but she holds back because he's studying the photos again and she sees a glimmer of interest in his eyes, a sudden alertness, an inkling of something he's trying to grasp more fully.

"Aren't you a little bit curious?"

But her hopes are dashed when he shakes his head. "Frankly, I'm not getting any messages from the beyond here. Must be a flaw in your sister's lens. Or you made a printing error."

"Forget it," she says, snatching the photos back and turning to the window. The blacked-out Quarantine Zone looms nearby like a tumor with its abandoned buildings and menacing security drones prowling its perimeters.

"It's like a scab on the city's soul," she says to herself.

The waitress slides by to find out if Miki wants more pancakes, if Mathis wants more coffee. He answers. She doesn't.

"Just the check," he says after Miki shakes her head.

"Coming right up, sweetheart." The waitress turns slowly to give him a good rear-view before she moves off.

"You only had the coffee," Miki objects.

"You can call me Sir Galahad."

"I'll let her do that," Miki says, watching the waitress sashay away.

Outside, it's starting to rain.

"I'll walk you," Mathis says when they come out of the diner.

"Don't you have better things to do?" she blurts, nodding back toward the diner.

An eerie crescendo of misery wails in the distance. It's coming from the Quarantine Zone. Makes them both pause.

"Just the wind chasing itself down vacant streets," he says.

"You feel it, don't you?" she says.

"What?"

"This city. Something's gone wrong."

"And you're just noticing this now?"

"It's something deep, Mathis. Something foul and dangerous. Maybe something irreversible." She pulls her jacket collar tight around her neck. "Thank you for coming with me. I mean it. Thank you."

Mathis nods and watches her head off. For a moment, he thinks maybe he'll tail her. She'd never know, he's that good, but he resists. The last thing he needs is to transfer guilt feelings about her sister to this unmanageable stray. Who knows where that would lead?

"Be careful," he yells.

She never looks back.

11

Miki's in no hurry to get back to the loneliness of Jennifer's apartment. Besides, she loves the city when it's like this. Rain makes everything slightly out of focus. The lights shimmer. The buildings undulate. The city feels more abstract. The way she draws it in her sketchbook.

Her route is not even circuitous. It's aimless. After a few blocks, she has no idea where she's going, and doesn't care. A predictable path would allow her to go on autopilot. She would lose herself in thought and speculation, simply putting one foot in front of the other until she arrived somewhere. This way, she'll be more alert and observant. And who knows? Maybe she'll stumble upon the needle in the haystack. Maybe she'll catch a glimpse of Jennifer and reassure herself she isn't a faceless corpse on a morgue slab. Like Angela Rossi. She tries to banish the thought by scribbling in her journal.

"My sister spent her days and mostly her nights documenting what's come to be known around here as the Catastrophe. A modern-day Diane Arbus she was. She created a portrait of a population still unable to comprehend an event as mindless as it was mysterious. It made her

famous. It may also be the reason she disappeared."

Before she knows it, Miki has ventured far from wide boulevards and avenues into narrower residential side streets where it's unusually quiet. Except for the rainfall muting all other sounds with its wet white noise, Miki is reminded of a city buried by a heavy January snow. She can barely hear the slap of her Joe Rockets on the pavement. An off-duty taxi splashes by, but there are no other pedestrians around. No residents out braving the weather.

There's a sudden rustling behind her. Like wind disturbing branches of trees. But it doesn't subside. It crescendos, louder and louder, closer and closer, as if a stampede of monkeys was fleeing across this urban canopy in full fright. What the hell is that? The ruckus passes over Miki as she strains to follow it through the spray of raindrops pelting her face until suddenly an explosion of birds leaps into the sky. Miki is so startled she yelps out loud. Pigeons, crows, sparrows. From tree branches, rooftops, from under balconies, gutters, and gargoyles. An enormous black cloud of them, terrorized by some contagious hysteria, roused and shrieking, jerking en masse into the sky then swaying back and forth drunkenly, leaderless, until suddenly blown apart, like scattershot, to seek shelter elsewhere.

Silence again.

WTF!?

An odd scent wafts past her. Sour, slightly acrid. Miki can't quite place it, but she knows she's smelled something like it before. It's like the aftermath of burning electrical wires.

And that's when Miki sees it. The dark figure across the street. Standing at the corner. Tall, thin, vague. Staring at her? Miki's not sure. In fact, she's not sure if it's male or female. She barely catches sight of its mottled reflection in the closed bookstore window she's passing, and when she glances back, it's gone.

But there it is again! Up ahead, at the end of the next block.

How did it get ahead of her so fast? Miki has the strange sensation that it's floating, and she's suddenly seized by the memory of that weird thing she saw in Mrs. Deluca's vanity mirror. She casually crosses the street, adopting the traditional evasive maneuver all women in this city instinctively know. If whoever it is wants to stalk her, she'll know soon enough. And then ... what? Miki fingers the can of Mace she always carries in her coat pocket. She ducks into an alley between brownstones hoping it leads to a boulevard with more traffic and people at the other end. Safety in a crowd.

That caustic odor sweeps over her face again. Why does she think she's smelled it somewhere before?

She looks back. It's there! Staring at her. No doubt about it. Miki picks up her pace, but she's pissed at herself for doing it. It's her adrenal medulla overreacting with catecholamines. Flee the danger. Like those birds. She should turn around and confront the sleazebag. Problem is it's now up ahead of her. At the other end of the alley. How is that possible?

It's coming toward her. Fast. Miki backs up, grabbing for her Mace, unwilling to look away. She wants to look in the eyes of the creepy fuck before she blinds them. But there are no eyes. None that she can see yet. There's not much of a face either. Just some oscillating mass that could be male or female. There is a mouth, however. And it's opening. A hideous deafening shriek blares from that hole. Miki drops the Mace to cover her ears, but the pain pierces her skull and goes straight into her mind. There's insanity in that shriek.

Suddenly hands are all over her. Pulling her, dragging her. She flails but they won't let go. She's off her feet and through a doorway which slams so loud it kills the noise.

"Don't look back," a voice orders her.

She can't shake loose the hand that now has her by the wrist and is yanking her into some smelly dark corridor, then down some iron stairs, into another black passage, then down more stairs. Miki is completely disoriented, and she can't break the grip.

"Let me go!" she screams.

Whoever it is slams her into a wall and covers her mouth with a gloved hand.

"Be quiet!" the voice says. It has command but not menace.

Miki complies. She can barely see the outline of a young man, or maybe a teenage boy. Hard to tell. He's wearing one of those "plateau" Wyatt Earp hats Stevie Ray Vaughn made fashionable. The collar of his long coat is up around his chin, but the coat hangs open revealing an elegant Rubinacci vest underneath. And the fringe of a white scarf circling his neck like a priest's collar is sailing behind him on some intermittent breeze. He presses her to the wall with his body and Miki can feel the bony ribcage, the rippled abdomen, the flexed muscles of his thighs holding her there. Not an unpleasant feeling, actually. She wants to see his face, but he's turned away, listening, waiting.

"Okay, you got lucky." He pulls away and heads off into a dark tunnel without further explanation. When she doesn't follow, he turns back and she can see his face for the first time. He looks to be sixteen, seventeen, tops. Sparkling eyes. Smooth ebony skin that would make Miles Davis envious. If it weren't for the tiny soul patch beneath his lower lip, one might think he's not old enough to shave.

When he notices that she isn't following, he says, "Can't go back the way we came, now can we?" He doesn't wait for an answer. Miki has to hurry to catch up as the boy starts to evaporate in the tunnel's darkness. At times she only knows she's following him by the sound of his footsteps up ahead. She has no idea which direction they're going, and she loses all track of time.

"Who are you?" she calls out.

No answer.

"Why did you help me?"

Nothing but a sly chuckle from up ahead.

Miki can feel the roar of subway cars nearby, but she can also smell the rush of sewer water. Good thing he's got that white scarf on. She'd be lost in this labyrinth without it.

Finally they come to a metal ladder pinioned to the wall with rusty braces.

"Up!" the boy says, and it's not a suggestion. "You'll come out on Third Avenue. On your own from there, kid."

"Speak for yourself, *kid*."

Another wry chuckle. The boy is backing away into the darkness.

"Wait! Aren't you coming? You drag me through the catacombs and that's it?"

"You're safe now. What else you want?"

"How 'bout a name. An explanation. Where'd you come from?"

His face is blurring in the shadows. She can barely make out the finger he's putting to that bright smile. "Shhhh."

"Can I at least say thank you?"

"You may." And with that he bows low and elegantly, doffing his hat like D'Artagnan. A moment later he's gone.

Miki emerges through a broken metal door at the top of the ladder into an alley by Third Avenue. The rain has stopped. Miki steps out to find the city busy again with traffic and people. Everything is glistening, and she can hear the hum of everyone's nerves. She thinks she's never seen the city so alive!

As she turns west, back towards Jennifer's apartment, she catches a glimpse of white scarf fringe floating around the corner in the distance. But it's gone so quickly Miki isn't sure she really saw it.

Something is happening to us.
I can't be the only one who sees it.
The only one who feels its presence.
You can feel it too, can't you?
Maybe you don't want to admit it.
But just take a look around.
At the people next to you on the corner.
The ones driving by in their cars.
You'll see it.
Look closely, everyone.
It's time to wake the fuck up!

THE OMINOSITY

12

When Mathis arrives at Angela Rossi's apartment, he's disappointed to find a team from the department's Special Crimes Task Force already on site. A unit which officially doesn't exist. And didn't, in fact, before the Catastrophe. Just before he left the morgue with Miki, he made sure the Assistant Medical Examiner did a rush on prints to confirm the body was who he thought it was. He was hoping to get here before anyone else and have a look around. But the ME must have called it in.

"Well, well, look who's crawled out from under a rock," Detective Freddie Pierce says when he looks up, visibly displeased to see Mathis coming across the room. Mathis is hardly surprised to find him sitting on a fashionable recliner, feet up on the ottoman, polishing off a couple of food truck delicacies. The biggest slacker in Homicide, Freddie Pierce. As corrupt as they come, but far too slick for any shit to stick to his Gucci loafers. At forty-six, "Fat Freddie," as he's known among his colleagues, is just counting days until he can put in his papers, take the train outta Dodge, and live happily ever after, drinking Southern Comfort all day long while shooting small animals from the porch of the upstate cabin he's rumored to own. He has always resented Mathis's swift move up the ranks, and more than once tried to sabotage his cases with sloppy follow-up. When the Dickie Prince murder went down, Freddie was only too happy to make the arrest. Even though Mathis was cleared, he ended up busted down to Missing Persons while Pierce still shuffles his incompetent way to a full pension and major medical.

Mathis sees the stain as soon as he comes into the room. On the wall above behind Fat Freddie. Dark and rusty. Could easily be dismissed as a leak somewhere in the wall. That is ... if similar stains hadn't been showing up all over the city. An emblem of the mysterious accidents and sudden spontaneous violence that's been plaguing the city ever since the Catastrophe.

Which explains the presence of the Special Crimes Task Force.

"Techs say it's some kind of burn or residue," Freddie says.

"Residue? Of what?"

Freddie ignores the question. Because he has no idea and couldn't care less since he doesn't buy the "phantom on the loose" hysteria going around either.

"Bit off your turf, aren't you, pal?" Freddie smirks.

"Her file came across the desk."

"Missing no longer," Fat Freddie chuckles, allowing a rictus grin to pull at his lips.

"Looks like we picked the wrong Public Service, Freddie," Mathis says, looking around an upscale apartment decorated more elegantly than one would expect from someone at Angela Rossi's government pay grade.

"Speak for yourself," Freddie laughs, brushing taco crumbs off his Hugo Boss suit.

Mathis wants to slap the skinny fuck. Why he's called *Fat* Freddie is anyone's guess, because even at six feet he can't possibly weigh more than one hundred forty-five pounds soaking wet. He's an equal opportunity omnivore. Woe to the colleague who leaves even a morsel of food within range of Freddie's indiscriminate gaze.

"Anyway, thanks for the heads up from the morgue," he says,

crushing a greasy taco wrapper between his bony fingers. With his skeletal facial features and his dead stare, Freddie looks more like a predatory bird than a man. "We'll take it from here." In other words, "find something else to do with your life." Nothing Mathis can do except nod and leave.

The last person Mathis needs to see as he storms out of Angela Rossi's apartment is Joe Carlucci from *thedig.com*.

"And my day was going so well," Mathis mumbles.

"I love you, too," Carlucci says, shoving his iPhone in front of Mathis's face. "I wasn't aware you were part of the task force."

Mathis takes a deep breath. He's got to be careful. Anything he says will be repurposed into the narrative Carlucci already has in mind. If Mathis thinks he's on a short leash now, just wait 'til he's quoted in tomorrow morning's *Post*.

"What task force?" he asks without a hint of irony.

Carlucci smiles, keeping his iPhone poised and ready. "I know her from City Hall," he says, nodding toward Angela's building. "Awfully young to be head of the City's Planning and Development Office."

"Guess she had patrons," Mathis suggests not even trying to hide his sarcasm.

"Maybe you boys should be looking into a connection between our girl's recent departure from this life and a secret redevelopment scheme being cooked up over in City Hall. What d'you think?"

Mathis has to struggle to hide his surprise.

"What have you been smoking, Joe?"

"Soon as the quarantine is lifted, I hear. Gonna be a gold rush."

"No one knows how long the quarantine is going to be in effect, Joe. The QZ's a dead zone. Some people are saying it's Chernobyl in there for the next twenty-five years."

"Don't be suckered by conspiracy theorists, Mathis. Although I have to say, I am missing the eloquence of that blogger,

Ominosity. Haven't seen a post in a while. Whatever happened to him?"

"I prefer the rag press, Joe. That's why I read your column."

Mathis gently pushes the iPhone away and Carlucci watches him move off down the street. *Mission accomplished,* he thinks. Mathis has been seriously baited. "It's what they don't say," he says to himself.

13

At the precinct the next morning Mathis doesn't even get to his desk before someone yells his name.

"Mathis!" The voice sounds like something bilious seeping up through sand. "Get in here."

Captain Bartok is filling the door to his office, surveying the room with his basset-hound eyes, still wondering whose ass he forgot to kiss, what gods he forgot to genuflect towards, what simpering bureaucrat he offended that landed him in this purgatory of a precinct on the edge of the Quarantine Zone with its cast of hapless characters. Unlike Freddie Pierce, Joe Bartok is a true believer, a man dedicated to the motto *Fidelis ad Mortem*. *Faithful Unto Death*. No twenty and out for him. He never seems to leave the precinct, which makes goofing off around here a truly creative enterprise. More than one variation of a joke has circulated through the ranks about "Righteous Joe" being found dead at his desk *"although it took weeks before anyone realized he wasn't simply studying case files."* Most of the precinct can't stand Righteous Joe. But Mathis likes him. Always has. At least you know where you stand with Righteous Joe, which is usually at the bottom rungs of the respect-and-admiration ladder.

"What the hell were you doing snooping around the morgue last night?"

"A friend asked me to go with her. She thought the body might be her missing sister. I had no idea it would be Angela Rossi."

Bartok holds Mathis in his skeptical stare. "There's going to be a shitstorm when the news breaks," he continues. "I can't wait to hear our friends in the media cheering on rumors about young women being attacked by toxic mutants lurching out of the QZ."

"What about demons from hell unleashed by the explosion?"

"Don't be a jagoff. I'm warning you in the most sincere way I can, kölyök, all it's gonna take is one whiff you're off the res again and the Dickie Prince case goes back up on the board."

Mathis knows he's right. Even though the fingerprints on Dickie Prince's murder weapon didn't stand up to scrutiny, Bartok had to use a shitload of his political capital and goodwill to convince IA to shelve murder charges. Still, most everyone remains suspicious that Mathis somehow got away with it. Fat Freddie's constant innuendo hasn't helped.

"Look, Captain, while I was following Dickie, I saw him with Rossi. Cozy little conversation in a dive down in Chinatown. A payoff gabfest, I'm sure. A fat envelope changed hands."

This gets Bartok's attention. "A payoff gabfest?"

"And I'm not surprised. You should take a look at her apartment. Now we all know Dickie used to do the odd job for Emeril Benedict ..."

"Okay, stop right there." Bartok lets go a long-suffering sigh. "Just the name makes me want to drop my badge on this desk and go join a seniors' bowling league. Isn't it enough you want to peddle conspiracy theories about what happened New Year's Eve, now you wanna cast the city's biggest Capo in the leading role?"

Mathis knows how this sounds. Bartok thinks he's trying to turn a breeze into a hurricane. Benedict is the acknowledged overlord of the city's criminal enterprises. Poor boy made good. Up from penny-ante crap games downtown to four star restaurants and private clubs uptown. Benedict believes in the equal opportunity of corruption, and he has parlayed that conviction into a multimillion-dollar business. He's one of the untouchables now. The kind who has graduated from mere thuggery to more creative and sinister means of persuasion. Why would he be involved in a botched explosion in a downtown nightclub that's turned the city upside down?

But that very question is what pokes Mathis's spidey sense.

"Connect the dots, Captain. Dickie's meeting up with the head of the City's Planning and Development Office to pass along a little goodwill. Then, he's going around town shooting his mouth off about the Club Nightshade explosion, trying to impress everyone with what he might or might not know. Someone then makes Dickie dead. All of a sudden, Angela Rossi turns up stuffed into a subway drainage gutter. Something about it has to strike you as just a little bit hinky, right?"

"The whole city is hinky, you want my opinion."

"And now I'm hearing about secret redevelopment plans being cooked up for the QZ after the quarantine is lifted."

Mathis detects a frightened tension starting to sweep up Bartok's spine.

"And you're hearing this where?" the Captain demands.

Mathis reluctantly coughs it up. "Joe Carlucci ..."

"Oh, Christ on a cracker. You're getting leads from that cockroach now? Next you're gonna tell me Emeril Benedict orchestrated the New Year's Eve explosion ... in a building, by the way, that just happened to be sitting on a chemical weapons storage dump forgotten for seventy-five years ... so he could cause a quarantine and take over the neighborhood."

"What am I supposed to think!?"

"You're supposed to think if I don't behave myself, my ass is going down! And then, you're supposed to do what we agreed. Which is stand down! Quit freelancing. Your daughter was at the right place at the wrong time, Levi. Like a lot of others, I might add. And my heart truly aches. For you, for everyone who lost someone in the Catastrophe. But you're not out of the woods.

You keep this up, I won't be able to protect you. The long-knives are out."

"What does that tell you?"

"It tells me to keep my head down. You better do the same."

The Artful Dodger

"He had about him all the airs and manners of a
man. His hat was stuck on the top of head so
lightly that it threatened to fall off every moment …
and would have done so, very often, if the wearer
had not had a knack of every now and then giving
his head a sudden twitch, which brought it back to
its old place again. He was, altogether, as roystering
and swaggering a young gentleman as ever roamed
the city's night."
—Charles Dickens

14

Dickens could have been describing Willy G. A second-story man, which, tonight, is the literal description of his activity because he has chosen to burgle a loft/condo on the second floor of a converted warehouse instead of the Midtown brownstones he's been invading recently. The police call him a cat burglar, but Willy resents the term. It's low-class and lacks the appropriate respect for style. And if there is one thing Willy G prides himself on it's his style. Clean, silent, purposeful. Sometimes it takes people several days to discover they've been visited by Willy G. He has a strict moral code. He redistributes wealth only from those he knows won't really miss it. He hates violence. He won't victimize his own. And he's never stolen anything he reckons might have precious or sentimental value. Except once, when he took a Picasso sketch, not knowing what it really was but simply because he liked the look of it. He fenced it to Johnny Waffles for a hundred bucks but then found out later the owner valued it at over two hundred thousand. Willy was mightily pissed off. Should have asked Johnny for a grand. What was worse, though, was when the bereft octogenarian owner tearfully told the media that he couldn't have cared less how much the painting was worth. To him it was priceless because Picasso himself had given it to him when he was a twenty-year-old GI in postwar Paris pursuing the love of his life. He was a dirt-poor Delancey Park kid then and had no hope of impressing this wealthy Sixteenth Arrondissement debutante. After listening to his tale of woe over multiple Pernods in a Montmartre café, Picasso took pity and drew something on the spot. With this sketch, which Willy G read later foreshadowed Picasso's neo-Expressionist period, the great artist promised the young man he could win the girl's heart. It worked, and they stayed happily married for sixty years until she died. The story appealed to Willy G's sense of valor and chivalry against all odds. He always imagined himself to be a romantic rebel. So, he stole the sketch back from Johnny Waffles, snuck back into the elegant Browns Hill apartment where he'd taken it, and put it back on the wall.

Willy can get into the most secure townhouses, the most exclusive clubs, the most expensive hotels to steal. Most times he keeps his ambitions in check. Loose jewelry is best, the easiest to fence, and cash is best of all. He will also steal things of relatively little value, like a full roast beef from the kitchen of a fancy restaurant with which he'll feed his crew of teenage gypsies for several days.

He's chosen this converted loft tonight because it looks easy to get into. He knows this because he's been scouting the place for several weeks. He knows what the couple who live here eat, when they are awake or asleep. He knows the woman has nice jewelry. He knows the man always has cash. And most important, they retreat to a country home they own somewhere else as often as they can to escape the city's post-Catastrophe malaise. A perfect opportunity for Willy to initiate his protégé into the craft of helping oneself.

He discovered little Shivers one night trembling in a condemned empty apartment building by the river where he'd been hiding for almost twelve hours. Willy had been detouring through the decrepitude after one of his reconnaissance missions.

"You with the Dukes?" the boy asked jumping to his hands and knees like an Olympic sprinter ready for the starting gun.

Willy understood right away why the boy had been cowering like some rat evading a tomcat in this smelly basement.

"Ringolevio, huh?" Willy laughed, referring to the street game every kid in this city learned before they were ten years old. After Willy reassured the boy that he was not from the enemy tribe, Shivers identified himself as one of the Bluff Park Sparrows. He'd been watching the Dukes' den across the street, counting the number of his teammates who had been captured.

"Almost got us all, now. I may be the last man out. And not for long."

"Then we better get to work," Willy said, and he confidently led Shivers out a boarded-up door and gave him the strategy.

"I got these bootleg mixtapes in my pockets, see? I'll bribe the Duke jailors and get them to leave the premises for a coupla minutes."

"Ain't that illegal?" Shivers asked.

"Frowned upon, I'll admit, but a perfectly legal gambit," Willy answered with such obvious confidence Shivers just nodded and went along. "Once they come with me to see the swag, you run in, call out 'Free All' and vamoose with your teammates."

It worked, and Willy later heard chatter on the street that the Sparrows regained the advantage and crushed the Dukes, acquiring bragging rights and many serious challenges in the months to come. From that night on, Shivers was in awe of Willy G. He'd follow him everywhere, making such a pest of himself that Willy finally had to "adopt" him into his crew.

When Willy found out that Miki Preston had come to the city to look for her sister, he chose Shivers as the one to anonymously deliver the flash drive Jennifer had entrusted to him.

But tonight is the first time Willy has allowed Shivers to accompany him on a job. They slink across the roof of the warehouse, Willy dressed in his customary black jeans and hoody under which a silk balaclava obscures all of his face except the eyes. Shivers has on a dark sweater and grimy Beastie Boys cap which is too big for his head. A small pouch of tools is slung over Willy's shoulder with an old belt. Simple tools which he has acquired over many months pilfering hardware stores and apartment dumpsters. Several small screw drivers, a wrench, some lockpicks he five-fingered when one of his competitors wasn't looking, some wire cutters for the alarm system connection, if any, a pair of ultrathin latex gloves, and his most prized tool, a center hole punch and porcelain chip. Tiny, quick and effective. He's been teaching Shivers how to use it for the past week. The kid is a fast learner.

Willy lowers Shivers over the ledge by one arm until the boy can reach the narrow bathroom window. With one crack of the hole punch a frosted pane of glass shatters softly and the boy reaches in to unlatch the lock. He slips inside like a ghost as Willy follows down a drainpipe. The lingering scent of cigar smoke permeates the atmosphere and makes Willy pause, but only for a moment. He knows the owners are away. Saw them leave for the country yesterday. They don't have to rush.

He finds Shivers just beyond the bathroom door staring reverently at luxury and comfort he's never imagined.

"Yo," the boy whispers, "people really live like this?"

"You have no idea," Willy says.

"Where do we start?" He's a kid on Christmas morning.

"First, we eat," Willy says, pulling the boy to the kitchen where they help themselves to hunks of aged cheddar, a couple of fresh Granny Smith apples, and two of those small green bottles of Pellegrino. Willy also pockets a couple of Menendez Y Garcia Montechristos from the humidor he finds in the wine cooler. Good for bribes, if necessary. And he makes sure to grab a Hefty Ultra Strong Kitchen Trash Bag he finds in the cabinets under the sink.

"For our trash," he instructs Shivers. "Never ever leave anything behind." As they feast, Willy takes a moment to savor the view across the open-plan layout. The decor is an eclectic mix of minimalist modern chic, exposed early twentieth-century brick, and ash wood plank. Not his taste, except for the one-hundred-inch LED backlit 4D curved TV screen above the gas fireplace. That's something he could covet. But not tonight.

He finishes his Pellegrino, stashes their empty bottles in the Hefty with the apple cores and cheese crumbs, and pads quickly through the great room to the master where he intends to show Shivers how to sweep the closets for jewels, perhaps cash. But as soon as he crosses the threshold, he sees it. That scorch on the wall the color of dried blood. Next to the mirror above the massive bed. Willy freezes as if caught in the glare of a policeman's flashlight.

"Outta here!" Willy mutters, backing out the door in fast rewind.

"But we didn't get nothin'," Shivers complains as Willy hurries him to the bathroom where they came in.

"Zip it," Willy hisses. "Get up on my back."

Willy climbs to the ledge of the window, quickly tapes a piece of plastic over the pane Shivers broke, and pulls the curtains closed. No one will notice they've been here until they try to figure out why the security alarm malfunctioned and discover where he snipped the phone line. Instead of scurrying back up to the roof, he shimmies down between the walls of this building and the next like a disturbed spider. Barely enough space for his slim body and the growth of the little boy now attached to his back, but enough to make a quick descent to the alley where Willy slips off his balaclava, reverses his hoody and hurries them into Friday night traffic empty-handed.

A few blocks later, he disposes of the Hefty in a dumpster then ducks with Shivers into the old hotel from which they emerged only an hour ago. They slink past the front desk before the clerk looks up from a baseball game on TV. In the basement, Willy finds the neglected door which leads to abandoned steam tunnels below the street. Twenty minutes of urban spelunking later they arrive at the forgotten locker room and showers Willy believes were once used by city sanitation workers. This is where he keeps his other personality. He stashes his satchel in one of the lockers and changes out of the dark burglar uniform back into his trademark long coat, vest, hat, and white scarf, angry with himself for the aborted mission tonight.

"We get up to the street, we separate. You let the others know there's no party tonight."

"What happened, Willy? Why'd we break off?" Shivers asks, slightly scared and not understanding why.

"I'll explain later. But this was a good lesson, kid, so remember it. Caution is the key to a thief's survival."

What he doesn't say is that it's always better to leave money on the table than confront the city's golems. That way you'll live to steal another day.

A few moments later, they emerge from a utility corridor into the Beal Street station, and after Willy does his routine survey of the platform to make sure no familiar cops are loitering about who might harass him, he and Shivers hurry up to the street and head off in different directions. Willy is still so spooked by that ugly stain he saw on the condo bedroom ceiling that he never hears the footsteps skipping out of the shadows behind him until it's too late.

"Past your bedtime, Willy," Mathis says with a sardonic grin as he pulls Willy into an alley.

"Ah, Mathis. It would be you," Willy sighs.

"Off on a little late-night scavenging, huh?" Mathis asks, doing a cursory pat down for effect.

"Nah. Can't sleep is all. You know how that is, don't you?"

"Why I was thinking of you."

Willy takes a step back. He can see it coming. "Oh no, Mathis.

Not this time. You're kinda toxic these days, case you hadn't noticed."

"It was you who put me on to Dickie Prince and the Silver Street boys in the first place, Willy."

"All I said was that my crew heard he was running his mouth about the New Year's Eve explosion. Never thought you'd barge into his kingdom and nail his hand to a table with his own knife."

"It was self-defense."

"That's what they all say."

"He came at me. I reacted."

"In front of his whole crew. So when he ends up with a shiv in his spine, who do they think of first?"

"I didn't kill him, Willy. But I think I know who did. If I'm right, it makes perfect sense he'd want his errand boy out of the way."

Willy can't help laughing. A humorless, almost frightened chuckle. "Man, you must have a death wish, Mathis. Why would an uptown Lucifer like Emeril Benedict need to blow up a chump-change slum squat like Club Nightshade?"

"That's what I'm asking myself. Something truly fucked is going on."

"No shit. Just take a look around. Somethin's gotten loose in this city, Mathis. And it's gettin' worse every day."

"C'mon, Willy, you're too smart to be peddling mumbo jumbo."

"There are more things in heaven and earth, Horatio, than are dreamt of in your philosophy," Willy says with a frown.

"You consistently surprise me, Willy."

"What, you think I can't read?"

"Oh, I know you can read. It's *what* you read that amazes me."

"Yeah? Well, maybe you should listen to what the Bard has to say." Willy's eyes dance around the dark alley behind Mathis, as if scanning the area for something dark and dangerous that might suddenly come oozing out of the walls.

"The only boogeyman I'm interested in is Emeril Benedict," Mathis says.

"And good luck with that." Willy doffs his hat and tries to move off, but Mathis holds him there.

"You've got eyes and ears all over this city, Willy. You and your crew. No one pays attention to you. You're ghosts."

"And I intend to keep it that way. That's how dodgers like us survive."

"All I want you to do is hang around, listen to the street. Let me know what you hear. Anything about the QZ, anything about New Year's Eve. If Benedict was involved, there's a reason. He doesn't do anything without a payoff. And this one would have had to be big." Mathis steps back, giving Willy some space to think about it.

Willy just glares at him. "You know, man, I like you. You're straight up, even though you are a cop. But you gotta let this go."

"I can be helpful, Willy. You know that."

Willy is feeling trapped. Yeah, Mathis can be helpful. They've had plenty of encounters over the years some of which might have gone down rather badly for Willy if Mathis hadn't intervened. He's always appreciated Mathis's style. The man definitely has his own moral code. Just like Willy. But this, this is crazy even for Mathis. "I ain't promisin' nothin'," Willy says, hoping it's enough.

"There's no scorecard here, Willy. I'm just asking for headlines. If there are any."

Willy finally nods. Satisfied, Mathis heads back up the alley to the street.

"What are we gonna do about the sister?" Willy calls out. This stops Mathis, but he doesn't turn back. "I've been keepin' an eye on her now and again."

"Feeling guilty?"

"Something like that."

Mathis finally turns. "I haven't told her," he says, "if that's what you're worried about."

"She don't belong here, Mathis. Not now. It's too crazy. You need to tell her to go home." Willy waits for Mathis to agree.

"I've tried. Your turn," he says, vanishing around a corner.

"Shit," Willy mutters to himself. Yeah, he's feeling guilty all right, and he's going to have to do something about it. Sooner than later.

15

The face in Miki's sketch is deliberately unremarkable.

It's clearly a young man, but generic, like the leading man in a graphic novel. More a type than a person. But the long coat and broad hat give it away immediately as the nightcrawler who rescued her from her stalker the other night. The one who led her on that creepy odyssey through the fetid underground of the city. Miki retouches the area around the mouth. That she remembers well. The smile, the bright teeth. Confident, slightly arrogant even. No, wait. Not arrogant.

Erasure. Redraw.

Not arrogant. Fearless.

It would be silly in the extreme to think she'll ever see him again. So why bother even considering it? She draws a big question mark in the margins next to the words, *"My Hero."* Her calligraphy is extravagant. The penmanship equivalent of sarcasm. Maybe if he was a few years older ...

The shadows in her sister's kitchen make Miki tense. Long abstract shapes thrown across the floor and cupboards by the buildings in the Quarantine Zone as the sun retreats behind them. They sway and slide as the light refracts every time a breeze pushes against the windows as if they were alive. She can spend the better part of an hour tracking their movement, sipping tea, while dissonant melodies in the city's ambience accompany their slow-motion choreography.

"There is more truth in dissonance than harmony," her sister used to say. Miki sketches Jennifer's words next to the nightcrawler's face.

Outside, the lights of the QZ perimeter barricades are coming on. Garish dual-arc sodium beams aimed not at the desolation inside the Quarantine Zone but at the streets bordering it instead. A blinding shield to obscure the bleakness beyond. Vague silhouettes of dark, evacuated buildings are the only evidence there ever was a life beyond the perimeter wall. HazMats and security are the only ones roaming around in there at night, hiding whatever that work is behind the glow of those beams. Authorities insist they're simply trying to gauge residual contamination levels, but the social media that escapes official censorship suggests something more sinister, much of it insinuating that a supernatural phenomenon has been released in there. Amazingly, Miki finds herself considering the notion. If it weren't for Jennifer's photos, she might be able to dismiss those phantoms she's seen as mere figments of a sleep-deprived, emotionally overwrought brain. But then, there are these pictures. And those odd figures hovering in the backgrounds.

"Ridiculous," she mutters, shoving the photos aside. Mathis is right. Specters do not exist. Period. The supernatural, in all its incarnations, is simply a narrative chimera humans have used since the dawn of time to explain their fears and failings. We've invented gods and monsters, she reminds herself, to exonerate our intellectual limitations. Still, who's to say the post-Catastrophe contamination hasn't birthed another kind of terror, something mutant, something predatory, something *real* plaguing the city that's now finishing off the tenuous social order that used to exist?

The darkening sky makes Miki remember she hasn't eaten a thing all day. She's been sitting here musing over her sister's disappearance and her inability to divine the meaning of the clues left behind in her photographs. Time to brave the streets for some of Mrs. Oh's noodles. Who knows? Maybe she'll catch sight of her *hero*'s white scarf sailing in the wind.

Before she gets to Oh's Deli, she hears it. The white noise of an angry crowd, interrupted occasionally by amplified commands to *move along*, to *disperse*, to *leave the area immediately*. She comes around a corner and sees the mob. It's gathered at the QZ checkpoint, confronting a barrier of flak-jacketed security personnel just inside the gates. A dozen of those hideous drones hover above the fence with their maddening buzz and blinding halogen beams aimed at the crowd.

Some of the protestors are throwing trash at the fence, or over it, but the sentinels inside remain passive and unprovoked. For the moment. Which only pisses the rowdies off even more. The cacophony grows louder, more profane, more personal.

Miki slinks along the edges of the crowd trying to get a glimpse of what's provoked the outburst. Inside the fence, full-suited HazMats congregate in clusters, shielded from the anger but clearly worried about how long they'll remain that way.

Suddenly, there's surge in the crowd, a wave of emotion pushing it closer to the fence. More debris is hurled. Miki finally gets close enough to see what has caused it. At one of those decontamination tubes that snake through the barrier into the QZ itself, several bodies are being rushed on stretchers to black unmarked ambulances. These are not official EMS vehicles. They're deliberately nondescript. A squad of HazMats and security personnel follow behind, escorting a handful of dirty and exhausted civilians out of the Quarantine Zone, wrists tied with plastic "cobra" cuffs, being shoved unceremoniously toward idling troop carriers where ominous-looking men in black suits are making notes. No one inside the gates even pauses to acknowledge the shouts of protestors on the streets demanding to know where these captives are being taken. Names are screamed in the hope that someone among the detained will answer back. Perhaps someone previously thought to be missing, lost, or deceased. But only one responds. He raises his arms and shouts toward the protestors *"LIES! ALL LIES!"* before he is brutally shoved to his knees.

The crowd becomes enraged. A few try to scale the perimeter fence before being knocked back to the ground by vicious baton blows to their fingers and feet. And that's when a Molotov cocktail sails over the perimeter fence, exploding in a shower of liquid flame right in front of the military blockade. One of the soldiers staggers back, on fire, while several of his compatriots throw him to the ground to smother the flames.

Inside the fence, soldiers line up and start firing tear gas and rubber bullets. At the back of the crowd, horrible screams make everyone turn to see the arrival of personnel carriers disgorging masked troops who immediately wade forward cracking skulls. Miki tries to snake her way through flying fists, thrown bricks, flaming beer bottles, and rifle butts. Tear gas fogs the entire street. It's impossible to see more than a foot or two in front of one's face. The stink is acrid and corrosive. She starts to gag and retch. Everything is a fragmented rampage of violence and panic. For all she knows, she could be running towards the QZ perimeter instead of away from it.

Something hot and stinging knocks her off her feet. She looks down to see a small tear in her pants leg and the welt from a rubber missile instantly blooming on her thigh. She tries to crawl behind a parked car, but a bloodied protestor holding his face staggers into her path and steps on her ankle, nearly breaking it. Miki screams in pain and goes fetal. Her eyes burn and blur. She's disoriented by the crush of frantic bodies and the flare of spotlight beams, but as she tries to cover up she catches sight of something moving in the mayhem that makes her freeze.

Shapes moving through the chaos. Dark translucent figures, vaguely humanoid but mercurial. For a second, Miki tries to convince herself they're just the swirl of tear gas and smoke from the mob's firebombs. But they don't evaporate or disperse, and Miki is seized by a frightening sense of déja vu. These *things* resemble the mysterious shapes in Jennifer's photographs. They seem to be coagulating among the crush of adversaries, as if animated by the hostility, as if breeding in the toxic tide pool of this pandemonium.

Before she can hobble to her feet to get a better look, Miki is grabbed from behind. Someone is dragging her away from the gas and the violence. She struggles to get away, but whoever has hold of her is too strong. She catches a glimpse of those unmarked ambulances rushing to the perimeter gate, wedging themselves with the help of baton-wielding soldiers through the melee until they reach the boulevard and speed away.

"Stop fighting me!" a voice yells into her ear. "You got no business out here. You just gonna get your head cracked."

And Miki knows instantly who it is. Her "*hero*." She twists on her good ankle to face him.

"Who are you!?"

"We need to talk. But not here." Just like last time, Willy G yanks Miki into an alley and through a bent metal door that leads to darkness. Miki is immediately overwhelmed by the stench of old sewers and rotting garbage, but this time Willy keeps a firm grip on her arm, and Miki surprises herself by not resisting.

"I'm not going to hurt you," Willy promises.

"I know," Miki answers, which makes Willy slow down ever so slightly.

After about fifteen minutes and several excursions through tight crawl spaces and up and down various wall ladders, Miki can see a dim light up ahead. The sound of voices drifts through the darkness toward them. Small voices. Kids' voices.

"This is my crew," Willy says as he leads Miki into a dingy

room lit by several bare bulbs strung together by a long extension cable that recedes into the ceiling and some unseen power outlet there. There are a half dozen boys sitting on a couple of threadbare couches and legless chairs. Stained mattresses littered with comics and graphic novels line one wall. Old video-game players, CDs, and DVDs are scattered thoughtlessly everywhere. It's a clubhouse of the dispossessed.

"That's Red over there," Willy says. "He's my numero uno." Then pointing to each boy in turn, "Ronny, Matchbook, Louis Uptown, Mac." The boys just glare at Miki, not even a nod or hint of a friendly smile.

The little kid from Willy's earlier B&E excursion sidles up to his mentor, keeping a wary but curious eye on Miki. "And this here's Shivers. He's our newest member. Go get her some water," Willy says, and Shivers scampers over to a small dorm-room fridge with a broken handle. "We gotta douse those eyes," Willy tells Miki. "Get rid of the gas." He leads her to a chair away from the others and holds her head back while dripping water onto her face.

"Becoming a habit, isn't it," she says, "you always showing up just in time."

"You sure know how to borrow trouble, girl. Just like your sister."

Miki lurches up, knocking the water bottle out of Willy's hands.

"What? What did you just say?"

Willy's crew freezes.

"I been wanting to tell you," Willy finally answers.

"You know my sister? You know w ... w ... where she is!?"

"Yes. And no. I mean, I know where she went, but I don't know what happened after that."

"What the f ... f ... fuck, man?"

"I was going to explain. I was standing outside your apartment trying to figure a way, but I waited too long. Fate intervened. You came outside and ended up in the middle of that shitstorm."

"So explain now!" She's almost screaming at him.

"She and her boyfriend ..."

"Jonas."

"Yeah, him. They paid me to take them. Not together. Separately."

"Take them? Take them where?"

Willy glances over to his crew, looking for moral support. All he gets instead are "told-you-so" shrugs.

"The QZ," Willy admits.

"You took them into the Quarantine Zone?"

Willy is almost offended by her disbelief.

"Hey, I can get from one end of this city to the other without ever coming up for air."

"But why? W ... w ... why would you do that? Why would they w ... w ... want to?"

"To find out what really went down New Year's Eve."

Miki is stunned silent, unable to get control of the fears now rampaging through her brain. Images of bodies being brought out of the QZ on stretchers flood her thoughts. "Oh, God ..."

"I tried to talk them out of it," Willy continues. "But Jonas, he was sure there was more going on in there than the government was saying. And when your sister found out I'd shown him the way, she made me show her, too, so she could go find him."

"There's not supposed to be anyone in the QZ."

"So they say."

"It's c ... c ... contaminated!"

"Yeah, they say that, too. But you saw those people coming out tonight, right?"

"So maybe they've caught up to Jennifer, too. Maybe the government has her. Is that what you're s ... s ... saying?" Miki's hope is restrained by trepidation at the thought.

"There'd be worse things that could happen to her," he mutters with a furtive glance toward his boys.

Miki can sense the tension in the squat suddenly rising. Fidgeting, whispering, and averted eye contact.

"Wait a minute," she says, revelation sweeping over her. "You've seen them! Those ph ... ph ... phantoms. The ones they make fun of on the news. They were there tonight. In the middle of that riot. You must've seen them."

"Yeah, I seen 'em."

A claustrophobic dread descends, and the subterranean ambience down here transforms into an almost menacing growl.

"What are they? Where do they come from?"

All eyes are on Willy now. It takes him a moment to decide how to answer.

"There are places everywhere in this city where hostility gathers ..." he finally says.

"Sounds like something that blogger Ominosity has said."

"Ominosity knows," Willy agrees, repeating the graffiti phrase scrawled all over the city.

"My sister photographed them! They're real."

"Oh yeah, they're real. And there's more of 'em now. Ever since the Catastrophe," Willy says, throwing a cautioning glare over his crew. "We call 'em Paramentals."

"I have to get out of here," Miki says, lurching to her feet.

"Good idea. This is no place for you. Take Mathis's advice. Get out of this city and go home."

Miki turns abruptly and levels him with a stare that could freeze fire. And across the room, little Shivers whispers to Red.

"Oooops."

Mathis is at his usual perch in McBride's, tormenting himself with the customary untouched glass of Laphroaig when the door slams open and Miki storms across the room. As soon as he sees

Willy sheepishly shambling in behind her, Mathis knows what's coming.

"You son of a b ... b ... bitch," Miki snarls. "You knew all along and you wouldn't tell me."

"I told you your sister went places she shouldn't have."

"Conveniently leaving out the part about it being the f ... f ... fucking Q ... Q ... Quarantine Zone!"

"You think I haven't made inquiries? You think I knew she bribed her way into the QZ and never followed up? There's nothing. No record of her being found there. Alive ... or dead."

A deep shudder sweeps over Miki. "What about Jonas, then? What happened to him!?"

Mathis throws a hard look over to Willy who puts his hands up in surrender.

"A patrol found him in there," Mathis says. "He was wounded trying to escape."

"Escape?"

"He was with some scavengers, apparently. His office said he's had some kind of breakdown. In a hospital ever since. Recuperating."

"H ... h ... hospital where?" Miki demands.

"His office won't say. Patient privacy, and all that."

"He was a public servant, for Chrissakes. Press Officer for the Public Affairs Office. He's wounded in the QZ with a bunch of looters and no one is talking about it?"

"State of Emergency protocols. Authorities are censoring all news coming out of the QZ, case you hadn't noticed."

"This is b ... b ... bullshit. Jennifer went in there looking for him. What's happened to her?" She's shouting now.

"Look, Miki, if your sister was caught sneaking around in there, you'd be visiting her in lockup. Everyone they've found who refused to leave, or anyone detained after sneaking back in," he said, narrowing his glare at Willy G, "is removed to biocontainment isolation for evaluation."

"Then where is she!?"

Mathis almost reaches for his Scotch. Jennifer Preston is either still wandering the QZ looking for her boyfriend, unlikely, or she's hiding somewhere, sick with contamination, a possibility, or she's hunkering down somewhere no one can find her for reasons only she can understand. The most plausible explanation. But none of them will satisfy her bereft sister, and Mathis knows it.

"I have no idea." That's all he can muster at the moment.

"Why didn't you tell me, Mathis? Why shine me on like you have?"

"I wanted you to go back home. I wanted you to stay out of this mess and let things sort themselves out on their own. Your sister is going to turn up. Sooner or later." And he feels he has to add, "One way ... or the other."

Miki's fighting back tears. "You should have t ... t ... told me."

"What would you have done if I had?" he says.

"What I'm going to do now!" She wheels around and heads for the door, brushing past Willy, still there watching, without so much as a nod.

Willy looks back at Mathis who just sighs and slides off his stool to follow her.

16

Miki is waiting in the cavernous lobby of the city's Public Affairs Office feeling slightly gamey. She's been sitting in these purposefully uncomfortable hard chairs ever since they allowed her in at seven this morning. Before that, she'd been camped outside on the cold marble steps all night, ignoring Mathis who kept bringing her coffee and crappy deli sandwiches, which she refused the few times she even acknowledged his presence.

She looks small in this expansive space. She *feels* small in this arena of indifference. It's designed this way deliberately, she decides, to intimidate, to diminish. After signing in, no one has acknowledged her. Not one of the seemingly purposeful bureaucrats flitting in and out of offices with their severe, self-important grimaces, has ever glanced in her direction. Even the security guard perched behind his podium like a Roman Praetorian has never looked up at her. So here she sits, the only one in the place, staring at muted soap operas playing on wall-mounted TV monitors. No images of the wild faces and shaking fists of protestors gathering outside for their daily shouting matches with city authorities. No news footage of the riot last night at the QZ perimeter. The quarantine of truth appears to be working just as well in the media as the one in the streets.

Mathis is sitting nearby, trying not to nod off, and Miki fights the urge to soften her anger at him. She wants to remain on edge when, *if*, someone consents to speak with her. At least he made it clear to the robot at reception that he represented the police in this matter, and that Ms. Preston was not to be ignored, delayed, or otherwise dismissed. She ought to be slightly grateful.

She picks up her diary again. Flips pages until she comes to a sketch she's made of Jennifer. With that afterthought hairstyle, that penetrating but nonjudgmental stare, that enigmatic half-smile slightly tugging at her mouth. Miki's thoughts cascade down the side of the drawing in her elegant, runelike handwriting.

> *"She had everything,"* Miki is thinking.
> *"Good looks. Smart. My*
> *parents' pride. She was going to*
> *change the world. Last any of us*
> *heard, one brief text. 'Left on*
> *assignment. Will be in touch.' She*
> *was gone, poof, vanished. But I*
> *was the one who was invisible."*

Miki remembers the day she told her mother and father she was going into the city to find Jennifer. They hardly objected, and she still can't decide if it was despair or indifference.

"Miss Preston ..."

Finally.

A slender woman carrying a file folder comes out a security door, waiting to be sure the lock triggers as soon as she closes it behind her.

"Sorry for the wait," she chirps as she approaches and extends a hand. "Brenda Watkins. I am ... I mean I was Angela Rossi's executive assistant. I hope you can appreciate how busy this office is these days. It's a difficult time for all of us." She has one of those patronizing "I feel your pain" expressions, and the way she avoids eye contact has Miki spooked. She keeps looking over at Mathis, who is roused now and hovering a respectful distance away.

"Perhaps you would like to come with me?" Brenda says, indicating that security door with her file folder.

Miki hesitates. The term "emergency protocols" flashes through her mind. One might go in but never come back out. As if intuiting Miki's reluctance, Brenda steps closer to quietly reassure. "Officer Mathis can accompany us, if that would make you feel more comfortable."

Miki finally acknowledges Mathis behind her and nods. She may still be pissed at him, but maybe it's not a bad idea to have a cop on her side of the table. Brenda leads them to the door and punches in her code. A moment later, the seal is breached and Brenda heads off down an intersecting corridor to a small conference room. She holds the door open for Miki and Mathis.

"Please, sit down, Ms. Preston." She takes a chair opposite Miki and begins a review of the report in that file folder.

"Look, Brenda, mind if I call you Brenda?" Miki asks but doesn't wait for an answer. "My sister has been missing for over six weeks." She drops her sketch of Jennifer on top of Brenda's file to break the woman's concentration. "Missing, Brenda. Ever since she managed to sneak into the Quarantine Zone. To look for her boyfriend, *Jonas Flack*! He was arrested in there."

Brenda looks up from the file. But not at Miki. At Mathis. An accusatory scowl. "That is privileged information, Miss Preston. The reasons for Mr. Flack's alleged excursion into the QZ are …"

Miki interrupts. "I want to speak with him! He may know where Jennifer is."

"Jonas Flack is currently under doctor's care. He's not allowed to see anyone."

"Where?" Miki presses.

"I'm not at liberty to discuss that. I'm sure you can understand, there are privacy considerations here."

Miki can feel the stutter tic surging. But she doesn't care. "I don't give a s ... s ... shit about p ... p ... privacy. Or your so-called p ... p ... privileged information. Jonas worked in this office." She shakes her head violently to dispel the tic and get control. Her voice descends to a low whisper. "He was a friend of your former boss, Angela Rossi. Who was found in a subway ditch and is now laid out in the city morgue."

Brenda flinches visibly, throwing another dirty look Mathis's way.

"She found that out on her own," he pushes back.

"I want to know why Jonas was in the QZ and why my sister went after him," Miki says. "And I want to know where she is now!"

For the first time Brenda holds Miki's stare, and this time a genuine compassion sweeps over her. She slowly lifts the sketch of Jennifer off her file and sets it aside.

"Miss Preston, at Officer Mathis's insistence I have made inquiries. Frankly, I've had to pull some strings and violate more than a few conditions of my employment. But I've located these files." There's a pause. The kind you hear before the axe falls. "I am very sorry to tell you this. Your sister, Jennifer, is deceased."

Miki goes rigid. Her eyes refuse to blink. But her hands curl involuntarily into white-knuckle fists.

"Soldiers found her on a routine patrol some weeks ago. Her body was brought to one of our quarantine facilities where an autopsy was performed. Customary protocol for all victims found in the QZ. Your sister had been exposed to fatal amounts of contamination."

"What kind of contamination?" Miki's voice is cold as arctic frost.

"We're still trying to determine the exact nature of the toxins. However, the autopsy is consistent with other victims retrieved inside the QZ. There were indisputable indications of severe tetra paresis and central nervous system collapse. Your sister became paralyzed. Her entire body locked up. I'm afraid she suffocated."

"I don't believe you," Miki says with a chill that borders on the menacing.

Brenda sighs and passes a morgue photo across the desk. A photo of Jennifer on a surgical gurney, dead-glass eyes, still open, mouth gaping in a silent scream, muscles strained like overly taut guitar strings.

"Why weren't we notified?" Miki's voice is starting to quiver.

"We try to notify next of kin as quickly as possible. But, frankly, we're still overwhelmed. The emergency protocols ..."

"FUCK THE EMERGENCY PROTOCOLS," Miki yells, slamming her fists on the table.

Brenda maintains her calm and soldiers on. "Emergency protocols require that we fully vet the circumstance of any individual's demise before releasing information. This requires extensive testing and lab work. It's a matter of public safety. And in your sister's case, there are additional complications. She was trespassing in the QZ. Criminal procedures must be followed."

"Gonna throw her body in jail?" Miki laughs sardonically.

Brenda glances nervously at Mathis. He seems to know what's coming.

"What?" Miki demands, glancing back and forth between them.

Brenda's posture stiffens. As if getting ready for fight-or-flight.

"She's been cremated, Miki," Mathis finally says.

"It's required by law, Miss Preston," Brenda adds. "In the aftermath of the Catastrophe. For anyone succumbing inside the QZ, anyone exposed to the contamination."

Miki deflates. If she were liquid, she would spill out of the chair into a puddle on the floor. Mathis reaches for her, but she still has enough energy to swat him away.

"I will make every effort to expedite the return of her remains to you and your family. If you'll just allow me to make a few notations where you can be reached ..."

Before Brenda can finish, Miki is on her feet, shoving her chair back so violently it hits the wall and overturns. She ices Brenda with a homicidal glare, then turns it on Mathis.

"I'm sorry," he mumbles, but she doesn't hear him.

She's out of the room before he can close his mouth.

17

It's calm now inside the QZ perimeter. Soldiers are engaged in routine patrols along the fence, but their vigil seem casual, even bored. The HazMats are sitting on crates by the operations tents, drinking coffee, smoking cigarettes, recalibrating their environmental monitoring gear. With their headgear off, it's easy to clock their exhausted expressions. Conversation is curt and monosyllabic, the hollow dialogue that follows an all-night shift.

There is no traffic, human or vehicular, in the vicinity. Connecting streets have been cordoned off ever since the riot the other night. An eerie quiet has descended over the area. Most of the detritus from the mayhem has been swept away, except for the pile of abandoned personal belongings and wrecked camping equipment piled carelessly on a sidewalk waiting for ignominious removal by the Sanitation Department. The street has been hosed down, but it's still glistening slightly, and there are oily puddles here and there, the water brownish with what might be leftover blood.

In the distance, if one looks hard enough, those annoying drones can be seen hovering throughout the Quarantine Zone. Manic mechanical hummingbirds, flitting this way and that, surveying every street, every building, every alley, every doorway, peering into every window, open or shut, searching for anomalies, sending back digital reports to some unseen command center from which come orders to seek out and recover. Or detain. Or ...?

It's like a scab that won't heal, Miki thinks as she glares at the QZ, this plastic-shrouded dead zone in the heart of the city, ringed by a perverse necklace of clinical barricades. She's been here almost an hour, unmoving, just staring at the sterile, lifeless void in front of her, trying to decide what to do next. How is she going to tell her parents? Up the street is the main perimeter gate where those unmarked ambulances shoved their way through the mob, carrying bodies on the way to ... where? Only a few weeks ago, one of those hearses might have had Jennifer in it. While Miki was sitting with her parents in their comfortable suburban home, her sister was suffocating on those streets. Contaminated, they said. Nothing left of her now but an urn of ash and bone fragments.

But that's not exactly true. There are photographs. Jennifer's visual essay of her last days. There is a narrative there, Miki is certain, a trail hidden among the images that Jennifer wanted someone to follow. *"In Case Something Happens To Me."*

There's suddenly movement in the corner of Miki's vision. In the window of a building just inside the QZ. A shape. A person, maybe. Tall, thin. Oscillating in the window frame like some vertical wave form. Miki comes forward a few steps, the first time she's moved. The thing starts to congeal, taking on vaguely humanoid form. Is it staring at her?

Suddenly, she's distracted by flocks of pigeons taking flight. Where have they come from? The noise of so many birds leaping skyward all at once is so startling even the soldiers and HazMats beyond the perimeter fence pause to look up. The pigeons scatter aimlessly, then join together in an organic cluster to speed away from the QZ.

When Miki looks back to that window in the Zone, the ominous figure has vanished.

But she remains there. Staring at Jennifer's graveyard. Contemplating the emptiness.

JOHN HARRISON

The city's.
And her own.

Something is on the loose among us. Something bad.
Something unimaginable.

Look closely and you'll see it. Leering in the reflections of
apartment windows, grinning hideously from the shadows of
doorways and alleys...

...insinuating itself among crowds of oblivious human
traffic, just waiting its chance to cause confusion, chaos and
death.

Look closely, don't turn away.

Something wicked this way comes. Something vicious.
Something malevolent. Something we are not ready to
understand.

THE OMINOSITY

PART II

TO: ███████████████ , OFFICE OF DIRECTOR
NATIONAL SECURITY AGENCY

FROM: ████████████████

RE: ████████ PROJECT

23, March, 1963

EYES ONLY

As you know, the purpose of project ████████ has been to
develop and maintain operational capabilities in the area of
███████████████████████████████ . Through the use of
cerebral stimulation, psychological stress, and other
biochemical and neurophsysiological inteventions, we have
attempted to provoke and then measure these ██████████
with the intention of ██████████████████████████
██████████

The possibilities for strategic and military planning as well as covert intelligence operations would seem to be obvious.

Per your directives, the existence of this project has been confined to a select team of specialists and clinicians who have carried out all the experiments at our designated ███████ laboratories.

Unfortunately, the efficacy of these experiments has proved elusive. Further time and expense does not seem warranted at this point.

Because, as discussed, the procedures used here could be considered controversial, even unethical by some, I am recommending that we terminate Project ████ at the earliest possible moment. ███

Please advise of your thoughts. Time is of the essence.

████████, Project Director

18

The video is grainy. The camerawork shaky. An iPhone POV rushing toward the confusion. Emergency sirens are blaring inside the Quarantine Zone checkpoint. The halogen beams atop the perimeter wall have turned night into day. A cluster of security drones hover above, buzzing like angry wasps. Security patrols and HazMats are emerging from their operations tents in a state of high alert, answering to the emotionless, mechanical alarms blaring from unseen speakers about a "Perimeter Breach." The iPhone is zooming now. Pushing in on the entrance to one of the decon tunnels that snake their way through perimeter wall into the QZ dead zone. Security patrols have surrounded the plastic sheeting of the orifice and are waiting tensely with overkill firepower. The sirens unexpectedly wind down and an unnerving quiet quickly descends. No one knows what to expect. Especially not the wet and frightened nomads now staggering out of the tunnel. Led by a young woman stumbling under the weight of a dazed young man who is bleeding profusely from a visible wound to his midsection.

"Don't shoot," she screams as weapons are immediately trained upon her and the others. "Please, we're unarmed. Don't shoot us!"

A handful of men and women and one preteen girl follow

behind her. Filthy and ragged, they look like refugees from some terrible Mideast civil war.

"Survivors!" The shout goes up among the crowd pressing against the perimeter gates, and immediately the Commander of the Security Patrols dispatches a handful of his men to block their view and begin confiscating phones and cameras. But this one avoids their reach and continues to record.

The young woman staggers forward, propping up her boyfriend. Camera zooming in. Focus blurring. The frame whip pans trying to find its subject, finally stabilizing as it settles on her. Although at this magnification the frame is annoyingly jittery. "He's wounded," she yells at the Commander. "He needs an ambulance. Please. He's been shot!"

The Commander seems momentarily paralyzed. He keeps glancing back at the crowd and the camera that has evaded confiscation.

"My name is Jennifer Preston," the young woman continues to scream. "This is Jonas Flack. He is the Press Officer for the city. He's hurt, for Chrissakes! Help us." The other "refugees" are cowering behind her, eyes wide with terror. More heavily armed security teams, clearly in pursuit, are now emerging out of the decon tube behind them, trapping them in a crossfire. As if sensing their fear, the young woman who called herself Jennifer Preston turns back to them. "Don't be afraid. They're not going to hurt us. They can't. Not in front of everyone." She defiantly stares straight down the barrel of the iPhone camera until a gloved hand covers the lens suddenly, and the electronic futz of circuitry shorting out makes everything go dark.

In the back seat of his SUV, Hollings Keller switches off the video monitor nestled in the seat in front of him and leans back to meditate. He needs clarity, he needs calm. But his thoughts are chaos. He can't focus. He keeps imagining the columns of that empty garage last night, the ones that reminded him of the mosques he used to infiltrate in Iraq when he was embedded with Special Forces there. Gray spaces he found ominous, not inspiring. Alien redoubts where he'd linger after the shuffle of stockinged feet had evaporated, listening for conspiracies that might have been left behind in the echoes of prayers. Certain Cathedrals in Europe evoked the same dread in him. They were places suspended in time, disconnected from the world around them. That was their raison d'être, Keller assumed. He hated them.

He'd been waiting for one of his weekly catch-ups with Stewart Whitfield. The man was pathologically incapable of meeting in a normal place. Always ready to play the role of spook, like some character out of a Le Carré novel. And he was usually late. Which is why Keller had time to ponder something that moved in the corner of his eye. Something ephemeral. Obscured by the shadows. Keller had glanced out the window at his driver to see if he'd noticed it, but the man was relishing a lungful of nicotine and wasn't interested in anything except the serpent of smoke slithering out of his nose.

But it *was* there, quivering like reflection in a shaky mirror. A wraith, hovering, trying to become something corporeal but never quite congealing. Keller felt his heartbeat accelerate. Was he really seeing this? Or was the light down here playing tricks? Could he simply have been projecting his own desperate hope that Project Morpheus might have been on to something?

A face suddenly appeared at Keller's window. A vague approximation of a face. A simulacrum, deformed and elastic, with a maddening stare and a mouth widening into a shriek. But it was only there for a nanosecond, because after all this was only a human face. Stewart Whitfield's face. Keller's "boss," although Whitfield preferred in his Ivy League noblesse to call his colleagues "brethren."

"May I join?" he asked with that toothy grin and practiced

patrician civility Keller loathed. Keller released the lock button and Whitfield oozed in. "You seem startled, Hollings."

"I wasn't expecting you for another fifteen minutes," Keller mumbled, glancing casually past Whitfield to see if he really saw something or was imagining it.

"Yes, well I ducked out early. Results?" He greedily eyed a data file in Keller's lap.

"I'm afraid not. Just a review of the project's history."

"The lads are getting anxious, Hollings."

"Trying to piece together fragments of research from almost sixty years ago takes time, Stewart." Whitfield nodded. Faux sympathy. What he really meant was *we don't give a shit.* "Our goal," he smiled, "was to prevent the discovery of so-called unethical and illegal experiments, not start them up again."

"It was your idea to engage Emeril Benedict, Stewart," Keller reminded Whitfield, not even trying to mute his disdain.

"Yes, when one sups with the Devil, as they say. That's why we need to wrap this up. As long as the quarantine remains in effect, he remains a stone in our shoe."

"What's he going to do? Go to the press? 'Hey, a shady group of intelligence spooks bribed me to blow up Club Nightshade on New Year's Eve, and now they're holding out on me?' Really, Stewart?"

"I'm reminded of the fable about the frog who promised to ferry a scorpion across the pond if the deadly little beast wouldn't sting him. Which of course, it did. 'But why?' asked the frog as they both sank to their deaths. 'Because it's my nature,' the scorpion answered."

Always ready with some stupid homily, Keller couldn't help thinking.

"So what am I to report back?" Whitfield persisted.

"Maintain the fiction of contamination from the weapons dump. 'Until we can be assured the area is safe for people to return ... blah blah blah.' No one is going to want to go back in there as long as they think they'll end up like the incredible melting man."

"Perhaps we could circulate some images of a victim or two?" Whitfield contributed, warming to the idea. "Suggest what happens when one is exposed. Vomiting blood, skin falling off, that sort of thing. You still have a few trespassers under observation, yes? Use one of them. A child, perhaps. A child is always good. Reliable emotional trigger."

A stupid idea, of course, but Keller nodded anyway. He'd have agreed to just about anything to get Whitfield out of this car.

"I'll let the lads know," Whitfield said as he opened the door and stepped out. "But, Hollings, please understand, the risk-reward ratio is narrowing. A few of the brethren are not in the mood to tolerate much more."

"Fools," Keller grumbles to himself, watching Whitfield evaporating in the darkness like a stale smoke. He glances back down at the 1963 memo about Project Morpheus, aborted and abandoned as if nothing had been accomplished. If they only knew. But Keller's "colleagues" don't care. They just want the whole thing gone, forgotten. Erased so that no pain-in-the-ass government investigation will ever be able to uncover it, destroying carefully curated careers and comfortable lives. Memories of the Church Committee Hearings terrify certain segments of the intelligence community. And Snowden's recent treachery is still causing blowback.

He told them their scheme was ill-conceived. Why anyone thought trusting a thug like Emeril Benedict to help them cover up an experiment like Morpheus was beyond imagining. Instead of trying to understand what Morpheus scientists inadvertently achieved, they have allowed a self-aggrandizing megalomaniac to blackmail them instead. And now, for all of his warnings, Keller's been rewarded with leading the shovel brigade. Of course, their blinding stupidity might eventually provide a silver lining. So far, no one in the group really knows what he's doing out on Oyster Bay.

They may believe he's trying to find some kind of antidote to the leaking biochemical stimulants used in those forgotten experiments, but he has a more ambitious agenda. What if Morpheus's technicians truly had stumbled upon the means to *"provoke electromagnetic emissions of the mind"*? The mind boggles with possibilities.

Up ahead, the Oyster Bay facility looms. Keller tries again to slow his breathing and drift into that reassuring embrace of thoughtless awareness. But his mind just won't stay still. His eyes continue their spastic dance behind his lids as thoughts careen involuntarily from one problem to another.

"Fuck it," he mutters and gives up.

Dr. Lewis Cameron is already waiting when Keller's car descends a ramp into the underground warren of covert facilities he grafted on to this otherwise ordinary psychiatric clinic. The work upstairs is a perfect camouflage for what he's asking Dr. Cameron and his team to do down here.

"Sorry to drag you out at this hour," Cameron smiles as Keller steps out, "but I was sure you'd want to see this."

A shudder races down Keller's spine. Why does this man give me the creeps, he wonders?

Inside, Keller follows Cameron to a small exam room where a sheet-covered body is laid out on a surgical gurney.

"A rookie," Cameron says. "On routine patrol the other night when he was attacked."

"Attacked?"

"He got separated from his CO when the two of them were sweeping a building. The CO heard him scream and start firing, but when he got there, this is what he found." He pulls the sheet back to reveal the naked corpse of a young soldier. And though he's seen this kind of thing before, Keller can't help wincing. The boy's skin is mottled around the face, stretched unnaturally tight across the skull. The mouth is twisted into a strained grimace, made even more horrible by a bloodless, waxy complexion. Something very bad has happened to this young man.

"Blood toxicology shows abnormally elevated levels of norepinephrine, and we found significant amounts of neuromodulators in the cerebrospinal fluid."

Unbelievable, Keller thinks. *The man sounds positively excited.*

"Was he given the antidote before the patrol?"

"Made no difference as far as we can tell."

Which means they still don't know what they're dealing with, Keller thinks.

"But we still have the other avenues to explore," Cameron continues.

He picks up a remote from a nearby table and aims it at the video monitor on the wall. The screen surges to life with observation views of a small room somewhere else in the complex. A young woman in a hospital gown is lying on a bed with her back to the room.

As if sensing someone watching with this digital eyeball in the ceiling, she suddenly turns and sits up, staring directly up at the camera with a hard, unforgiving expression. There is no doubt who it is.

Miki Preston's sister.

Jennifer.

Very much alive, if not exactly well.

19

The room is pitch-black. Has been for hours. At least she thinks it's been hours. In fact, she has no idea. It seems like they keep her isolated like this longer and longer. No sound. No smell. Nothing to touch. Total sense deprivation. Where time quickly becomes irrelevant. Leaving her trapped in the density of her own mind. Until the torments begin, that is. Right now, she's simply floating. Doesn't even try to think logically, or chronologically, or narratively. Perhaps that's what they want. She's reminded of what that asshole Keller told her last time he showed up, about meditating, about how he's learned to absent himself from the world in order to cleanse his mind and restore his chi. His way of befriending her, no doubt. With that sickly smile and his not-so-subtle suggestion how to endure these procedures. Fucking cunt!

She can feel the "cap" tight around her skull, and the pin pricks of probes piercing her scalp. Not painful, really. More of an annoyance. Like an itch that can't be reached.

She doesn't fight these moments.

She uses them to plan her escape.

But then, the drugs start coming. She can feel the slight burn in the crook of her arm where the intravenous needle is nestled. They must be ready to put her on the rack again. She steels herself for the effects. It always starts with some kind of sedative. Diprivan, maybe. They used it to put her under when she had an appendectomy a couple of years ago. Really good shit. Except it killed Michael Jackson. This is the way death-row patients must feel during lethal injection. A sense of dissolving. Might as well enjoy it while it lasts. Because what comes next will take all of her mental vigilance to keep from going mad.

And here it comes. The burning in her brain. Like an acid liquefying her rationality, dispersing her thoughts to the pandemonium circus. Disconnected images, phrases, and sounds. Senseless, uncontrollable feedback loops competing for attention. Even if she could isolate one and concentrate on it, which she can't, the sheer inanity of it would drive her bonkers sooner or later.

Ultrasonic frequencies that would drive any dog to think it was a cat begin stabbing straight into her brain, making her teeth grind uncontrollably. Intermittent, concussive shock waves rock her nervous system even further. And merciful moments of silence are abruptly obliterated by deafening bangs, shrieks, and unidentifiable howls.

That's just the hors d'oeuvres.

Here come the flashing lights. The blinding strobes. Turning her every movement in this sterile space into a palsied marionette performance. And then, without warning, another impenetrable blackout. Latent images on her retina persist, disorienting her even further.

And that familiar terror returns. The worm growing inside her. The awareness. Her, and yet not-her. Creeping along her central nervous system. Trying to penetrate the membrane of her consciousness. This slithering malevolence, this poisonous jinn that's trying to escape her.

The hallucinogens they're pumping into her are taking hold now. The real and the surreal are merging, abetted by the awful atonal sonics being sprayed down on her from multiple speakers. They must be everywhere, pulsing toward her, trying to envelope her with their unnatural ambience. Maybe the walls themselves are speakers. That would be cool, wouldn't it? She's losing it. And she knows it. She tries to rationalize by thinking of Varese's music, or Messiaen's, but this sound is too sinister. She screams along to mute its power, or at least turn it into something of her own, but her voice sounds like the squeal of a rat caught in the jaws of a trap, and she bursts into lunatic laughter. Which doesn't last. Because now she's melting. Her essence is leaking through her pores, joining the evanescent phantasmagoria all around her. Vaporous, vaguely human shapes. The phantoms in her photographs, or the one that was hovering in front of her in the QZ before they captured her. The things she called Paramentals in her blogs. Mutants? Ghosts? Demons? Parts of herself? For some reason she can smell burning electrical wires.

Finally, the electroconvulsive shocks. A tsunami of seizures makes her body jump and buck. She devolves into nothing but a twitching mass of muscle contractions. She has no more thought now.

Areas of Jennifer Preston's brain are lighting up like storms on Jupiter. Dr. Cameron is fascinated. Hollings Keller is becoming nauseated.

"Are you trying to kill her, Lewis?" he complains.

"We're following the Morpheus protocols. A few technological enhancements, of course. We're over fifty years on, after all. And we've tweaked the pharmacology. Added some new psychotropics of our own devising with very promising potential."

They're staring at a bank of fMRI monitors displaying multiple images of Jennifer's brain, accompanied by continual readouts updating her vitals.

"I hope you remember your elementary neuroscience, Hollings."

"How do you think I ended up in intelligence work?"

Cameron is either oblivious to Keller's sarcasm or he deliberately ignores it. "You'll recall that the brain is a global workspace. Millions of interconnected networks functioning separately and together. In other words, a collection of distributed specialized grids, most of which do not support conscious experiences. Those are the ones we're interested in." He points to a section of Jennifer's brain that is throbbing with color. "Notice what is happening to alpha range frequency oscillations in the amygdala."

On the monitors, areas of Jennifer's brain are igniting like lightning strikes in the middle of a Dakota thunderstorm.

"We're using aural and visual stimuli to set off maximal anxiety and fear triggers. In other words, inducing extreme stress and mental disorientation to intensify electromagnetic emissions of the brain."

Keller is weary of the man's pedantry.

"But you still can't duplicate the phenomenon."

"Unfortunately, no."

"So Morpheus failed. That's why they shut it down and abandoned it ten stories underground. They failed."

"Did they, Hollings? Did they fail? You and your colleagues thought something was seeping out after all these years causing disturbing behavior and violence. Provocateurs like that Ominosity fellow were blogging about malicious supernatural entities that might be behind these incidents. Is that why you tried to bury their labs under a block of city rubble? Is that why I'm here? Because they failed? Or because they simply lacked the tools to understand what was really happening?"

"She's our most promising subject. We have video of her in the QZ, before she was captured. The phenomenon was visible. Right in front of her. How did that happen, Lewis? *That's* what you're here for!"

"And I remain convinced that if we understand where and how those electromagnetic emissions reach critical mass,"

Cameron exalts, "we'll be on a path to understanding the phenomenon. We'll be able to manipulate it. Perhaps even able to train an individual how to … pardon the sorcery metaphor … how to conjure it." He has that Messianic gleam in his eye that creeps Keller out.

"*If* that's where it's coming from," Keller says, turning back to the monitors and the pitiful figure of Jennifer Preston in that isolation chamber, quivering and twitching as her convulsions subside. "If we're wrong, we'd better be certain no one ever finds out what we've been doing down here."

WHO IS WINDING THE CLOCK?

By Joseph Carlucci

Columnist/Editorial Board Member

This city is like a gigantic clock, its gears and springs oiled and synchronized, hidden from view essential to the complex functioning of the mechanism but apparent only as numerals and sweep hands. Even digital timepieces have complicated entanglements of diodes and transistors at their core which must be perfectly harmonized.

Have you ever wondered how things get done in this city? Have you ever truly pondered the hidden but synchronized relationships that must exist for even the simplest of routines we take for granted to exist?

Who winds the clock? Who charges the battery?

Remember William 'Boss' Tweed? He spent his entire life building and managing complex, often camouflaged relationships that dominated his city.

According to biographers, "Tweed's 'ring' was an engineering marvel, strategically deployed to control key power points: the courts, the legislature, the treasury and the ballot box. Their methods were curiously simple and primitive. They would buy up undeveloped property, then use the resources of the city to improve the area thus increasing the value of the land, after which they sold and took their profits."

Sound familiar?

20

Emeril Benedict, aka "The Baron," is standing at the chef's table in the kitchen of the Black Orchid, his uptown but modest Thai restaurant, his pride and joy, using the back of his hand to peel the skin from a perfect filet of wild Chinook Salmon. Flown in fresh every night. Having "encouraged" the previous owner to abruptly retire, Benedict spends the better part of everyday here enjoying chores like this. The majordomo. Proverbial poor boy made good, up from the dismal streets of harbor town. No door is closed to him. But despite the "Baron" nickname, Emeril Benedict is not ostentatious. Witness his "offices" here in this steaming Thai kitchen where he dispenses wisdom, influence, and occasional punishment to the city's movers and shakers who make dutiful pilgrimages to pay homage and sample his indisputably world-class cuisine. No conspicuous trappings of wealth for this Baron. No chauffeured cars, no sycophant entourage, no extravagant jewelry. His black-tie attire every evening is a visual reminder to respect his food, not an advertisement of his personal status. His power is indirectly applied and no less potent because of it. He can waltz unannounced into virtually any bank, any corporate office, any government bureau and expect to be treated with courtesy. He can also swagger down the darkest alleys or through the most depraved neighborhoods and expect to be feared. Those aware of his pervasive and profitable criminal enterprises refuse to acknowledge them. The status quo is well oiled. Emeril Benedict believes in the equal opportunity of corruption. And thus, he is one of the untouchables.

"You are two of the sorriest goddamn mooks I've ever had working for me, you know that?" he growls as fish epidermis finally separates from flesh with a wet *pop* and is discarded on a page of *thedig.com* displaying Joe Carlucci's snide Boss Tweed insinuations.

Two of Benedict's lieutenants, Frank and Hank, stand across from him stoically tolerating a gale of cigar breath and venom. "What the hell do I pay you for? Why do I allow precious minutes of my time to be wasted in your company? Do you revel in your incompetence? Do you practice your inadequacy?"

"We've got eyes and ears everywhere, Mr. B.," Hank sputters. "It's like it just went poof."

"Poof, you say?" Benedict snorts.

"Yeah, you know, like a magician's trick. Poof."

"What say you, Hank?" He's nailing the other man now with an icy stare.

"Frank, Mr. B."

"Whatever." He couldn't care less what their names are. Frank, Hank. He hired them precisely because the names were similar. And these two have proven the wisdom of his decision by often answering to the other's name or even simultaneously when Benedict yells something that sounds simply like "Ank."

"We know she went to work that morning," Frank continues. "One of our guys saw her in a bar over on Amsterdam that night. But after it closed, she left. No one knows what happened to her down in that tunnel."

"Or to the briefcase she was carrying, hmmm?"

Hank and Frank's silence is damning. Benedict picks up a gleaming carving knife. With expert strokes, he quickly renders the salmon slab into multiple chunks of sashimi.

"Let me explain this to you one more time, fellows. Angela Rossi was a bacterium. She performed a beneficial function essential to the health of exciting new enterprises I've planned. But bacteria can mutate. If she had become pathogenic, I would need to know. I would need to know yesterday! Do you understand what I'm saying? Do you understand the stakes here? Angela Rossi knew things. Things that *must not be known to others*."

"We're doing our best, Mr. B." Frank says.

"Said the one-armed basketball player to his coach," Benedict mutters. "Get out."

Frank makes the mistake of reaching for a salmon chunk as he gets up. Without warning, Benedict's knife spears his hand to the chopping board. Frank gasps but he doesn't scream. He knows better.

"Leave it," Benedict says so softly Frank almost can't hear him. But he doesn't need to. He nods vigorously. Benedict withdraws the knife and waves him away.

"May I take a napkin?" Frank pleads through gritted teeth.

Benedict pulls the napkin from his own collar, wipes the knife clean then tosses it to Frank who hurries away with Hank. No one in the kitchen bats an eye. If they heard any of this conversation, they're already busy erasing it from their memory banks. The only person in the room who is paying any attention is Detective Freddie Pierce. Fat Freddie. Lingering by the sous chefs, enjoying a bowl of yum woon sen.

"I expect you'd like some of this fish to go with that, Freddie," Benedict says, summoning him.

"No one in this city has fish as good as yours," Freddie smiles. He carefully avoids the drops of Frank's blood on the block and takes one of the bigger chunks while Benedict wraps up the salmon skin in the pages of the Post.

Speaking of skin, this Carlucci character is getting under the Baron's. Why does he have to remind everyone what a cesspool this city is?

"*They would buy up undeveloped property, then use the resources of the city to improve the area thus increasing the value of the land, after which they sold and took their profits.*' Sound familiar?"

"Who does this guy think he is?" Benedict says to no one in particular as he dumps the paper in the garbage.

"Can turn a phrase," Freddie observes between chews. "Him and that blogger, Ominosity, they really know how to stir things up."

"I need to know what happened to those documents, Freddie. They are my leverage."

"My money is on wind and rats, boss," Freddie says, helping himself to another piece of fish. "But even if a few turn up, and someone tries to put two and you together, you can always enlist your pal out there," he said, nodding to the dining room. "He and his snakes can suppress it."

Yes, Benedict has no doubt he can manage Hollings Keller and the rest of those clubby spooks. Fear can be an effective management tool. It's Angela who disappoints him. Her betrayal caught him up short. Who knew she had a conscience? She never exhibited any second thoughts while taking the payoffs he sent over with Dickie Prince. Never questioned his plans for the properties in the QZ he told her to secure with forged title transfers and fraudulent deeds. He was going to make her rich.

"So what happened, Freddie? What turned her?"

"People are doing a lot of unpredictable things these days, boss. It's like it's contagious."

And it's a good thing Freddie is on that task force investigating it, Benedict thinks. *He can misdirect anything that starts to get too close for comfort. Including alcoholic, drug-fogged former homicide detectives.*

"So Mathis is back on the prowl," he mentions casually while filleting another piece of salmon.

"He won't be a problem," Freddie says. "Most everyone still

thinks he did Dickie Prince and got away with it. His credibility is shot."

"Still, a hungry lone wolf can be dangerous."

Freddie nods. He's got his orders. "When the opportunity presents itself, boss."

"Don't wait too long for it," Benedict decrees as skin slides off flesh once again.

Hollings Keller is at his favorite table. A small banquet near the back, full view of the room and all its entrances: front, back, kitchen, bar, restrooms, and the nearby access to a service exit. Just in case. At the moment, however, the only thing on his mind is the surveillance video playing on his iPhone. The one of Jennifer Preston the night she snuck into the Quarantine Zone looking for her boyfriend. The streets are dark and empty. The plastic sheeting that covers the buildings expands and contracts like breathing. *She moves like a damn burglar,* Keller thinks. *Cautious, almost tentative. Alert to every ripple in the atmosphere.* She knows she's being watched. Keller is sure of it. When she reaches the Five Points intersection, she halts abruptly. A noise, perhaps. That's when she pulls the gun.

And there it is. That thing, whatever it is. A vapor, at first, but quickly solidifying, taking shape. Hovering there as if trying to complete itself. The girl is awestruck. Raising her goddamn camera to photograph this ephemeral, oscillating *thing* drifting toward her now. Closer and closer. Still vibrating, trying to finish its transmigration from nothing into something that's starting to look suspiciously like a photonegative of the girl herself!

Unfortunately, that's when someone grabs her. The girl. Charlotte. Twelve, maybe thirteen, with her gaunt frame, stringy hair, and haunted eyes. Not wearing any protective gear. *She knew there was no contamination,* Keller muses. Her intervention ruined everything. Whatever it was that was happening on that street evaporated like smoke in the wind. And Keller's team hasn't been able to duplicate it since they captured them.

"Put that goddamn thing away, Hollings," Benedict barks as he steps up to Keller's banquet with his meal. "You know I don't allow them in my restaurant!"

Keller has heard it many times before. As far as Benedict is concerned, all those iPhones and iPads with their TikToking and Facebooking are nothing but foolish diversions from real life. Mere toys to entertain empty souls. If you can't look someone in the eye and get his measure, he maintains, no amount of texting, emailing, or Googling will inform you. Besides, being off the electronic grid has its advantages. It makes people come to him. Like tonight.

"You're not joining me?" Keller says, pocketing his phone as Benedict sits opposite him.

"You eat. I'll talk."

Nice way to ruin a guest's appetite, Keller thinks. But he won't give the bastard the satisfaction of knowing it. Instead, he spears a forkful of the salmon. "I can probably quote you before you do, Emeril," he says, savoring the fish with genuine delight.

"So you better not tell me again to be patient."

"Emeril, please, don't play the fool with me. I know how smart you are. You're a long-game man. Six months is just a blink for you."

"But you see, Hollings, when I blink I expect my vision to clear."

"We're still making sure the area is safe. What good will those properties be if everyone's afraid to go into them?"

Benedict allows one of his infrequent smiles to tug at his lips, more menacing than friendly. "So here we sit. Each with a gun to the other's head. Mine loaded with the truth about what happened New Year's Eve, and yours aimed at the future of my enterprise."

"You asked me not to use the word patience, so I won't.

Instead, I'll suggest self-interest. We're making progress, Emeril. I just can't give you a timeline that will clear up your vision."

"I want that quarantine lifted, Hollings."

"I know you do," Keller says, taking another bite and trying not to think of the fable Stewart Whitfield told him about the scorpion and the frog.

Are we too afraid to consider the possibility this terrible tragedy, this Catastrophe and the scar we live with every day called the Quarantine Zone could actually have been good....for someone? Why is no one is asking...

Who benefits? Who comes out ahead?
Who profits from the suffering?

If you're not asking the question, you're simply being complicit.

Remember, the twin of catastrophe is opportunity, people.

So...
Here's the real question:
If we know where to look for the answers, do we have the guts to go there?

THE OMINOSITY

21

The ringing in her ears has finally subsided. The Xanax they pump into her to calm the nervous system after these sessions is starting to wear off, too. She'll begin to feel alert soon, and the anger, the fear, and the relentless despair will return. Until then she's content to drift on a lake of drugged tranquility. She tries to review her escape plan, but she can only get to the part where she subdues her "minder." And even that is a bit confused. Is she supposed to hit the bitch over the head when she comes to take her to the shower, or is she going to use the plastic knife she's hidden from one of her meals?

"Welcome back," the voice says, and Jennifer recognizes it immediately.

"Jonas?" she whispers, trying to force her eyes open. The room is a gray abstract. Nothing seems to fit together properly. There are no right angles. Walls throb. The floor undulates. But there he is, sitting alone on a folding chair in the middle of this empty space. Wearing some kind of monochrome jumpsuit, hands folded in his lap, hair wild, face unshaven. A bit of a blur, but there's no doubt it's him. Smiling at her with that warm, slightly impish grin she fell in love with the first moment she saw him.

"They wouldn't tell me what happened to you," she

whimpers. "They wouldn't let me see you." She tries to sit up but only gets as far as one arm.

"Bit of advice," he says. "Don't ever get shot. It's nothing like in the movies."

"Oh, God, Jonas, I'm so sorry. This is all my fault."

"Shhhhh. It's all right."

She falls back, tries to will herself into clearheadedness. But the drugs still have a grip on her.

"Is this for real? Are you really here, or is this just the drugs?"

"What do you think?" He leans over and kisses her. Soft and tender. And brief. Over and over. The way he always did. The way he always made her want him, driving her crazy with anticipation. No one had ever kissed her like that.

"How long has it been?" she sighs.

"I don't know. No one will say."

"What about the others?" she asks.

"What others?"

"The ones who found you. The ones we came out with. The little girl, Charlotte. What happened to her? No one was supposed to be left in there. Everyone was supposed to have been evacuated."

"They want to know why we were there, Jen. In the QZ."

"Because it's a lie, Jonas," she shouts so "they" can hear her. "New Year's Eve, the contamination. All of it. A fucking colossal lie."

But Jonas doesn't move. He's frozen in place, just staring at her with limpid eyes. As if studying her.

"I've been dreaming about you," she says. "About you being here before. In my room."

"I didn't think you were aware of it."

"I thought maybe it was the drugs."

"Know the feeling."

"You saw them, didn't you? The Paramentals. Before they shot you. You told me. You know they're real." And then, shouting again, at hidden cameras she can't see but knows are there, "You know, too! That's why you're keeping us here!"

Jonas's smile hasn't changed. "I had a breakdown, Jen. It was bad. But I'm getting better now. I think."

Something is hollow here. She can feel it. Something incomplete. This conversation. It's counterfeit. An imitation. Maybe she *is* hallucinating.

"This is all wrong," she says.

"They haven't been easy on you, have they?"

"What are they doing to us, Jonas?" she moans.

He comes over and takes her hand. He's in the shadows again, and she can't see his face anymore.

"They've emptied me out," she says, starting to cry.

"We'll be away from here soon, Jen." He leans down and kisses her again. She closes her eyes as his fingertips glide down across her breasts and into her pants. She gives in. She wants him to make love to her right here, right now. So what if they're watching? She'll be so lost in passion, she'll forget where she is. Where they are.

But when she opens her eyes, he's no longer there.

"Jonas?" Was he really there? Or was he just another narcotic dream? She can still feel his touch. His scent lingers. He was here. She's convinced. Otherwise, how did that folding chair end up in the center of the room?

And how did that small syringe find its way into the clutched palm of her right hand?

22

Rush hour. And raining. Hard. A goddamn downpour. Shit. Traffic is already a mess and now this. Why do these assholes laying on their horns think it will make anyone move out of the way? There's nowhere to go. Crowds are pushing and shoving into intersections. Heads down, ignoring their fellow man, no one stepping aside. Some don't even bother to wait to reach the corner. They simply rush into the street between cars, with newspapers, briefcases, purses held over their heads, expecting vehicles to avoid them, not the other way around. Umbrella duels are breaking out everywhere. Those without have to bat away eye-gouging canopy spines. There are shoving matches over taxis.

The bus driver stares out at this sea of human selfishness and feels his despair morph into rage. He's at the end of an extended shift, and now he definitely knows he's not going to make it back to the terminal for another hour. Forget the kid's wrestling match at school this evening. Just another Dad missing. Is this all there is? This is his reward for his ten-hour shifts and a measly fifty-two K? A two-bedroom semidetached dump across the river where he and his cafeteria worker wife are trying to raise three kids? That's it?

The Town Car idling next to him is the last straw. One of

those Russian oligarch's kids who never pay their parking tickets, sitting in the back, dry and warm and content as a prince, latest smartphone in one hand, drink in the other. Can't be older than thirty-five. Gorgeous woman sitting next to him, flashing Tiffany, maybe Bulgari, working his pants so she can go down on him. Hell, who cares if traffic isn't moving? He can get a nice long blow job while they wait.

The bus driver has had enough. He jerks the bus to the curb. "Get out!" he yells turning to his full load. "Bus is broke. Ain't goin' nowhere."

Disbelieving passengers start grousing.

"Service won't get through this traffic for an hour at least. And you can't sit here. So, get off. Another bus'll be coming through."

People are now cursing. This is just great. Someone yells at the driver. "What the hell'd you do?" As if it was his fault. Another hollers, "You can't just put us out in the rain!"

"Not my problem," the driver yells back. "Your tax dollars at work, folks. They won't maintain these crates properly, this is what happens. So like I said, get out!"

Reluctantly, angrily, the passengers file out the doors into the streets.

The driver could walk away. Just get off himself and keep going. Leave it behind. All of it. Never look back. Just walk away. But where's the fun in that? Instead, a darkness sweeps over him, and a hideous smile bares his teeth. He jumps back behind the wheel, slams the bus into reverse and jams his foot down on the pedal. The people who just got off don't have a chance to be surprised. He flattens a half dozen and knocks that many more into the street. Then he grinds the gear box into drive without even stopping and speeds over the curb, crushing even more who have been felled. The bus lurches over the bodies, smashes past the cars in front of it and takes out a city mailbox. Clear sailing ahead. Except for the swarm of pedestrians who are so startled by this behemoth surging down the sidewalk toward them they can't get out of the way fast enough. The ones the bus doesn't hit are trampled by their fellow man. Just trying to save my own life, fuck you very kindly.

The driver's adrenaline is really pumping now. He hasn't had this much fun since his teenaged son taught him how to play Grand Theft Auto. Couldn't believe how fast he got good at it. Chaos and violence. What a great way to let off steam after a long day. But the carnage on his TV monitor was nothing like this. This ... this is AWESOME!

People are screaming. Blood is splattering the windscreen. And the noise! He can barely hear that vaporous phantasm behind him any longer, the one slithering around his shoulders, whispering into his ear. His personal Iago. His imp of the perverse, egging him on. All day. Shit, all week. That creepy shadow following him around. Reminding him what a loser he is, what a shit-swamp his life is. Why not go out with some dignity, dickhead. Make 'em remember ya! He can feel it seeping through his skin now, into his soul, devouring his conscience, leaving nothing behind but homicidal fury. And ecstasy.

Pedal to the metal, boy. Really picking up speed now. Might even hit fifty. This bus is a goddamn battering ram. Twisting metal and breaking bodies in its wake. What a rush! And there's a red light up ahead.

He clips a light stanchion as he aims for the gridlock. But when he tries to veer away from the subway stairs blocking his path, he loses control. The bus slides on the wet pavement and sideswipes an UberX trying to pick up a businessman. The impact tips the empty bus over and it crushes a motorcyclist who can't get out its path. Twenty tons of screaming steel careen into a light pole, sheering it in half. The top drops like a dagger, penetrating the driver's windscreen, impaling him to his seat.

Something dark and slimy seeps out of his pores. The driver tries to decide if the laughter he's hearing is his own. But then, he can't hear anything anymore.

By the time Mathis arrives, Freddie Pierce and other members of the Special Crimes Task Force are already managing the scene. Several uniforms make a show of blocking Mathis's way until he flashes his shield and tells them to fuck off.

"Just another day in paradise, eh, Freddie?" he says, coming around to the front of the overturned bus. Fat Freddie is kneeling there, finishing a Sabrett's frankfurter, staring in at the dead driver slumped against the window.

"Just can't stay on the reservation, can you, pal?" Freddie asks between chews.

"Dispatch said all hands on deck."

"Nothing left but the cleanup."

"There a story to this?"

"According to a couple of passengers, the guy said the bus was disabled, kicked everyone off. This was followed by a scene out of a bad Bruce Willis movie."

"Malfunction?"

"Causing this much damage?" Freddie shakes his head. "Looks like suicide by bus, with a side order of mass murder."

Mathis leans in to get a better look at the driver's face. "What are those?" he asks, pointing to the thin black spider-veins around the man's eyes.

"Postmortem blood flow maybe," Freddie answers. "Some weird drug residue. Who knows? Guess we'll have to wait for the autopsy. Hey, you really want to be of service, go over and give Marshall a hand with the interviews."

Mathis backs up to scan the area. Lookie-loos snapping pics with their phones being corralled behind crime-scene tape, pissed-off drivers still in the street arguing with impatient police. *Who is going to pay for this damage and how am I supposed to get home now?* Not much sympathy for the bodies still laying where they fell or the bloody survivors being attended to by paramedics.

Detective Paul Marshall is talking to a cluster of passengers and witnesses at the back of the bus.

"Give you a hand, Paul?" Mathis mumbles coming up behind him.

Marshall eyes Mathis suspiciously, but a nod from Pierce at the other end of the bus gives the okay. "Take this group here," he says, sawing his interviewees in half with a wave of the arm.

"Come on over here, folks," Mathis instructs, and a half dozen people move with him to a spot several yards away.

"What happened to the other one," a young woman with a bandage around her forehead asks.

"The driver?" Mathis asks, pulling out his notebook.

"No, the one with him. The person behind him," she says.

"There was someone else still on the bus with the driver when it lost control?"

"Couldn't see him too good. He was kind of a blur."

Another wounded passenger pushes forward. "Wasn't no one else in there. Everyone got off. You's imagining it!"

"No, I'm not. He was there. I saw him. Right behind the driver."

"Are you sure, ma'am?" Mathis asks writing down what he's hearing.

The woman puffs up, indignant that she's being challenged. "I have very good eyesight!"

"Can you recall what he looked like. White? Black? Tall? Clothes?"

The woman hesitates, suddenly flummoxed. But afraid of losing the limelight, she forges ahead. "Actually, he was more of a shadow. You know the bus was moving pretty fast. But I swear it looked like he was encouraging the driver. The two of them, laughing like a coupla teenage thugs."

"Anyone else see this?" Mathis asks surveying the crowd.

"Wasn't no one else," the man behind her says.

This provokes a chorus of voices. Pro and con. Several insisting there *was* someone still on the bus with the driver when he went crazy, most of the others denying it, accusing their fellow witnesses of being in shock, or trying to exaggerate their importance. Or worst of all, parroting those silly theories on the internet about mutant phantoms escaping from the Quarantine Zone. Things get heated.

"All right, calm down, or none of you will get a say." He starts taking down names and addresses, assuring each one that the police will be in touch to get a thorough statement once the shock of this tragedy subsides a little. He urges them all to write down what they think happened. "It will help each of you to think more clearly. And it will be extremely helpful to us," he promises.

"I know what I saw," the woman with the bandaged head insists, and her conviction gets under Mathis's skin.

Before he leaves, he takes one last tour of the scene. Various techs have congregated at the front of the bus to debate the best way of extracting the driver's impaled body, giving Mathis a brief chance to get up close and personal. And that's when he sees it. The thing he missed before. The stain. Another one. A rust-colored scorch. On the seat behind the driver's back. Like the one in Angela Rossi's apartment. Like the one in Jennifer Preston's.

Only this one is moist. And thin wisps of gray smoke are seeping out of it.

23

It's almost midnight. The bitch is late again. This is what it must feel like in a nursing home. Trapped. At the mercy of minimum-wage attendants for whom you're not an individual, just a resident.

"Ready for a relaxing bath?" Here she is. Coming across the room with her honey voice and pert little ass.

If Jennifer wasn't always so limp from her sessions with Dr. Lewis, she'd slap the robotic smile right off that Botox-fattened face. But not tonight. Tonight, Jen, be pliant. Be a good girl. Get to the shower first.

Down the corridor to the bath. Putting on a good show for the security cameras. Shuffling as if under the influence of her nightly meds, which she spit out earlier under camouflage of a cough. Hopefully, no cameras in the shower. They couldn't be that perverted, could they? Find out soon enough.

Jennifer waits until the door is closed and the electronic lock *clicks* before she moves. Her minder goes to the stalls to test the water.

"Let's get it nice and warm for you, okay?"

The prick of the needle at her neck paralyzes her.

"Don't make a sound," Jennifer hisses.

"Jennifer, please."

"Too late for that." Jennifer presses the syringe. The minder leaps away like a startled cat.

"Sorry," Jennifer says, almost genuinely, watching her minder stagger to a wall for support. The drugs take effect instantly. The woman's eyes are rolling. *"Shit, what did Jonas put in there?"* Jennifer thinks. *"Do I care if it kills her?"*

"Take your clothes off," she barks.

The minder hesitates. Jennifer brandishes the syringe again, and the woman complies. But she fumbles with her buttons like a two-year-old. By the time she's down to her underwear, her legs give out. She sinks to the floor.

"Fuck," Jennifer growls as she kneels down to finish the job, because the bitch is no longer compos mentis.

***

Jennifer comes out of the shower dressed as her minder and uses her security badge to relock the door. She's about the same size as the woman, same hair coloring. With the woman's clothes on, Jennifer hopes she can fool security long enough if she keeps her head down. Problem is, she doesn't know her way out of this maze. And time is not her ally while she figures it out. She's going to have to get lucky.

First things first. Jonas!

But there's no one in any of the other rooms that line this sterile tunnel. Just a solitary tech in one of the exam suites calibrating an MRI machine like the one used on her. She wants to rush in and smash it, but survival instinct wins out, and she slips past before the tech knows she's there.

There's a stairwell exit at the end of the corridor. Jennifer uses the security card to access it. Alarms don't sound, lights don't flash. Stairs only go up. If she wasn't sure before, she's now convinced she's been confined in a basement.

When she emerges from the stairwell, she's shocked to find herself in the hallway of what appears to be a psychiatric care facility. The lights are dimmed. The decor is monotonous. Wheelchairs are scattered carelessly. The smell of bleach is oppressive. But there are windows here! And the outside beyond. Broad, well-manicured grounds, almost like a park. And not well-lit.

Jennifer abandons caution. She's going to make a break for it. Once she's free, she can make so much noise, they'll have to release Jonas. But she passes a common area where several "residents" are still awake. Some passively sequestered in front of a giant TV. Some isolated in corners, carrying on private conversations with themselves, others slumped over in medicated stupor, staring at nothing. But among them, there's a girl. Maybe twelve or thirteen. Sitting between two elderly ladies by the television.

The girl is clearly medicated, too, but her eyes blink rapidly as she focuses on the woman suddenly kneeling in front of her.

"They ... told me you died," the girl mumbles as Jennifer puts a finger to her lips.

"I'm here. I'm really here. Do you know where Jonas is? I saw him. He came to my room. I know he's here somewhere."

The girl shakes her head sadly.

"The others, then. Where are they?"

Charlotte looks away. "Gone."

Nearby, Jennifer senses tension. People are fidgeting. A few are making nonsensical sounds. It's as if these people have a primitive sixth sense. Danger approaching.

Staff is scurrying about in the halls.

They know I'm on the loose, Jennifer thinks.

"We have to go, Charlotte. Right now. C'mon." She pulls the girl off the couch, but one of the elderly ladies grabs her by the wrist, holding her back.

"It's okay," Jennifer says tenderly. "I'm going to take care of her. I promise."

Charlotte tries to pull away, but the woman holds on. Jennifer can hear anxious voices in the distance. They've got to get out of there now. Finally, something on TV distracts the old lady, and she lets go with a jerky laugh.

Jennifer rushes to the doors and glances both ways. A couple of orderlies are conferring nervously at the far end of the hall.

"Don't look back, Charlotte. Just hold my hand like I'm taking you to your room."

The girl slips her fingers between Jennifer's and the two of them head down the hall the other way, around a corner past a reception office where several nurses are on the phone. Jennifer swipes the security card at the entrance and waits for the lock to release. She can hear running footsteps somewhere behind her now.

The lock finally lets go, and Jennifer pushes Charlotte outside ahead of her.

And that's when the alarms go off.

"The woods. Over there. Run, Charlotte. As fast as you can. I'm right behind you. *Run!*"

INTERIM REPORT OF SPECIAL CRIMES TASK FORCE

Executive Summary

Summary Statement

In attempting to analyze the current rash of atypically violent incidents plaguing the city, and the extreme civic anxiety and unrest they are causing, it is necessary to review certain events preceding this turmoil which we feel have had a catalytic effect.

THE EXPLOSION AT CLUB NIGHTSHADE, New Years Eve: Commonly referred to as The Catastrophe, this tragedy continues to haunt the daily life of our city. Since no perpetrators have yet been apprehended, and no motive has been conclusively confirmed, an alarming cynicism about the effectiveness of authorities to resolve this crime has impeded efforts to restore calm and equilibrium to the community.

The effect of this 'lack of closure' should not be underestimated.

THE QUARANTINE ZONE: The continued segregation of major neighborhoods of our city has become an intolerable irritant to our citizens, whether directly affected by evacuation or simply peripheral to it. The diaspora of evacuees is becoming increasingly volatile as witness the recent demonstrations and riots around the Quarantine Zone perimeter. Sympathy for their plight is becoming ever more outspoken and insistent. The "QZ" is, as many have called it, a 'scar on the city's psyche'. The longer it persists, the more damaging psychologically it will be.

This is not a situation that can be sustained. Until authorities are able to reassure the public that contamination has been mitigated, and that the Quarantine will lifted within a reasonable time-frame, the relationship between public and civil authority will continue to be strained.

Fear breeds in uncertainty.

PRELIMINARY OBSERVATIONS AND CONCLUSIONS:

SURGE IN VIOLENCE: At the moment, there is no simple explanation for the spikes in aberrant behavior we have seen throughout the city: seemingly unprovoked murders, baffling nervous breakdowns and impulsive suicides, a variety of mysterious accidents and fires, and a rise generally of sudden, spontaneous and motiveless violence. Although a recurring anomaly at certain crime scenes (a STAIN of unknown origin) suggests some kind of linkage among these incidents, our analysts cannot yet identify its source or meaning, if any. It appears to be the result of some kind of Pyrolysis, or decomposition due to elevated temperature. But no evidence of contingent fire or combustion in the area would seem to support this. Therefore, we continue to believe this is coincidental, not germane.

This report is unwilling to imply that any connection among these violent episodes exists.

Furthermore, there is no absolutely no evidence to suggest there is any kind of contagion emanating from the Quarantine Zone that could be responsible.

PARAMENTAL SIGHTINGS: Contrary to anecdotal accounts of a supernatural influence occurring at the site of these events (what some eye- witnesses and the media have taken to calling Paramentals) this Task Force has found no substantive evidence to explain these observations. It is possible that gases released by the pyrolysitic process (however it is occurring) could be responsible, and that a kind of smoldering is what is being perceived.

It should be assumed, therefore, that these sightings are the result of a kind of collective hysteria and should be forcefully disputed.

This report recommends that an immediate and concerted public outreach effort should be mounted to counter and discredit the incendiary and alarming provocations in the media and cyberspace that encourage these fantastical distractions and suggest a conspiracy among government authorities to hide the truth about the Catastrophe and subsequent Quarantine. Such provocations only fuel civic unrest, encourage more violence and delay a return to normalcy.

We refer in particular to the website 'theominosity.com', which is authored by someone who calls himself Ominosity. As long as the misinformation and incitements perpetrated by Ominosity and his cult of devotees are allowed to persist, we believe the plague of violence this Task Force has been asked to investigate will only get worse. Given the state of the city, we feel this is a matter of some urgency.

24

Miki is almost finished packing up Jennifer's apartment. For the first week after she was told her sister had died, she barely got out of bed. She made arrangements to have the ashes shipped to her parents, then crawled under the covers and didn't come out except to eat a few bites of food she can't remember or go to the bathroom. Finally, though, she couldn't stand the sound of her own crying anymore. She could hear Jennifer scolding her, from wherever she was, telling her to pull herself together and get on with it. It's taken the better part of another week just to get things organized. Now stacks of books and videos are neatly arranged against walls. All of Jennifer's photographic gear is gathered together at her workstation. Dishes are methodically arranged in the kitchen, and clothes are laid out in segregated piles on the floor of the bedroom. All that's left to do is figure out where to send Jonas's things, then hire movers to pack everything and get it out of here.

She's sitting by the window, staring out at Quarantine Zone, that goddamn QZ, when she notices two hoodied kids sprint out of the shadows onto the railroad trestle up the street. They scurry down a utility ladder on to the catwalk where one of them retrieves several tubular cans from the backpack he's carrying. Spray paint! With synchronized moves, the duo works in tandem across the trestle's frame, adding baroque graffiti to its steel panels. One of the boys lays out the basic outlines while the other follows with elegant shading. Then the first leapfrogs behind his partner to add flourishes of color. And the second then mimics this maneuver, filling in gaps to complete the legibility. Miki is fascinated by the performance. A shrill whistle from the street signals the artists to skedaddle. They toss their cans and scamper back up the ladder, leaving behind a decorative message for all to see in the next hours and days.

OMINOSITY KNOWS

Someone is knocking at the door.

Mathis. Slightly taken aback by Miki's defeated posture and sleep-deprived pallor.

"Thought I'd stop by to see how you were holding up."

"Guess you better come in, then."

While he waits for her to finish making the coffee she's promised, he tries to think of a way to ask her. If he's too abrupt, or "too much cop," it might open her wounds. He'd seem to be insensitive. On the other hand, if he makes the request too casual, he'll only seem ghoulish.

"You're all packed up," he ventures, attempting an indirect approach.

"Been on autopilot. Figure I owe it to our parents. Let them have a say in what to do with it all." She delivers the coffee, and they sit there in silence. Considering the emotional trauma of the past few weeks, Mathis is surprised that it's not uncomfortable. He wonders if she feels the same.

"The place was such a m ... m ... mess. Just like her," Miki finally says with a voice so quiet Mathis has to lean in close to hear her. "She was everywhere I looked. I could stare at her things, her clothes, her pictures, and feel she was here. Somewhere. Like she was going to walk back through the door at any moment. Now, it's all neat and tidy, everything arranged and organized. She's not here anymore. The place is empty. Like m ... m ... me."

She's barely holding it together, Mathis realizes. An instinctive urge to comfort her wells up inside of him, but he resists. The last thing he wants her to think is that he's come to prey on her vulnerability.

"I'm not angry anymore, Levi," she says as if reading his thoughts. "I was pissed at first because you wouldn't help me find her. But Jennifer ... Jennnifer did what Jennifer ... d ... d ... did. I guess I shouldn't be surprised what happened. She always ran toward danger, not away from it."

More silence. Mathis can't help staring at her. She surely feels it, but she doesn't meet his eyes.

"Must have been hard," she says and finally looks up. She can see that he's confused by the non sequitur. "Finding out you had a daughter," she clarifies. "Missing all those years with her."

Mathis is surprised that he's actually grateful for someone to talk to about Louise. He has no one else. Not Joanne. Certainly not his fellow losers over at St. Eustace.

"Actually, she was my redemption. While it lasted." He stops abruptly. Now it's her staring, boring into his soul with unblinking eyes. "Didn't end well."

"I can take it if you can," she says, knowing he wants to continue.

"I was working a Molly scam at some rave clubs downtown. Bad scene. Lots of underage kids. Horse tranquilizer being peddled to e-tards too whacked to know any better. I finally had enough evidence to bring the walls down. I set up a major bust one night at a pretty hip club. Turns out my daughter was there. Not doing drugs, just slumming it with some friends. Only fourteen, but the assholes at the door let 'em in. She got caught up in our net. I had no idea. That was the first time in fourteen years I'd heard from Joanne. She begged me to help get her daughter out. But she didn't tell me I was the father. Said it was her niece."

"How did you find out?"

"I didn't. My daughter did." He drifts off again. Miki lets him. "Whip-smart, that one," he says, returning to the present. "Said something about the way I looked when I showed up with her release, the way I talked, it got to her. Tell the truth, same thing happened to me. I shrugged it off, but not her. She started pestering Joanne about who her real father was, but Jo wouldn't say. Anyway, the little snoop got hold of her birth certificate. My name was on it. She tracked me down. One thing led to the next. Good little detective, that one."

"Like father like daughter."

"I wanted to resist, but she wouldn't let me. And something happened inside. I'd never felt that way before. Life seemed hopeful, actually. But Jo was pissed. Wanted me to back off."

"Felt threatened?"

"Yeah, I guess. So Louise had to sneak around sometimes to see me. And I let her. I needed to. We had a lot of fun, actually. Being sneaky." He doesn't finish. "Sorry," he says. "This is not the reason I came to see you."

"I know. But it would have been all right if it had." Giving him permission.

"She wanted to be with me New Year's Eve when it struck midnight. A new year. A new life. For both of us. But I was drunk and high. Woke up on the floor of some hotel room I didn't recognize with a couple of gorgeous Czech tourists who didn't speak a word of English. Didn't need to either." He almost laughs, but the rest of the memory intrudes. "I still have the voicemails she left, trying to reach me, begging me to come get her at Club Nightshade so we could be together and have fun. I never made it." There's another dreadful pause while he fights back his rising bile. "I kept them. The messages. I listen to them sometimes, so I can see her face."

He's clutching his coffee cup so hard Miki is afraid it's going to shatter. She reaches out and gently takes it away from him. But she keeps hold of his hand. And now they're both looking at one another. And there's no reason to talk about what they each know comes next.

———

Mathis is staring up at that stain above Jennifer's bed while Miki's peaceful breaths caress the pores of his chest. It had been passionate, desperate lovemaking. Hard and fast, both of them furiously trying to exorcise the pain with which this ugly world had infected them. Racing together and apart toward some cathartic, exhausting release that might, even for just a moment, allow them to sink into an endorphin oblivion where their losses couldn't find and torment them.

"So what was the reason?" she whispers. "Why you came to see me? The real reason."

"Can I see those pictures again?" he finally asks, and so tentatively he's afraid she might not understand him. But without even asking which pictures, she gets up and goes to a box by Jennifer's workstation. Doesn't even bother pulling on clothes, which is fine by him. A moment later, the same photos she showed him at the diner are laid out on the bed. The same photos with that weird anomaly in each. Sometimes an approximation of a face, sometimes just a vague shape in the background, hovering near the photo's primary subjects. Mathis studies them one by one, trying to rationalize what he's looking at, reason it out. But the explanation won't come. Jennifer Preston captured something in these photos that he can no longer dismiss.

"I don't believe in ghosts either, Levi," she says, reading his thoughts again.

When the bed starts to tremble, they know instantly that something terrible has happened. In the Quarantine Zone. As they rush, naked, to the windows, clutching on to each other, they can see the smoke rising a couple of miles away and the buildings in the QZ engulfed in flame.

Last night was only the beginning.

THE OMINOSITY

25

The lads, as Stewart Whitfield refers to them in his best Anglophile geniality, have gathered in a basement room of an estate on the bay. No one knows who owns it, and Whitfield won't say. Store-bought sporting-lodge decor. Parklike grounds surrounded by thick forest marred only by frequency-jamming towers disguised unartfully as pine trees. An upscale safe house.

Everyone arrived separately over the past few hours, and they have since busied themselves with billiards or cards until Hollings Keller finally shows, Dr. Lewis Cameron in tow. Keller knows and dislikes them all. Except for the anorexic thirty-something off by himself at the back of the room. Never seen him before. Ill-fitted suit, hasn't said word, and won't or can't make eye contact with anyone in the room. One of Stewart's "protégés," no doubt.

Remains of a light meal, mostly untouched, are scattered around the tables. Liquid refreshment should have been limited to iced tea and coffee, but the full bar of open bottles in a corner is evidence some have already wearied of the chitchat. Servers were dismissed over an hour ago.

The sabotage in the QZ the other night has added urgency to tonight's inquisition, and insinuations about Holling's fecklessness have hardly been veiled. It's a good thing none but Whitfield are fully briefed on what he had been doing to Jennifer

Preston out in Oyster Bay, especially now that she's escaped. That would surely compromise his narrative of things.

"I think we can conclusively rule out leakage of biochemical stimulants from the Project Morpheus labs causing the phenomenon," Keller says, concluding the presentation to his Torquemadas.

"Well, if it's not coming from those old experiments, then where is it coming from!?" Xiao Hua's English is sinking into the goo of his native accent, which means he's either angry or drunk. Several others, especially Bertrand, because he's a snob, and Andreyev, because he's a bully, demand Xiao repeat himself. Dr. Cameron decides it's time to insert himself into the discussion.

"We have opened a Pandora's box, gentlemen. Our attempts to put the Morpheus genie back in the bottle may have instead aggravated some dark psychic energy surrounding us."

"I give up," Bertrand huffs turning to Keller. "Really, Hollings? I thought the point was to bury that 1960s ooga booga under a thousand tons of city rubble."

"Apparently its ghosts are restless," Keller says, trying to add a bit of sardonic levity to the proceedings. It doesn't work.

"I'd like to see us explain that to the great unwashed!" Andreyev grumbles as if Keller had been serious. "Might as well set up shop at Stonehenge."

"Lighting some incense while we're at it," Xiao mumbles, although it sounds like he's saying *writing some tennis why we had it.*

Keller despairs as he looks around the room at these products of the last century with their devotion to the covert, who claim duplicity and anonymity as articles of faith. Information as power. The lack of it, subservience. That's their catechism. What people don't know, as they say. Separates the haves from the have-nots, don't you see? Must control the narrative, chums. Trouble is, Keller knows that world has expired. Technology and attitudes have seen to that. Privacy, secrecy, they're archaic concepts now. Any attempt to restore the glory days is simply fighting a rearguard action. Today the best way to navigate full disclosure is to participate in it. Perfect the illusion of transparency then weave one's way through it. Nothing to hide is the best camouflage. One's motivations are what matters, and those can be disguised until things are fait accompli. Exactly what Keller is doing out in Oyster Bay.

"So how bad is it, Hemmings?" Whitfield asks, trying to guide the conversation back to a more practical direction. The anorexic looks up from his laptop like a startled teenager caught logging on to porn sites.

"We've been intercepting all media mentions of the phenomenon since the Catastrophe," he says, pushing glasses up his nose and trying to lower his pitch to a more authoritative timbre. "In social media alone, there's been a thirty-two-point-six percent rise in sightings the last two weeks. Descriptions vary, but my analytics still strongly resist any kind of collective obsessional behavior at work here."

"English, please, Hemmings." Whitfield smiles.

Hemmings quickly scans his memory banks for the vernacular while continuing to stare at the walls six inches above everyone's heads "So," he finally sighs, "this is not a case of mob hysteria brought on by contagious suggestive triggers like rumors, media buzz, SM posts and such. Even blogs by Ominosity that have suddenly reappeared referring to so-called Paramentals don't seem to have provoked more sightings. Instead, it seems people are spontaneously and genuinely seeing something ... real." Hemmings's eyes quickly descend back to his laptop screen and he appears to shut down, or at least withdraw from the present. The eyes of everyone else turn toward Keller.

"At some point, gentlemen, we must own the existence of Project Morpheus. But not until we can claim it for our own benefit." Not what they want to hear, but need to. "Unless someone has a better course of action," Keller concludes.

Of course no one does, and frustration succumbs to the lure of the bar.

"We're not bulletproof, Hollings," Whitfield says as he walks Keller back to his car. They had separated from the others on the pretense of getting air and enjoying the grounds, and Stewart has been unravelling the raw subtext of the evening's discussion. "We better get a handle on things before our various masters in the C-suites decide to pay attention. Otherwise, we are all rather fucked."

"But why do I get the feeling I'm the one being curried as sacrificial lamb, Stewart?"

"You stepped up, Hollings. Bared your throat and dared them."

"I'm just trying to help us hang on to the wreckage," Keller responds, careful to reveal only part of his motivation.

"You see, that's the point. The brethren don't even want to admit there's been a wreck. As far as they're concerned, opening this "psychic warrior" can of worms has been nothing but a pyrrhic enterprise."

"A bit late for buyer's remorse, Stewart. Something is going on out there. And we better understand what it is." He neglects to add that by understanding it, he intends to manipulate it.

"What about the Preston girl?" Whitfield asks. "Any idea where she's gotten to?"

"Could be living on the streets for all we know. We have eyes on her old apartment and the sister that's living there. If she shows, we'll know."

"You said she had promise, Hollings. What have we got now that we don't have her?"

"We'll find her. I think Jonas Flack will be helpful there." But he keeps his plans about how he intends to use Jennifer's former lover to himself.

"And if someone else gets to her first?" Whitfield asks.

"We're inoculated. When she turns up, *if* she turns up, she'll come off as a mad Cassandra. Cameron has already prepared the proper documentation."

"And the sabotage?"

"We're pushing out stories about looters and scavengers to our friends in the media. We're increasing patrols inside the QZ. Deadly force authorized."

"Preferred, I would think," Whitfield mutters. "What about Benedict?" he presses.

"Ironically, the violence in the QZ works in our favor. As long as there's still chaos, he can't push too hard to have the quarantine lifted."

"Grateful for small favors, eh?" Whitfield says.

26

Miki still can't shake the feeling. The nagging suspicion that has been creeping up on her ever since she left the apartment this morning with Jennifer tucked safely in her JanSport backpack. *"I'm being followed."* Even at the FedEx office where she carefully repacked what was left of her sister for the guaranteed overnight shipment to their parents' home, that vague paranoia has been gnawing at the back of her mind. *"I'm being watched."*

She had stepped outside FedEx and suddenly realized she had no idea what to do next. She had no more purpose. Nowhere to go, nowhere to be. Mathis left the apartment the other night right after the explosion in the QZ. Who knows when she'll see him again. Does she even want to?

She's been wandering, trying to get control of her emotional havoc. Her dead sister. Her new lover. How to make sense of any of it.

"I'm being watched."

On impulse, she abruptly changes direction and jukes into the street, dodging traffic until she makes it across and descends into the first subway entrance she sees. Good thing she topped up her Metro Card earlier. She barely makes it on the train, hoping she's lost whoever is tailing her. *If* there is anyone tailing her. She tries to distract herself by pulling out her sketchbook diary to work on the face she'd been drawing before she left the apartment. Mathis. Not a bad depiction, actually. Maybe he isn't quite as gaunt as she's drawn him, but his character is all there. Especially in the eyes. *He's got the enigmatic stare down perfectly,* she thinks. The only time she saw that ambiguity disappear was when he was talking about his daughter. Even during their sex, Miki had no idea what he was thinking when their eyes met. He was there, and then he wasn't. He was in the moment, and then he was somewhere else.

She flips the page. Foolish girl. It was a spontaneous tumble, that's all. Two lonely drifters looking for any port in the storm. Nothing more. Don't seduce yourself with fantasy, you silly sap. In this world, fairy tales end tragically. Just look at the unnerving drawing she made of the dead woman at the morgue. The one Mathis called Angela Rossi. The one without a face. The monster of that tale sucked away her beauty, her personality, probably her soul. The image still freaks her out. Who, or what could have done that? She has to look away, and the creepy feeling of being watched surges back down her spine again.

It's the girl in the denim jacket in the car up ahead. Turning away before Miki can see the face. She's been staring at Miki! No doubt about it! And now she's pushing through the crowd in a hurry, as if afraid of being caught. Her back is turned, but everything about her, the hair, the way she moves, startles Miki so much that she drops her sketchbook.

It's Jennifer! She's sure of it. How can that be?

The train is pulling into its next stop. Miki grabs her sketchbook and backpack and elbows her way to the doors through a crush of passengers already shoving to get off and on at the same time. A strident, amplified voice admonishes everyone to "stand clear of the doors, please," but Miki jams herself into the gap and stumbles out to the platform. The station is crowded. She rushes up the stairs, then turns back to look down on this chaos. No sign of the girl in the denim jacket. A train on the downtown line pulls in and a mass of humanity heaves toward its tracks. Miki fights her way back down the stairs, racing up and down the platform, shoving disembarking passengers out of her way, but there's still no sign of the denim jacket. Until the doors close, and the train pulls out. There she is. In the last car, with her back to the windows. Miki races alongside of the train, and the girl, as if sensing her pursuer, finally turns. But she's swallowed up in the darkness of the tunnel before Miki can see her face.

"It was her. I know it was. It was definitely Jennifer." She's marching up the avenue, oblivious to everything around her, almost yelling into her mobile.

"Listen, are you sure this is not wishful thinking?" Mathis's voice at the other end is calm and patient, but she can hear shouting and arguing in the background. Caught him at a bad time apparently.

"What the f ... f ... fuck, Levi? I told you I've been followed all day." She's desperately trying to suppress her stutter tic, but she's too wound up. "God ... d ... d ... ammit. I know it was her. She's not d ... d ... dead. They lied to me."

"Why? And why would she be following you? Why wouldn't she tell you she was okay?"

"I don't know." Her voice cracks. She's on the verge of hysteria. "Am I going crazy, Levi?"

"Okay, where are you?"

Miki looks around. "Corner of Lafayette and Walker."

"Listen to me, don't go anywhere. The tension's worse than usual around here. Ever since that explosion in the QZ. We got some trigger-happy assholes down here just looking for an excuse."

"I've got to find her, Levi!" she shrieks.

"Okay, okay, wait for me. Okay? Don't leave. I'm coming down there. Please, Mick. Don't go running around in a panic."

That's exactly what she's doing. He's right. She's a mess of excitement, fear, hope, and confusion. And deep down, she wants him here, to help her make sense of this. "All right, but hurry up. I don't think I can just stand here doing nothing."

Mathis clicks off. Now what? She can't stop pacing. She's throwing sparks. The world has become a technicolor exaggeration. Her thoughts are ricocheting. Wonder what her parents are going to do with those anonymous ashes she FedExed them? Maybe they can use them on the steps out front next time it snows. *Wow,* she thinks, *I'm really losing it.* And she remembers she hasn't had anything to eat yet. Maybe she was hallucinating Jennifer in the subway station. Mrs. Oh's deli is up the street. Better put something in her stomach before Levi gets here. He already thinks she's nuts. Better not give him any more excuses to dismiss what she saw.

Miki opens the bag of cashews and shoves a handful in her mouth before she gets to the counter to pay for it. She continues down the aisle looking for some decent fruit, or at least a box of raisins. But she's distracted by the sound of a news conference on a TV above the soft drink coolers.

"The Quarantine Zone is still an extremely dangerous place. I just happen to be one of the lucky ones."

The voice is so familiar. Miki moves around the corner to see the TV. It's Jonas. Jennifer's boyfriend. Standing in front of a microphone array outside what appears to be a nursing home.

"It's been quite a struggle to regain my health, physically and mentally. But thanks to my good friend Dr. Lewis Cameron, I'm on the mend." With a nod to a creepy-looking doctor standing right behind him, murmuring encouraging words.

He doesn't look well, Miki thinks as she stares transfixed at the TV. *Not at all like the photos Jennifer has sent her.* His suit doesn't fit him. His complexion is sallow. There are dark circles under his eyes which are blinking too often. There is something placid and apathetic about him. His eyes are unfocused, his voice is monotone. *He's a zombie,* Miki thinks. *Like a ventriloquist dummy being manipulated by that Mephistopheles behind him. This is not the man Jennifer used to tell her about.*

"Mommy, what's wrong with that man?" Miki turns away from the TV to the little girl and her mother shopping in the next aisle.

"Shhh, child, you keep your eyes to yourself, and help me carry these bags," the mother says, turning her daughter around so she meets Miki's stare. It's not the man on TV she's referring to. It's the man at the end of a slow checkout line, visibly frustrated by the time it's taking Mrs. Oh to check another customer's lottery tickets.

"Think you could work any slower up there? Maybe we could all finish a novel or two while we wait."

The customers ahead of him pretend he's not there. One with earbuds sways to her favorite tunes. Another feigns interest in her text messages. No one acknowledges him or each other.

"Hey, you deaf? Or just retarded?" he shouts over them at Mrs. Oh. "We could get arthritis standing here waitin' on the likes of youse."

Miki wants to say something, get in his face about what a moron he is, but Mrs. Oh can handle herself, she decides. The woman is deliberately ignoring the man except to move even more slowly.

"Mommy," the little girl says, tugging at her mother's sleeve, "what's wrong with him?" The mother barely glances at the counter.

"He's just being an asshole, honey. You pay him no mind." She's seen it all before.

But there *is* something wrong with him. And Miki can see it now. A strange gray smoke is wafting around him. Hovering over him like some toxic shadow. A faint, translucent vapor seeping into his shirt, his pants. The customers in front of him don't see it because they refuse to acknowledge the jerk. Which pisses him off even more.

"No wonder this world is so fucked up. People like you ... wasting time ... taking up space." Everyone around him is tensing up, but none of them is willing to call him out and give him the satisfaction of their unease. "I am so sick of this shit!!!!!"

Miki sees him lurch forward. The texting woman in front of him yelps. A cry of surprise, as if suddenly stung by a bee she didn't see coming. But then Miki sees the flash in the man's hand, and this time the woman howls in agony. He is stabbing her with a knife. Repeatedly. She stumbles into the woman behind her, flailing to ward off his blows. Miki jumps back in disbelief, almost knocking the mother and child to the floor. Texting woman goes down, and the man steps on her as he lunges at earbud lady who is too slow to realize what is happening because of the music blaring in her ears. Texting woman tries to crawl away through a pool of her own blood, but earbud lady collapses on top of her with an awful groan. Mrs. Oh is so shocked she's momentarily paralyzed. Just enough time for the knife-wielding man to leap over the counter and slash her face.

The little girl shrieks before her mother can cover her mouth. The man with the knife whips around to glare at them, his face contorted with rage. There is no way out. He is between them and the door. His eyes are sinking into inky black holes. A mottled web of ugly dark veins is shrink-wrapping his skull. His body jerks and spasms as he staggers toward them. He is being warped and contorted by something inside him.

The mother covers her daughter with her own body. Miki jumps forward, putting herself between the man and the mother. She grabs cans and jars from the shelves and starts pelting him with them, but he swats them aside and keeps coming, raising his knife, about to strike.

A violent noise explodes behind him that freezes everyone where they stand. Time slows down. The man with the knife sinks to his knees as a scarlet bloom spreads across his chest.

Behind him, the blood-soaked Mrs. Oh is aiming a pistol, waiting, hoping it's over. But it's not. With an inhuman howl, the man leaps to his feet with a final mad burst of energy and rushes toward Miki, slashing the air with his knife. Three more explosions from the counter concuss the air as Mrs. Oh empties her gun into the man's back, and he finally goes down for good, leaving only the ringing in everyone's ears, and the heartrending whimper of the little girl.

27

Miki is sitting in the back of a paramedic van, wrapped in a blanket, sipping coffee, when she sees Mathis approach the crime tape and flash his shield. After a quick conversation with the uniforms there, he hurries over to her.

"I'm fine," she says, preempting him. "Except for my nerves."

"You out lookin' for trouble, or is it just followin' you around?" There's that smile. The one she struggled with in her sketch. Warm and gentle. And cautious.

"Little lady here is a hero." Miki's African paramedic friend, Baako Kenyata, emerges from inside the van. "Witnesses say she saved a mother and daughter in there. Got in the way of the bad man before he could hurt them."

"Yeah. Big hero," Miki says. "Throwing cans of Vienna sausage at him."

"Slowed him down 'til the owner could stop him permanently," Baako laughs.

"How is she, Baako, Mrs. Oh?" Miki asks.

"All stitched up. But she's going to have a conversation piece of a scar. The other women will make it, too, but they're going to need surgery."

"She really okay?" Mathis asks the big man about Miki.

"She's fine. I gave her a good all over. But the girl needs to rest. Slow down this crazy odyssey she's been on. Not healthy."

"She's alive, Baako," Miki says. "I know it was her. In the subway. They lied to me. Jennifer's alive."

Mathis and Baako exchange a furtive glance. "Then you'll hear from her, my girl," Baako says. "No use runnin' around these streets looking for her, especially these days. Let her come to you."

"He's right, Miki," Mathis adds.

"Who asked you," she says, managing a slight smile which quickly turns into a wince when she tries to stand up. Mathis looks to Baako.

"Couple of bruises when she fell, that's all. Gonna make her stiff for a few days. Here," he says, handing her a packet of pills, "you take a couple more of these when you get home and sleep until next week. Baako's orders." Then to Mathis, "Better that you take her home." Mathis nods and puts an arm around Miki to lead her away from the scene. "My guys say they took your statement," he tells her. "Once the investigation gets organized, they'll want you to come back in and talk to them, but we can leave now."

"I saw it, Levi," she says, lowering her voice to a whisper. "One of those things. Just like in Jennifer's photographs." And this time he doesn't challenge her. "Like a shadow, hanging on to him. He kind of sucked it in somehow, and then he went c ... c ... crazy." Either the drugs or the shock of what she's been through is kicking in hard now. She leans into him for support, and for comfort. He's virtually carrying her by the time they cross out of the crime scene. But not before he spots Fat Freddie Pierce coming out of Mrs. Oh's deli with another member of the task force. He and Mathis eye-fuck each other as Mathis commandeers a black-and-white to take him and Miki away from here.

At about three in the morning Mathis decides Miki is sufficiently tranquilized that he can leave for a while. He'd like to flatter himself that his lovemaking skills are the reason, but he knows better. She clung to him all the way home and wouldn't let go even after they got to her apartment. At first, he thought it was the shock, or the drugs hobbling her better judgment and undermining her inhibitions, but she was persistent and urgent. And besides, she was all he'd been thinking about since the other night, so he wasn't hard to persuade.

"Please, Levi, I can't be alone right now," she whispered as she was pulling on his pants. "Take me someplace else." So he did. And they both got lost. For a few minutes anyway.

He's been sitting by her bed ever since making sure she doesn't surface from Baako's Lorazepam, disoriented and afraid. But Willy G texted him an hour ago to say they needed to meet. The cryptic lure was a single word. "Benedict." He makes sure she's covered up, then leaves a small note under the glass of water he's put by the bed. *Call me when you come back to life. We'll figure this out. L.*

<hr>

Images are careening around Willy G's mind while he hurries to meet Mathis. Fragments of memory. The subway. The perfect pickpocket playground. Two of Willy's crew. The veteran, Red, and the newcomer, Shivers, smallest and youngest. The "stalls." Hanging by the doors, feigning interest in an iPhone game. Next to them, the "mark." A man in an expensive suit. Reading the Wall Street Journal. The station. The train pulling in. Red and Shivers making quick eye contact with Willy, the "tool," at the other end of the car. A nod of approval. Red and Shivers moving toward the doors. Willy slowly coming up behind. The train slowing to a stop. The stalls flanking the mark. Doors opening. Passengers surging forward. Red getting in front of the mark. Turning back to show Shivers something funny on the iPhone.

Shivers pausing to laugh, forcing the mark to veer around them. Right into the tool's path. Willy angrily bumping the man. "Watch it, dude!" Everyone carrying on as if nothing happened.

Willy can't help smiling. The mark had one hundred dollars in his wallet. The crew had steak that night. But Willy's smile quickly fades as he remembers what came next. Shivers had been badgering Willy into letting him participate in more and more cons, and Willy was running out of creative reasons why Shivers wasn't ready for the bigger and better. The real reason was simple. Shivers reminded Willy of the brother he lost on the streets a few years back, and for which Willy still blames himself. But Shivers was nothing if not persistent. So after Mathis "enlisted" Willy to spy on Emeril Benedict, he partnered the kid with Red, and the two of them have recently infiltrated one of the Baron's crew led by those two losers, Hank and Frank. Willy can only hope this hasn't been a big mistake. Maybe what he's come to tell Mathis will get him off the hook, and he can pull Red and Shivers out of danger, and they can all go back to the cons they know best.

It's only taken Mathis twenty minutes to get from Jennifer Preston's apartment near the QZ to his favorite noodle bar food truck, always parked under the train trestle near the station. Best Nabeyaki Udon in the city. He used to bring his daughter here after she tracked him down. It's also where Fat Freddie arrested him for the murder of Dickie Prince, so sitting here watching Mr. Abe work his magic allows Mathis time to contemplate the linkage. But tonight, all he can think about is Willy G's cryptic message.

"I'll have one of those. Put it on his tab," Willy tells Mr. Abe as he slides on to a stool next to Mathis. "So, another citizen goes crazy for no reason, eh?" He produces his iPhone and the TikTok imagery lookie-loos have been posting. Someone, probably one of the first responders, has even gotten a few shots inside Mrs. Oh's convenience store. The two women bleeding on the floor, crying for help. The dead perp lying face down a few feet away. Willy shakes his head. "Ominosity's got it right, Mathis. Somethin's definitely happening to us. That's for sure."

"Let me see that," Mathis says as he takes the phone, using his fingers to enlarge the perp's photo. Sure enough, there it is, on the floor near the counter. One of those dark, ominous stains. Could be confused with dried blood. Or possibly some kind of scorch. But blood wouldn't have dried that fast, and how would burn residue end up on the floor? In another photo, Fat Freddie is standing over it, staring down at it.

"Our girl okay?" Willy asks.

"Couple of bruises and some frayed nerves. So?"

"Okay, so I got a couple of my boys into one of the Baron's crews. Run by these two mooks, Hank and Frank."

"Yeah. I know 'em."

"The Blanks, we call 'em. Losers Benedict uses for small-time shit. Deliveries, pickups, occasional muscle. So stupid they took my guys in without much never mind. And anyway, they may be only twelve and ten, but Red and Shivers are twice as smart as the Blanks, who like them because they're just kids, and cops like you don't hassle them as much. So the other night they're delivering some powdered entertainment to a fancy party uptown, and when they bring back the cash, they overhear the Blanks bitching about some woman named Angela Rossi."

"Went under a train a few weeks ago," Mathis says, becoming intrigued.

"The Baron wants to know what's happened to a briefcase she took with her when she left work that night. Had some papers in it he wants bad. And he's royally pissed the Blanks haven't been able to find it. Used a sushi knife to make a pincushion out of one of their hands."

Willy reaches into the pouch he's carrying and produces a small bundle of papers. Some of them torn, others just fragments, all of them filthy and stained. But enough of the text is still legible. He hands them over.

"Red and Shivers decided to do a little urban archeology. Now, no one can get around this city underground better than me and mine, so they figure out where Ms. Rossi took her last ride and they start looking around." He points to the documents Mathis is intensely studying. "Scattered over the better part of a mile. Under tracks, in culverts, a couple shredded on air vents. Your CSI boys probably thought they were just the usual trash. Not my boys. Like I said, they're sharp. And I train 'em well."

Certain words leap off the pages at Mathis. *Deed, Title Transfer, Escrow, and Loan.* "These addresses are all in the Quarantine Zone," Mathis mutters as Willy starts slurping his Udon.

"Angela Rossi, Emeril Benedict, property inside the QZ," Willy says between mouthfuls. "You're the detective, Mathis, but even I could make a some kinda case out of this."

And Mathis knows he's right. Circumstantial at the moment, lacking smoking gun certitude. But if it walks like a duck and quacks like a duck, as they say.

28

The Lorazepam is wearing off. Miki is having hallucinatory nightmares. The knife-wielding man from the convenience store is stalking her on the streets. Except he doesn't really look like a man now. He's more of a phantom. An oscillating humanoid shape without a face. A shadow on the wall, drifting in and out of focus as the sun comes out from behind a cloud or slides behind one. But there is no wall. And there is no sun. It's a moonless night, and this thing is freestanding, three-dimensional, and brandishing a very large blade which slashes the air like a broadsword. No matter how fast Miki runs, the thing keeps pace. Her feet sink ankle-deep in swampy muck with every step. The people watching across the street make no move to help. They're transfixed, halos of gray smoke gathering around each of them, a sadistic audience turned on by this torment. Behind Miki, an orifice appears in the middle of the thing's faceless head, a mouth perhaps, an endless tunnel gleaming with concentric rings of spiky teeth. The shriek it makes shatters Miki's mind. She sinks to her knees.

The knife comes down.

The world goes black.

Miki's eyes flutter open only to see that ugly stain on the ceiling above Jennifer's bed. She finally notices Mathis's note on the table when she grabs for the water he left there, but she's still parched even after downing the entire glass in one gulp. She stumbles to her feet and tentatively navigates the spinning rooms to the kitchen. The cupboard is bare. She should wait for Mathis to come back. She doesn't.

Outside the crisp predawn air helps clear away the dream residue. The streets are empty. People are reluctant to go out at night lately. Too many stories about incidents like the one at the convenience store. Too much inexplicable violence randomly erupting. Too many rumors that something mutant and dangerous has been set loose. Too many people reading Ominosity blogs. Even protestors have cleared out of the Quarantine Zone perimeter. The area is lifeless except for the HazMats and heavily armed mercenaries on patrol. The abandoned buildings of the QZ now seem like harbingers of the city's future.

Mrs. Oh's deli stands as mute testament to the possibility. Closed up. Lights off. Crime tape still barricading the entrance. Miki has to detour to the convenience store several blocks away. Open, thankfully. She hurries to collect a bottled coffee drink and several energy bars. The minimum-wage clerk behind the counter watches her every move suspiciously, and it pisses her off. Loud K-Pop leaks into the store from his earbuds.

"Your music is shit," Miki says as she drops three dollars on the counter. She actually likes K-Pop, but for some reason she just feels like taunting him. Whatever it is haunting this city is getting to her. He offers a middle finger along with her change.

Back on the street Miki finishes off an energy bar with a couple of bites then washes it down with cold coffee. She feels only slightly better, and the sound of those hideous drones surveying the QZ nearby don't do much for her mood. The awful experience in Mrs. Oh's store earlier almost erased the shock of seeing Jennifer in the subway, but now a torrent of emotions comes flooding back. Her sister is still alive! Why was she told she was dead? What are they trying to cover up? And what has

Jennifer been doing? Why hasn't she contacted her like Mathis and Baako think she should? She tosses the energy bar wrapper to the street and unwraps another. This one, too, is gone in a few chews. The carbohydrate sugars and caffeine hit the nervous system like an electric current.

"Slow down, girl," she says to herself. "Gotta get logical here." And she is surprised by the food wrapper she left on the sidewalk. "I can't believe I did that. What is wrong with me?" She reaches down to pick it back up and takes it to a nearby trashcan.

But when she passes that elevated subway platform and the "Ominosity Knows" graffiti spray-painted there, a familiar feeling returns. The same gnawing at the back of her neck she felt yesterday. Before things got crazy. *I'm being followed.* She deliberately picks up her pace, then slows it back down, then randomly crosses the street back and forth and turns up side streets. The feeling remains. Maybe it's Jennifer. Maybe it's been her sister all along.

Miki turns the corner to a quiet residential street, and now she can hear the patter of other footsteps keeping pace with her. If it is Jennifer, Miki decides, then it's time to confront her. If it's not, well then Miki isn't sure what she'll do. But this silly cat and mouse can't go on. She whips around.

There, in the shadows, a girl is staring at her. Not Jennifer. Too small and too young. Maybe only twelve or thirteen.

"Miki," the girl says. Soft and unthreatening.

"How do you know my name?" Miki shouts. "What do you want!?"

The girl approaches calmly, hands up as if to show she means no harm. "It's not what I want. What *she* wants," she says.

She nods toward a small park across the street. A private retreat for the association of condos in the surrounding buildings. "Member's Only." But the gate is unlocked. "My grandparents used to live over there," the girl says, pointing to an elegant mid-century building, now dark and lifeless. "They used to bring me here to play. No one plays here anymore, though. Not since the

Catastrophe. Too close to the QZ." The gate swings closed behind them with a definitive *click*. As soon as she steps across the threshold, Miki can feel the urban ambience fade away. It's eerie, this oasis in the middle of the city, like a fragment of a parallel universe slipping though time-space, a madness-free zone. She follows the girl to a bench nestled beneath a somber willow, but she's too keyed up to sit.

"Okay, what's your name?" Miki finally blurts.

"Charlotte." Matter of fact. No emotion, no qualification.

"It's Jennifer, isn't it? She sent you, didn't she?" And when the little girl nods, "How do you know her?"

"She rescued me. Twice."

Miki's heart is pounding so hard she feels out of breath. She paces back and forth, scanning the area with hopeful eyes.

"She's not coming," little Charlotte says. "She sent me instead."

"She's alive ... she's here ... she sent you ..." Miki pants.

"She wants you to go. Leave the city."

"Wait a minute! She t ... t ... told you that? She told you to f ... f ... find me and tell me that!?"

"She doesn't want you to be in any more danger. Like you were in that store."

"I was right. She's been following me!"

Little Charlotte won't confirm or deny.

"Okay, look, where the hell is she!?"

"Where you can't find her," the girl answers.

"Why? What kind of trouble is she in? Is someone trying to hurt her? Who is she hiding from? The people who told me she was dead?"

"There are worse things to be afraid of."

Charlotte's eyes are wide. Her posture is rigid. Fight-or-flight coiled.

"It's those things, isn't it!" Miki whispers. "In her photographs. They're real, aren't they?"

"It's not safe here, Miki. And it's gonna to get worse."

"I want to know what's going on. I want t ... t ... to t ... t ... talk to her! I need t ... t ... to talk to her."

"She said you'd be upset, but there's nothing you can do to help her right now. You must go home. It's for the best."

"No, goddamit! NO! What the hell ...?" Miki isn't talking to the girl any longer. She's running back and forth, shouting at the streets. "Talk me to me, Jen! I know you're out there. I know you're watching. How can you do this? Why don't you let me know you're okay? What the hell is the matter with you!?"

She turns back to Charlotte, fury raging in her eyes. She wants to grab the little shit and shake the answers out of her. But the girl is gone.

"She loves you, Miki." There she is, on the other side of the fence, staring back in at Miki. How did she get out there? "She loves you more than anything. It will kill her if anything happens to you. Her exact words. I memorized them. Please, go home. She'll be all right. She promises." And she's walking. Up the street, vanishing around a corner.

"Wait," Miki shouts, racing to the gate. It won't open at first, but that's only because Miki is fumbling with the handle in panic. "Wait!" The gate finally gives, and Miki lurches out to the street, racing to the corner only to find herself at the mouth of an empty dark alley. No windows. No doors. No Charlotte. Just three brick walls. There's no place that girl could have gone. But she has vanished into thin air. How can that be?

A low moan of wind howls up a twenty-story shaft, echoing Miki's bewilderment.

"I am not leaving," Miki says with such rigid conviction she even surprises herself.

"Why am I not surprised?" Mathis chuckles. He can't help it. When he got back to Jennifer's apartment and found her gone, he wasn't surprised by that either. So he lay down on the bed where they'd made love and fell asleep staring at the mysterious stain on the ceiling, thinking about what to do with the documents Willy showed him. And what to do about Miki.

He was so exhausted he never heard her return. She had to flick cold water on his face to wake him up. But here they are now, at that diner they visited after Baako showed them Angela Rossi on a slab at the morgue, both of them famished, trying to satiate a raging hunger roused by the last forty-eight hours of violence, sex, and unexpected revelations that might bring each of them closer to the answers they've been craving.

"When she realizes I'm not going anywhere, she'll have to show up."

"You seem pretty sure of that," Mathis says gently.

"I know my sister. She won't take no for an answer."

"But you intend to say just that," he says.

"In person."

That same waitress from before is keeping her distance at the moment, sitting on a counter stool pretending to be interested in the morning paper. Maybe because the intensity of their conversation cautions against any hovering, or maybe because of Miki's menacing "hands-off" vibe every time she glances over at Mathis.

"Hey, we could use more food over here," Miki calls out rudely, holding up her plate of applesauce and potato pancake scraps.

"What 'bout your *friend*?" the waitress asks, making sure Miki can't misconstrue the snark.

"More eggs and ham. He's gonna need his energy," Miki fires back. Game, set, match.

"Maybe you should take your sister's advice," Mathis says, pretending to be oblivious to the female headbutting.

"Are you kidding? I just find out she's alive, and you think I should abandon her?"

"Sounds to me like she's abandoned you, Mick."

Her stare almost wilts him. She's going lose it if he's not careful.

"Don't you get it, Levi? She's on to something. Something about the Catastrophe. And someone wants to stop her from pursuing it."

"How do you know that?"

"She goes missing while looking for her boyfriend in the QZ. She leaves photos behind with mysterious images in them. Authorities want me to think she's dead, but she's not. She won't c … c … come out of hiding, but she sends a child to warn me things aren't safe and going to get worse. Connect the dots. Something is being k … k … kept from us!"

She's right, he knows, but he can't let her get involved. There are too many ways it could all go sideways.

"You're not ready for this, Mick. You have no idea what you're up against," he says, wishing immediately he could take back that last part.

"Up against what, Levi? What am I up against?"

He has to walk it back. The last thing he needs is to encourage her with crazy theories about underworld crime bosses, bent cops, and government conspiracies. Not to mention the possibility of something unnatural roaming the streets.

"All of it!" he barks. "Lunatics with knives in convenience stores, madmen on buses, your sister and whatever it is she's gotten herself into. The city itself has turned. It's become a malevolent creature all its own!"

"Don't patronize me, Levi."

"This is no place for someone like you."

"Someone like me?"

"You know what I mean."

"No. Not sure I d … d … do." Shit. Goddamn tic. Undermining her at the worst possible moment. Deep breath. "But thanks for the vote of confidence."

"Think about it, Miki. You're not from around here. You don't know the city. You're better off waiting at home until

Jennifer decides to reach out and explain. What can you do about it now anyway?"

"I was hoping maybe you could help me figure it out."

The waitress arrives with more food.

"Your first spat?" she chuckles.

"Know what, you can have him," Miki says, getting to her feet.

"Miki," Mathis pleads, reaching for her.

"Sorry I'm such a disappointment," she says as she dodges his grasp and escapes out the door.

"Shame for all this to go to waste," the waitress purrs, hoping for an invitation. But Mathis ignores her.

I must be poison, he thinks. *First my daughter, now Miki.*

OYSTER BAY PSYCHIATRIC HOSPITAL

TO: Hollings Keller

FROM: Dr. Lewis Cameron

RE: Morpheus Project

In response to your request for an update:

It is becoming increasingly evident that the phenomenon we originally observed is real. However, we have not yet been able to replicate it under laboratory conditions. So the question remains: what are these entities?

- Are they some kind of residue of Morpheus experiments which we have released?
- Are they the product of a mass psychosis exacerbated by the Catastrophe and subsequent Quarantine?
- Are they a manifestation of individual cerebral emissions instigated by stress, fear, other factors (which we are duplicating in our experiments)?
- Or have we inadvertently stirred up some kind of dark psychic energy heretofore unknown and beyond our current measurement capabilities?

The paramount question we should be asking ourselves at this point is whether we're dealing with individual manifestations of the phenomenon or a collective disorder, i.e. "monsters" from the collective id, that has been exacerbated by recent events. The answer to this question will provide significant insight into how we proceed.

Going forward, I recommend we stay the course with our cerebral stimulations and drug protocols on available and newly acquired subjects, and continue our attempts to provoke observable incidents of the phenomenon so that we can understand what we're dealing with and ultimately facilitate positive operational capability.

29

Why do I have the feeling we're being watched? Hollings Keller is thinking as he looks up from Cameron's memo to stare out the window of his black SUV at the empty buildings of the Quarantine Zone. His convoy is flanked fore and aft by M1161 Growlers, those lightweight, fast attack vehicles with .50 cal BMGs mounted on each. A bevy of armed drones buzzes overhead like alien wasps monitoring the convoy's progress, surveying the area for any suspicious movement. A week ago Keller would have thought this show of force laughably extreme, but the explosion and the fires last night have changed the equation. What at first seemed like a few random acts of vandalism appear to have morphed into a kind of improvised insurgency. More of an annoyance than a serious challenge so far, but the media jackals are having a field day. Not to mention that anonymous blogger, Ominosity.

"This damn thing is stifling," Keller complains to his driver as he tugs at the neck of the portable HazMat mask he was given for the ride. "It obstructs my view." But he can see well enough the charred façades of buildings from last night's blaze. Whoever set off this conflagration knew what they were doing. The properties are nothing but burnt-out shells now. Several HazMat teams are already on site, moving in and out with monitoring devices and sample collectors under the watchful guard of heavily armed mercenaries patrolling nearby.

When the SUV pulls to a stop, Keller waits patiently as his bodyguards dismount the Growlers and form a shield perimeter by his door. Burkett, the team leader, emerges from the scorched carcass of a former hotel and approaches Keller's door.

"Clear for entry, sir," Burkett says.

"No need to maintain the charade any longer, is there?" Keller asks, impatient to be rid of the HazMat mask.

"No, sir," Burkett agrees. "No one outside the QZ can see this far in."

Keller is happy to fill his lungs with the uncontaminated air, but inside the hotel lobby the smell of charred walls, blistered paint, and some chemical residue Keller can't identify assaults him as soon as he steps through the door.

"They had accelerants on every floor, sir. By the time we got here, there was nothing to do except let it burn itself out. Our primary objective was to keep the fire from spreading too far."

The tour continues out the back of this building into an abandoned but unscathed multiplex movie theater in the next block. Keller has to pause when he sees the marquee above the box office. Someone has rearranged the plastic letters there.

NOW SHOWING
WELCOME TO HELL
PRICE OF ADMISSION...EVERYTHING YOU GOT

He follows Burkett into the auditorium where small emergency lights in the aisles are throwing bizarre shadows over the walls and movie screen. Keller can't help noticing how dirty the room is. No one ever thinks about this, he muses. We all just sit in the dark in our comfortable seats blissfully unaware of the sticky soda stains beneath our feet, the discarded candy wrappers, the spilled popcorn, the used napkins and other assorted nasties hidden by the darkness, ignored by the pimply faced staff cleaning up after each show. There are still jumbo drinks in the cup holders, dropped food in the aisles, even some coats and caps forgotten on the seats and floor. It's as though people just got up and left. Or were forcibly evacuated. The mess suggests no one has been in here since the New Year's Eve explosion. But Keller knows better. That's why he's been summoned.

"This way, sir," Burkett calls out from the front of the auditorium. When Keller joins him there, the man pulls back a small fly curtain allowing them to go behind the screen and into a utility area where more emergency lights are bordering a small encampment. A couple of tents, abandoned sleeping bags, some Coleman lanterns, a small grill. A surreal scene that could have been a set in one of the movies that once played here. Someone's squat, but clearly disrupted. One of the tents is partially collapsed, the grill is overturned. The detritus of people's belongings is scattered about. And there on the floor, a large, dried stain. Blood?

"How are they still evading us?" Keller asks, not even trying to mask his irritation.

"They're like roaches, sir. By the time we get a sighting and move in, they've scattered."

Keller steps carefully through the trash. *What is wrong with these people? They're being hunted like animals. What possible reason could they have for hiding out like this?* He trips over a small black bag, spilling its contents across the floor. Camera accessories. Two lenses, ND and UV filters, a couple of unopened DAT cards. Jennifer Preston! She was a photojournalist. What's the possibility this is where she's escaped to?

"Do we know how many we're dealing with?" he asks the Burkett.

"Hard to say. We've found a few other squats like this, but we can't be sure if it's the same group moving from one place to another, or several different ones. This one is interesting, though. Why I wanted you to see it."

"Interesting how?"

"We didn't roust this one. Whatever made this group flee, it wasn't us."

Keller turns back to that stain on the floor. It has a rust color consistent with dried blood, but the closer he looks the more he realizes the edges have a chalkiness to them. He drags the tip of a shoe through it, smearing it like old dust or the residue of some kind of scorch.

"It's only a matter of time, sir," Burkett assures. "If we don't get them first, something else will."

Keller admires the man's sangfroid. If he only knew what he's up against.

"Have there been new sightings?" he asks.

"Not since that rookie we handed over to Dr. Cameron," the team leader responds. "And we're still not sure what went down with him."

"Neither are we."

"My men are pros, sir. Takes a lot to spook them."

"What about Ground Zero? Any quantifiable activity?"

"None that we've been able to monitor. I have our equipment calibrated daily. If anything were emanating from those old labs, we'd get readings immediately."

Keller moves away. He's running out of time to keep Stewart Whitfield and the lads at bay. And the question remains.

"Where are they coming from?" he whispers to himself. He's not thinking about squatters.

But he is thinking about Jennifer Preston.

30

Mathis knows he's close. He can taste it. That iron tang in his saliva. Blood and adrenaline. The body calling to him. The mind racing to keep up. The answers he's been desperate for these past months, starting to become clear.

"Connect the dots," Miki had said. So yes, go ahead, connect them: the New Year's Eve explosion at Club Nightshade, Louise's death, the murder of the bomber, a small-potatoes mook named Dickie Prince for which he, Mathis, the alcoholic loser cop unable to cope, was the perfect patsy. Fat Freddie Pierce, Emeril Benedict. The Quarantine Zone. The creeping advancement of corruption. A Rorschach inkblot to some, maybe, but not to Mathis. It's a gruesome portrait of rot. Except it's still incomplete.

All this can't simply add up to a land-grab scheme, can it? Some mad conspiracy to drive people out of their homes and businesses so their property can be had for a song? The rich and powerful have been pulling that kind of shit for decades. They call it "eminent domain." Why resort to killing several hundred people and contaminating the area when a compliant court would have done just fine? Why risk the blowback, the public outrage, the conspiracy theories, the mysterious violence, and a special task force investigating? There must have been some quid pro quo. That's the missing piece. Something even more sinister at work here. Who is the phantom in the background, hovering over it all like one of those things in Jennifer Preston's photographs? Who is the puppet master?

Still work to do. Move up the chain of command. Don't get distracted. Not now. Not so close. And yet, and yet, what about Miki? Can't risk her getting hurt because of his carelessness. Once in his godforsaken life has been enough, and almost more than he can bear. What he's about to do is risky, no doubt about it. Got to make sure the chain reaction doesn't result in collateral damage. Take it step by step. Let the bad guys make the first mistake.

He takes the steps from the street into his precinct almost three at a time.

"Where'd you get this?"

Fat Freddie is sitting at his desk looking over one of the incriminating documents Willy G brought to Mathis.

"One of my CIs," Mathis shrugs. "Found it floating in the breeze down in the Canal Street station. Isn't that where they think Angela Rossi decided to take the train?"

"So?"

"Notice the name at the bottom of this deed," Mathis says, running a finger ever so slowly across the bold print: **Metropolitan Development Partners, LLC.** "Seems I remember that's the name of a shell company. A front for one Emeril Benedict, aka the Baron."

Freddie does his best to remain poker-faced, but Mathis knows his tells. That slight hint of a sneer tugging at his left cheek. It's the name, Benedict, hitting the target.

"What's this got to do with the price of peas?" Freddie mutters, dismissively tossing the document aside as if it were just another Human Resources memo about sexual harassment.

"Check the date," Mathis says, pushing the paper back into Freddie's line of sight. "Our uptown friend just happens to acquire title to these buildings just days before the New Year's Eve explosion. Curious, don't you think?"

"Bad luck," Freddie offers.

"The Baron doesn't trade in luck, Freddie. He makes plans."

Freddie stares at the paper on his desk, but Mathis knows he isn't really looking at it. He's calculating odds.

"Why are you showing this to me?" Freddie asks.

"Well, since I've been excluded from the task force, maybe you want to bring it up. Earn some kudos."

"Do I need them?"

"There's a brass ring to the guy who can close the Nightshade bombing, Freddie. The task force's mandate has its origins there, right? All the crap going on in the city these days. It all starts there. Everyone knows it."

"And you want a piece, then?"

Mathis isn't sure whether Freddie means credit with the task force or some kind of under-the-table remuneration courtesy of the Baron. He chooses option number one. Let Freddie think he's too square to see a sticky bribe sashaying his way.

"You could mention my name to the team. Yeah, that would be stand-up. Make me slightly less pissed off about my false arrest in the Dickie Prince murder." Make the linkage tight. Benedict, Dickie Prince, the New Year's Eve explosion. Make Freddie understand that dots are being connected.

Freddie meets Mathis's smile with an enigmatic one of his own. Both of them know there are ulterior motives at work here. But that's okay. They're just two scorpions in a jar, circling each other, waiting for the other to make the first move. Way the game is played.

"Who's your informant? Your CI?" Freddie asks. "He got any more of these?"

Nice try, Mathis thinks. *But clumsy, and expected.* "Wouldn't be surprised. I'll ask." Leave it at that. Don't oversell. He can feel Freddie's stare boring into his back as he leaves the bullpen. Good. The fuse has been lit.

Emeril Benedict is at his usual post in the kitchen of the Black Orchid, sitting on a stool watching his chef, Cho Prayut, dice coriander for the pot of broth that is simmering nearby, about to become the day's hot and sour soup. The Baron studies the man's technique as one would a pianist's fingers massaging a Rachmaninoff glissando. The man is an artist, and Benedict considers it a privilege to envy his skills.

"We have a problem."

Benedict is annoyed by the intrusion, but he knows he can't ignore it. Freddie Pierce does not offer warnings casually.

"It's that fuck, Mathis. Says one of his informants found this while spelunking under the city."

Benedict takes the document from Freddie's outstretched hand and scans it. Within seconds, his neck begins to flush. "Is there more?"

"No doubt. I'm sure he's holding on to it for future use."

"What's his game?"

"Not sure."

"Wants a taste?"

"I doubt it. He's too goddamn righteous for his own good."

"So then, this is just some accidental discovery? Mathis has some 'snout' on the leash who just happens to find trash in a subway tunnel and decides it's significant?"

"Not a likely scenario, is it."

"It is not! I need to know who this urban mole is, Freddie. I need to know where he found this and how much more of it there is. And I need to know what Mathis's agenda is."

Freddie is already plotting ways to lure his prey into a trap when the Baron's brightening mood unexpectedly changes the subject.

"Well, well, it's the future. Freddie, come see."

He's referring to the unwashed, malnourished street urchins coming through the kitchen door.

"Bringing you glad tidings, Mr. B." the taller one, Red, smiles. "The weekly honorarium, sir." He gives Shivers a slight nudge in the Baron's direction, and the smaller boy pulls a fat envelope from his pocket.

"With regards from Hank and Frank, Mr. B," Shivers says proudly.

"Good boys. Don't say anything to those morons you work for, but I've been keeping an eye on you two. You be patient and you'll be running a crew of your own one of these days."

Willy G's boys make a good show of gratified smiles and enthusiastic nods.

"Whatever you say, Mr. B," Red says. "We aim to please."

"Get your dirty little faces over here and sit down. Cho, spoon out some of that hot and sour for these young men. Get them spring rolls, too. I can't have people working for me who look like refugees from the Bakhmut."

Benedict opens the envelope and pulls out two five-dollar bills. Stuffs one each in the boys' shirt pockets.

"Thanks, Mr. B," Red says.

"C'mon, Freddie," Benedict orders. "You haven't picked up a morsel of food since you got here. Are you sick or something? Sit down here with our new apprentices."

"Hank and Frank, huh?" Freddie asks as he sits with the boys and watches them stuff their faces while the Baron moves away to count his cash.

"Crew we were running with couldn't cut it," Red volunteers.

"We do the odd bit here and there," Shivers adds.

"You've made quite an impression on the boss, I see," Freddie says, and the boys are too young and inexperienced to sense the malice in his tone.

"That's 'cause we're good," Shivers says a bit too casually. "We can get from one end of this city to the other without ever coming up for air!"

Which starts Freddie thinking. "That so?"

Mathis is sitting in a small coffee shop across the street from the alley behind the Black Orchid. He's been here the better part of an hour, nursing a vente latte, which he can't stand, but which he needed to buy to justify his apparent purposelessness. But his patience is paying off.

Fat Freddie steps outside the Black Orchid's kitchen door, finishing off one of Cho's inimitable spring rolls. First place he came after Mathis visited him at the precinct. To pass on the incriminating document to the Baron no doubt.

Connect the dots.

31

Miki has been concentrating on her sketchbook and the drawing she's made of the girl who confronted her on the street.

> *"Jennifer's errand girl. Who is*
> *she? Where did she come from? She*
> *said that Jen rescued her. Twice.*
> *What does that even mean? Can I*
> *even believe what she told me?"*

Miki thinks she's seen Charlotte since, staring out doorways or around corners, in a subway station crowd or in the reflection of a store window, but she can't really be sure. The girl is quick and clever. There one minute, gone the next. It would make sense, though, if she was stalking. Miki has made a purposeful show of herself on the streets these past few days. Hanging out at the QZ perimeter, taking long aimless walks just to be outside and visible, visiting Mrs. Oh at her deli now that it's reopened. If the little spy is still watching, Jennifer knows Miki has not left the city. Precisely what Miki wants her to know.

So why hasn't she shown up?

Mathis's deep breathing finally distracts her. He's asleep next to her on the bed. She tried to avoid him after what that bovine bitch at the diner called their *spat*. She even hid in the dark several times when he came to the apartment and pounded on the door. But he knew she was here. And this morning when she opened the door to go out, she found him leaning against the wall, nodded off. He'd been there all night. Such persistence destroyed her resolve. She gently nudged him awake and led him into the bedroom where she promptly wore him out and put him back to sleep.

She strokes hair away from his eyes. He snorts softly and rolls toward her. Sleep softens his face, erasing the torment and self-loathing that usually darkens his expression. For these precious few moments, the boy he once was surfaces through the pain. She could stare at him like this for hours, but she won't permit herself the pleasure. That way lies emotional peril. She can't take the chance. And neither should he.

She slips off the bed, wrapping herself in his shirt, and goes to the kitchen to make tea. Standing by the stove, waiting for the kettle to boil, still calmed by the intimacies of the past few hours, she almost forgets her mission: find Jennifer, find out what she's gotten herself into, find out who is trying to hurt her.

The girl staring up at her window from the street below brings it all smashing back. A jolt straight to the nervous system, as if someone just turned on a TV and it was still at volume ten.

Miki is dressed and out the door in moments, leaving Mathis still deep in his dreams.

She tries to make a furtive approach to the spot where Charlotte was standing, but the girl is no longer there. If she saw Miki clock her from the kitchen window, she probably decided not to stick around. Maybe she has simply moved to a different vantage point. Miki moves down the block, trying to look nonchalant while remaining hyperalert for any sign of her. Sure enough, she catches the girl's reflection in the window of a bakery she's passing. She's at the intersection behind Miki, watching with that feral stare. Miki keeps going until she can make a turn in that direction seem casual.

The girl is gone.

No, wait, there she is, down the street, just a small blonde head, bobbing through pedestrian traffic. This has gone on long enough, Miki decides. If Jennifer won't come to her, then she has got to go to Jennifer. She hurries across the street in pursuit, maintaining just enough distance to keep the girl in view. Charlotte's route seems aimless, uncertain. Maybe she knows Miki is following and is trying to shake her. This goes on for several blocks until suddenly Miki recognizes where she is. That quiet residential neighborhood with its small park where Charlotte introduced herself and told Miki her sister wanted her to leave town. But the girl isn't there either. Miki stifles an urge to call out her name. There are only a few people nearby. A businessman lost in the urgency of texting as he walks, a housemaid bringing trash bags to a dumpster then scurrying back inside, a woman jogging behind a baby stroller, holding tight her Doberman's leash as it yanks her toward a tree to piss. Each one self-involved. Each one avoiding eye contact with Miki. It's unlikely any of them has seen Charlotte or would be forthcoming if they had. The city is too tense for that kind of polite neighborliness. Best advice these days, avoid others. Mind your own business. Keep moving, never stop.

There's a flash of dirty blonde in the distance. Going into that alley where she saw Charlotte disappear the other night. Without hesitation, Miki hurries there and lurches to a stop. As before, the alley is empty. No windows. No doors. No Charlotte. The girl has once again vanished into thin air. How can that be? There is no place she could have gone. But there is a manhole cover slightly ajar at the far end of the alley. No one would even notice it unless one was determined to suss out the magician's trick. The damn thing is so heavy Miki wonders if Charlotte could have moved it by herself. But where else could she have gone? With great effort, Miki slides it back just enough to see a small ladder dropping into the darkness below.

"I must be crazy," Miki says aloud to the four walls. Crazy enough to squeeze herself past the heavy steel plate to descend into the city's guts.

It takes a moment for her eyes to adjust to the darkness. Even then, she can only see a few feet ahead of her. Miki waits, breathless, straining to hear any movement. Nothing. She gamely sets off, feeling her way along the wall, feet sloshing in a muck of mud and waste. She's afraid to call out because of who or what that might attract. People are rumored to be living in these subterranean warrens. And who knows what kind of mutant animals might be breeding down here? The muffled city din hovering overhead is a distorted reminder that Miki has stepped into a parallel universe. It's hard to keep track of time or distance down here. There are no points of reference.

After what she assumes has been about fifteen minutes, Miki comes out of the clammy corridor she's in only to realize she's stumbled into one of the city's subway lines. To her left a dim glow indicates some kind of light source. Miki heads that direction, careful to avoid the third rail, sensitive to any change in wind or sound which could signal an approaching train. By the time she emerges into a large, underground "yard" where several rail sidings venture off like spokes on a wheel, she knows she's lost. It's a catacomb of tracks and pillars here. Still no sign of Charlotte, visible or audible, in this gritty iron-greasy atmosphere. So now what? Which way to go? Back the way she came? Which way was that? She's completely disoriented by this dank mandala of crisscrossing tracks rimmed by the black holes of tunnels leading who knows where. Strange noises are seeping out of them. Agonized moans or impatient whines, or maybe just the low growl of forced air against old piping and brick. She needs to get back up to the street. She chooses one of the black holes at random and heads into it. She can sense things scurrying around and above her. It stinks down here.

She almost misses the crumbling concrete steps in the dark. In fact, if she hadn't tripped on a fallen brick from the wall, she would have passed right by it. She has no idea where these steps lead, but they go up, and that's good enough for her. The higher she goes, though, the narrower the staircase, the lower the ceiling. Definitely built during another era when people were smaller. It spirals around like the turret of an old castle. Miki has no idea how many floors she's ascending but she's out of breath by the time she comes to a broken gate that's swinging on rusty hinges as if someone had just pushed it open. Miki squirms past it and is finally able to stand up straight. She relishes the clean morning air so much that, for a brief instant, she doesn't even recognize the neighborhood she's entered. When she finally looks around and clocks the environment, her heart almost stops.

"You gotta be kidding me," she says, staring at the empty streets, the blacked-out buildings, the abandoned vehicles.

She has stumbled right into the Quarantine Zone!

The Quarantine Zone is a malignant tumor in the middle of our city.

As long as it exists, we are in danger.

Think about it this way.

The contamination in the QZ as a metaphor for the corruption everywhere.

The fear of it... a contagion. Impervious to medication.

And we are all becoming infected.

Unless ...

THE OMINOSITY

PART III

THE  OMINOSITY

Don't listen to them. The experts.
The professionals. The chattering classes.

They want you to think things are under control.

Things are not under control.

We have been lied to.
And we're going to prove it.

THE OMINOSITY

32

Miki can't hold her breath any longer. It's probably too late now anyway.

She steps further into a world devoid of color, into a landscape of somber and empty buildings shrouded in a grim haze as far as the eye can see. Stark and monochromatic, like her sister's photographs.

"I am legend. HA!" Miki blurts, thinking about Richard Matheson's iconic novel which she loves.

A strange hush has descended here, an unnerving stillness that's settled over the whole Quarantine Zone. No traffic noise, no hum of machinery or pedestrian clatter can penetrate it. Not even the sound of distant sirens wailing. There's only the occasional whine of wind gusts cruising through these forsaken urban canyons. Miki's footsteps sound to her like gunshots as she moves down the street to the intersection. Nothing but deserted avenues, abandoned vehicles, open doorways and broken windows in every direction. Is this where Jennifer fled? Is this where she's been all this time? And if it is, why? What would she be doing in here? What would she be looking for?

"I should get out of here," Miki says to herself. This is the QZ, after all. What if it really is contaminated? By something biological, or chemical, or who knows what? She could end up like those first poor bastards they sent into Chernobyl.

Something moves in the window of an apartment building up the block. Miki freezes. An animal? A person?

"Hey! HEY! Someone there?" It's foolhardy to call out like this, Miki knows. What if it's one of those armed security squads that patrol the borders of the QZ? What if it's one of those HazMat creeps?

What if it's one of those ... things!? "Paramentals," Willy G called them.

"Charlotte? That you!?"

No answer.

Miki moves down the street toward the apartment building where she saw whatever it was. One of the gilded doors at the entrance is swaying slightly as if someone had just pushed it. Miki can't help herself. She goes inside.

Nice place from the looks of it. At least it had been once. Now a visible layer of dust coats everything, and that musty smell of neglect is pervasive. There are magazines left open on the tables, some luggage forgotten by the elevator, a few coats haphazardly thrown over couches in the seating area. There's even one of those expensive Graco baby strollers overturned by the Concierge Desk. It's like people just got up and left. In a hurry.

Against her better judgment, Miki decides she wants to get a better view of the QZ. That means upstairs. But there's no electricity, so that means no elevator. She's going to have to hoof it. The building is only about ten stories tall. How bad can it be? Curiosity wins out over fear.

It's dark in the fire stairs. She continually stumbles as she climbs. When she finally gets to the tenth floor, she realizes there are two more to go. She's completely winded, and adrenaline is flooding her bloodstream so fast that she feels like she's floating. But what the hell, she's come this far.

A foggy ambience of daylight seeps in through a window at the end of the twelfth-floor corridor, allowing her to see apartment doors on either side. She chooses the west side of the building figuring the view there will give her the widest expanse of the QZ. Most of those doors are locked. *People expected to return,* she thinks. But one at the end of the hall is not only unlocked, it's wide open. Miki pauses in the corridor, listening, wondering if some evacuation refusenik could still be hiding inside.

"Helloooooooo? Anyone home? Pizza's here," she says with a chuckle. No one answers, so she steps inside and starts her tour.

The apartment is homey. Nothing designerly about it. Comfortable furniture comfortably arranged. Hardwood floors occasionally interrupted by department store rugs. An IKEA-style desk is sitting in front of floor-to-ceiling windows, still piled high with books and papers. Legal tomes and case briefs, some of them handwritten on long yellow pads. Gibberish to Miki. Other than that, though, there's a puzzling absence of personality here. No pictures anywhere. No family mementos cluttering tables or bookshelves. Maybe the tenant didn't intend to stay long. Maybe this place was only temporary.

Miki moves the ergonomically optimized desk chair aside and steps up to the windows. A sweeping view of a QZ boulevard lined with empty plastic-shrouded buildings spreads out in front of her. There's no activity on the streets of this desolate panorama, and a surge of loneliness sweeps over her. Do the buildings feel it? Do the streets? Does this entire quarter of the city miss the purpose for which it used to exist?

The bed is unmade in the bedroom. A few suits and dress shirts are left behind in the closet. Some dirty underwear and socks are on the floor. The bathroom is neat except for a dry bath towel hanging over the shower door. The toilet paper roll is just about finished. Interestingly, the kitchen doesn't smell. No rotten food left behind on the counters. No moldy garbage festering in the trash. No dirty dishes in the sink. But there's a place set at the center island. An empty bowl waiting for its cereal, a tall glass waiting for its juice, a large coffee mug parked precariously at the edge of the counter next to a kettle of water on a Sterno burner. The mug is half-full. Abandoned in a hurry, it appears.

"Guess they didn't have time to finish," Miki says quietly as she picks up the mug to move it a safer distance away from the edge.

"What the ...?" She almost drops it. The mug is warm! The coffee inside is still fresh!

Senses on high alert. Someone has been in here. And not long ago. What's she going to do if she's caught here? How's she going to explain? She quickly retraces her steps to the front door, treading as lightly as she can, hyperalert to any sound or movement not hers. When she's convinced that no one is lurking in the corridor, she takes a deep breath and bolts for the fire stairs. It's her only way out. But it's also anyone else's way in. What if someone is coming back? What if she runs into them? Miki decides she'll just keep on going as if it's the most common thing. She'll probably say something stupid, like *"damn elevator, always breaking down, huh?"* Hopefully she can put enough distance between them to get away on the street.

She doesn't encounter a soul on the way down. And on the street, it's as quiet and desolate as ever. She feels like she's standing in one of Jennifer's photographs. So strange, this quiet. Like in the movies when they turn all the music and backgrounds off. Not just down, but off. The dramatic effect always startles Miki. She's still freaked by that fresh cup of coffee. People are obviously still living in the QZ. The question is, how many? And why? And is one of them her sister?

A gust of wind sweeps across the street bringing with it dust, some scattered trash ... and *that smell*. The same scent in the air the night that dark figure was stalking her. Cordite and ozone. Like the air after a lightning strike. And suddenly she remembers where she smelled it first. On the subway. On Bike Boy. When he turned into a dick and wouldn't move out of her way. There's something slightly rancid about it. Creeps her out.

"Okay, tour's over," Miki mutters, trying to stave off a panic attack. "Time to get your skinny ass outta here." But which way to go?

In the far distance, through thick haze, she can see the faint glow of office towers on Seventh Avenue. That's north. If she heads in that direction she should eventually come out of the QZ somewhere mid-city. So she sets off, her pace verging on a jog. Those damn hard soles of her shoes reverberate off these empty buildings like cracked whips, but she can't very well tiptoe all the way out of here, now can she? An uncomfortable feeling sweeps over her after a couple of blocks. She's being watched. From windows. From doorways. From alleys. Feral eyes flickering here and there, tracking her progress. Animals maybe? Like in those TV shows about the Earth-After-Man where even the tallest skyscrapers are eventually claimed by all kinds of beasts happy to rule the planet again? But if birds avoid the Quarantine Zone, other animals probably do, too. Even roaches and rats. She hasn't seen a single one since she stumbled in here.

She finally comes to one of those roundabout intersections where five different avenues converge, created long before automobiles made them hazardous to one's health. A bird-shit-covered statue of some forgotten big shot from a century ago presides over a tiny memorial of dead grass and trash at its center. Miki pauses, trying to decide which way to go.

The wind is picking up. Feels like a storm coming.

"Shit!" Miki says out loud. "Just what I need." She's tired and frightened, and wandering down here alone and soaking wet is not her idea of a good time. Those buildings on Seventh Avenue don't seem any closer than they were a few blocks ago.

That's when she hears it. That eerie wail. The wind chasing itself down vacant streets, Mathis called it. Miki thinks it sounds more like the wind in pain. But it's not the wind. It's too unnatural to be that. There's something almost hostile about it.

And now she recognizes what it is. A drone! One of those mechanical flying bugs that patrol the QZ perimeter. Sounds like it's behind her. And getting closer. If it sees her, soldiers won't be far behind. Time to find shelter.

Too late. There it is. Coming straight at her from the north. Time to run. Back the way she came. Dashing between buildings, across side streets and through alleys. Trying to escape the damn thing, trying to outrun its hideous sound. But the fucking machine is agile and intuitive. It anticipates her every move, swooping down like a falcon on the hunt, cutting her off, driving her back. And like a panicked rabbit, Miki jerks one way and then another getting nowhere. Miki thinks it's trying to corral her, keep her penned in until a security team can catch up. Or maybe, it's just toying with her.

Miki jerks to her left, but she misjudges where she is and doesn't see the stone staircase right in front of her until it's too late. With an incredulous gasp, she tumbles forward, tripping over her own feet as she tries to pull up. Instinctively she tucks and rolls as her momentum sends her plunging toward another street thirty feet below. She hits the ground with an agonized groan. The breath is knocked out of her. As she lies there gasping, she can't tell if anything is broken, but she can't move to find out. She can hear that incessant monotone howl approaching. Like the distorted screech of an amplified bagpipe. This is it. They're going to get her now. And then, who knows what will happen? Whatever it is won't be good, she guesses.

Miki's vision is blurred and doubled, but she can see a tiny portal opening on the drone's underside. Something pokes out. Long, tubular. Like the barrel of a weapon. Are they going to kill her!?

Miki closes her eyes.

There's a loud blast. Like a gunshot. Reverberating down the canyon of these empty buildings. And then another. Miki can't figure out why she doesn't feel the pain. Maybe she's been paralyzed.

Above her, the drone's whine sputters. Then its pitch rises abruptly, almost like a shriek of agony. Miki opens her eyes. The thing is swaying erratically, tipping radically to its left as it tries to climb. Its gyro fails, and it veers into the side of a building, bouncing off in a cascade of brick and metal parts, making one last effort to ascend, but then diving straight down toward Miki. She can't move. It's going to impale her to the street.

That's when she feels fingers pulling at her. Yanking her away just as the machine smashes into the ground. Gray silhouettes suddenly descend upon the disabled drone, pounding it relentlessly with iron bars and two-by-four clubs. She can hear it coughing and chattering as it dies. And then everything falls silent.

One of the silhouettes looms over her. Miki's vision is blurred and doubled. Her head pulses with excruciating pain and she can hardly keep her eyes open. There's a hiss of hushed whispers as more of them crowd around, but they're quickly silenced by the straining growl of diesel engines approaching. Those fingers are suddenly pulling at Miki again. Except she can't really feel them anymore. She can't feel or see or hear anything anymore.

33

The room is a basement somewhere. Dreary, dim, lit only by slivers of hazy sunlight seeping through a small and grimy street-level window and a couple of Coleman lanterns turned down low. Miki is trying to orient herself. On one side of the room, unopened boxes of canned and dry foodstuffs stacked in a corner next to cases of bottled water. On the other, squat propane tanks, plastic gasoline cans next to a couple of portable Honda generators, cases of cleaning supplies and other household chemicals that surely aren't kept here for housekeeping. Someone's been looting Home Depot. The only concession to "normal" life is the makeshift computer workstation of keyboards, portable hard drives, monitors, and mess of cables haphazardly arranged on an old door supported by sawhorses, tied in to one of those small generators. Whoever stays here has plans.

"I asked you to leave."

Miki's head turns to the voice. She'd recognize it even underwater. A little hoarser now, a little more fatigued perhaps, but there's no doubt.

It's her sister, Jennifer.

"And maybe now you understand why," she says, pulling closer the chair she's sitting on.

"How l ... l ... long have I ... have w ... w ... we ..."

"Only a few hours. Had the wind knocked out of you. Nasty bump on the head. Had me worried there for a moment."

Miki sits up with some effort. Her whole body aches, and her head is still throbbing.

"You took quite a fall down those stairs, Mick."

"Anything for you, Sis."

Miki can see her sister now as Jennifer leans into the glow of one of those Colemans. Maybe it's the flickering of the lantern's mantle, but she looks almost spectral. Her complexion is anemic, her hair is uncharacteristically short and dirty. She's too thin and bony. Not the way Miki remembers her, not the way she's sketched her. Except for the eyes. Those are still clear and wide. The contrast is almost scary. *Jennifer has always been intense,* Miki thinks, *but down here she looks like some kind of fanatic.*

"This is no place for you, Miki."

"You sound just like Mathis. R'member him?"

Jennifer nods, but the gesture suggests she remembers in a way Miki would prefer not to think about.

"Why didn't you just go?" Jennifer presses.

"Would you have?" If it were me, she means.

The silence that follows is almost too much for either one of them. Miki breaks through first.

"They t ... t ... told me you w ... w ... were dead, Jenn. They gave me a g ... g ... goddamn box filled with ashes. Said it was y ... y ... you ..."

That breaks the spell. Jennifer lurches forward to pull her little sister into her arms. "I'm such an asshole," she whispers.

The two of them cling to each other and won't let go.

"I knew you were here," Jennifer says. "Well, not at first. I was a little ... indisposed. But after I escaped. I knew you were looking."

"Escaped from where? From who?"

"I could have told you, I should have told you. I didn't want you to think I was dead, but I didn't want you to get involved in this."

"This ... what, Jen? What is *this*!?"

Jennifer pulls back slightly and takes Miki's face in her hands. "It's not easy to explain. At least not completely."

"Well, you b ... b ... better start t ... t ... trying."

"Everything they've been saying, everything they're telling people is a lie, Mick. The New Year's Eve Catastrophe. The contamination. The quarantine. It's all a fraud. A cover-up for something they want to keep from us."

"What's in your photographs, right? Those things you saw in your pictures."

Jennifer nods. "But I'm not sure yet whether they're the cause or the result."

"So what good is sitting here in some stinky basement, hiding out from those-you-haven't-named, letting whatever it is go on? You've got p ... p ... proof, Jenn. You've got the photos. At least they'll start people talking."

"I'm already doing that." With a nod to the electronics across the room.

It only takes a second for Miki to add two and two.

"Om ... m ... inos ..."

"Deep breath, Mick."

"Fuck!" That's it. Expel the tic. "Ominosity. That's you?"

"Infrequently, I'm sorry to say. Gotta make sure the baddies can't triangulate our access nodes. Keeps us on the move."

"They do graffiti about you, you know." Miki sounds almost proud.

"Yeah, but most people still think we're the tin-foil-hat crowd. It's not easy to get people to believe in things beyond their own experience. Jonas and I had a couple of knock-downs over it. And I wasn't really sure what I had at first, so it was the only way I could think of to communicate. I had no idea how viral it'd go."

"But someone's gotta believe you. Someone with the 'th ... 'th ... 'thority to investigate. You can't just live like this. On the run. What happens if they c ... c ... catch you?"

"It won't be a pleasant experience, I can assure you."

Miki can hear the pain in Jennifer's voice, and for the first time her sister's eyes go slightly unfocused.

"What have they done to you, Jen? Where have you been? What's b ... b ... been g ... g ... going on?" She's upset. The tic urge is getting harder to control.

Jennifer's gaze jerks back to Miki. That hard, penetrating stare which could be misinterpreted as malevolence. "There will be time enough for that." There's a barely suppressed fury in her tone that frightens Miki. A darkness has descended. "But not for you."

"What do you mean?" Miki asks, backing away.

"I asked you to leave. Now I'm telling you."

"And I'm not g ... g ... going anywhere, in case you hadn't noticed. Not until I know what's g ... g ... Shit!"

"Miki, please, don't make this a fight. There is absolutely nothing you can do in this situation. Go back to Mum and Dad. Tell them I'm okay. Or if it's easier, tell them I've lost my shit, tell them I've gotten involved in a thing I can't get out of. Or better yet, let them believe I died."

"You're shitting me, right?"

"Please, Mick, keep my secret. For now. Let me do what I need to do."

"Which is what!?" Now it's Miki turning on the fury.

"For starters, rescue Jonas."

"Coming with you."

"No way! Fuck it, Miki, when did you become so goddamn stubborn all of a sudden?"

"The day you v ... v ... vanished and didn't tell me why."

"I couldn't!"

"Really? You go off into the QZ, chasing after phantoms and God knows what else, which may be worse, you won't say, you end up getting caught but you won't say by who or where, you escape, how, who knows, you're on the run from whoever, turns out you have an internet alter ego that gets thousands of hits, but you can't take ten seconds to send word? 'Dear Miki, I'm okay.

Don't worry. I'll be in touch!' Bullshit, Jenn. What utter fucking bullshit!"

Jennifer is so taken aback by her little sister's shouts, she's rendered speechless. But the aphasia is fleeting. "Jesus, Miki, you didn't stutter once."

"Maybe you should hurt me more often." As soon as Miki lets the words fly, she regrets it. She knows she should yank it back, she didn't mean it, sorry, just the anger talking. But it's too late.

A couple of the silhouettes from the street hurry into the room, drawn by the yelling, no doubt. A man and a woman. Middle-aged. Could be husband and wife. Dirty and unkempt like Jennifer, and like her, wearing the hyper-focused expressions of zealots.

"Everything okay here, Jenn?" the woman asks.

"Just a bit of sibling disagreement. This is Bob and Betty, Mick. They lived over on Eighth Avenue."

"Still do," Bob says.

"Most of the time," Betty adds.

"Pretty clever, these two. They've been dodging the HazMats since the Catastrophe. They've taught me how. It was their apartment you stumbled into."

"Good thing Bob saw you while he was having his morning coffee," Betty says. "Otherwise you'd have been drone fodder."

"He told the others and they came to tell me," Jennifer says.

"How many are there?" Miki asks. "I mean like you, still here, in the QZ."

"A few groups here and there," Betty answers. "They've gotten to most of us, but we still got enough to make trouble." With a nod to Jennifer.

"The press calls us refuseniks," Bob says, which elicits a dark chuckle from Betty.

"Because we refused to leave after the Catastrophe," she says. "The mercs keep scouring the neighborhoods for us, but we're too quick."

"Mercs?" Miki asks.

"Mercenaries. They've been hired to come in here and clean us out. Whoever they find they forcibly remove."

"Or worse," Bob says.

"Gonna be dark soon," Betty tells Jennifer. "Ulysses will be waiting."

Jennifer nods while staring at Miki, clearly pondering a dilemma that's just been introduced into the equation. She goes over to the computers and picks up a camera there, checking to make sure the battery is charged and that she's got the right lenses.

"If I show you something, will you promise to let us escort you out of here?"

"And go home?" Miki grumbles, already preparing a new mode of argument.

"I guess you'll have to make up your own mind about that, but I don't want you staying in the QZ. Maybe after what I show you, you'll know why."

34

It takes them the better part of an hour to get where they're going. A circuitous route above and below ground. Through buildings and tunnels, sprinting across avenues, scurrying through alleys, pausing in shadows to listen for signs of drones or HazMat vehicles. It's dusk by the time they approach the river, the only natural border of the QZ, fenced off by fifteen-foot-high chain link and constantly patrolled by armed paramilitaries in swift boats. Empty warehouses line the cobblestone streets of this once-thriving hub of commerce and crime. The occasional and anomalous designer boutique, loft restoration, and digi-tech shareconomy workspace presently abandoned are the sad reminders of the impatient gentrification that was aggressively sprouting here until the Catastrophe interrupted. And in the middle of it, a blackened tumor of rubble and bent rebar. A block-long pile of wreckage that could stand in for Fallujah, Gaza, the WTC. Segregated from the rest of the area by a wall of Jersey Barriers, industrial fencing, and razor wire. No wonder it's referred to as Ground Zero. This is where it all started on that terrible New Year's Eve when reality shifted and something emerged to drive the city crazy. The baroque neon sign that used to blink haphazardly above the garage-door entrance still dangles precariously from a stalagmite of concrete. *Club Nightshade.*

"We're not going there?" Miki asks as Jennifer leads the four of them toward the debris. "What about the contamination?"

"Do we look contaminated to you?" Betty huffs.

They huddle in the doorway of a small bake shop that advertises the *"Best Oatmeal Raisin Cookies In The World."* No cookies left, unfortunately. Nor any other tasty sweet. Just display cases of moldy roach-scavenged crumbs.

Across the street, a gray shape appears in the window of Poet's Corner, a decrepit tavern that looks like it hasn't heard a line of free verse in decades. Whoever, whatever it is just hovers there, swaying slightly back and forth.

"Don't move," Jennifer says as she pushes Miki deeper into the doorway.

"Where are you going?" Miki hisses as her sister hurries across the street without answering and disappears through the tavern's door. "What's she doing?" she demands of Bob and Betty.

"Checking to see if it's safe," Bob whispers.

"Is it one of those t ... t ... things!?"

"Hush," Betty scolds.

Miki's mouth is a desert and her heart rate is accelerating. Her instinct is to rush after her sister, but Betty's vice grip on her upper arm promises a nasty struggle if she should try it. The wait is agonizing until Jennifer finally appears in the tavern window, signaling them with a slight wave.

"Let's go," Bob says, and the three of them sprint across the street.

Inside the tavern, the fetid stink of stale beer, cigarette smoke, and urine-saturated sawdust is overwhelming. The windows here probably haven't been opened in years. The door closes quickly behind them and the room consumes them in a gray murk.

"Back here," Jennifer's voice calls out from a door behind the bar which is framed by a faint flicker of light. It leads to a wooden ladder descending into an airless stone cellar. When Miki climbs down behind Bob and Betty, the first thing she sees is a pallet of newspaper, cardboard, and threadbare blankets. One of those

Coleman lanterns is set up next to it on an empty liquor crate. A craggy Dunhill pipe still smolders in its dish there. Piles of books all around, some open, some bookmarked.

"Meet Ulysses," Jennifer says, moving into the light of the Coleman with that spectral figure from the window, six foot five if he's an inch, weighing no more than one hundred thirty-five pounds, with a beard that would shame Billy Gibbons of ZZ Top. "He's the only one who knows how to get into the labs."

"The labs?" Miki asks, not sure she wants to know the answer.

"Where the devil did his work," Ulysses croaks with a sandpaper-on-cement tenor. Miki can't take her eyes off this mad Rasputin who is holding an ancient twelve-gauge shotgun. Probably the one that shot down that drone, she speculates.

"Ulysses was a Morpheus volunteer back in the day," Bob offers without additional explanation. "Didn't go well."

"Have had some trouble adjusting ever since," Ulysses adds with a lopsided grin. "But I got me some good survival skills," Ulysses says as he pushes an old beer tap aside to reveal a hole in the wall behind it. "Time's a wastin'."

He takes the Coleman and slips through the hole. While Bob and Betty follow, Miki looks over at her sister who is staring back with a grim expression. *You asked for it.*

Another serpentine, claustrophobic journey, crawling through tiny man-carved openings in walls, sloshing through rank streams of water and other questionable effluents, until they arrive at a kind of underground cave-in. Mountains of debris and trash suggest they are directly below the bombed-out Club Nightshade. An entire city block has collapsed here, burying everything beneath in a grave of glass, steel, and garbage. An excavation would be pointless. Better to just build over it. Let the rubble and whatever is entombed with it slowly disintegrate with time so everyone will forget it was ever here. Maybe that was the intention. If so, the perpetrators didn't plan on someone like Ulysses. While Miki watches in astonishment, he climbs a mound of broken concrete and pulls away a slab that must weigh as much as he.

"No one knows about this but me. And now you," he says, eye-stabbing each of them individually to add an unambiguous if unspoken warning. *"Don't blab!"* A blast of foul wind surges out of a shaft below that descends several stories into darkness. A shit chute into some forgotten and forsaken netherworld. Ulysses extends a hand to Miki. "Ladies first."

"Where does it lead?" Miki can't help asking.

"Hell," Ulysses says with a confusing smile.

One by one, they follow his direction into the shaft and climb down a rusted metal ladder to the landing of a fire well of corrugated iron stairs which they also descend. In this darkness, Miki can't be sure, but she calculates they've gone down at least eight floors when Ulysses finally pushes open a security door swaying on broken hinges and guides them into a large, tiled room that could have once been a hospital or clinic surgical suite. Various medical machinery and monitoring equipment is scattered everywhere. Curtains dangle from twisted hangers around several tubular tanks the size of subcompact automobiles, the purpose of which can only be darkly imagined.

Almost as soon as they come through the door, Jennifer is taking photos. The flash of her camera strobes the room, shredding time into image fragments that conjure the horrors that must have gone on in this surreal chamber. With each disturbing flash, Miki sees Ulysses's expression contort with pain and anger, eyes wide and unblinking, teeth bared as lips pull back in a feral grimace.

"Is there more?" Jennifer asks when she finally lowers her lens.

"Oh yeah," Ulysses answers. "There's more."

He leads them through the room into a seemingly endless colonnade littered with more upended medical furniture and lab equipment. Their own shadows from his lantern make it seem like they're being followed, and the wind echoing down that shaft behind them reminds Miki of the wail she heard on the streets, the screech made by one of those "things," as she calls them. The Paramentals. Stains randomly scattered on these tiled walls add fuel to her fear. Dark, rust-colored scorches like the one above Jennifer's bed.

"What are they?" she whispers reaching out to touch the chalky edge of one.

"Residue," Ulysses says, "of what they did to us."

More flashing as Jennifer documents the stains.

Finally, Ulysses brings them into a bizarre crypt-like room. A columbarium of storage niches, some open and empty, others with rolling metal trays poking out like tips of a ballpoint pen, still others welded shut. It's beside one of these that Ulysses sets down his lantern and yanks on corroded latches to break the seal. A thin *swoosh* escapes the cavity, like the hiss of a pop-top soda can being opened. A gurney tray glides out as if propelled by the pent-up pressure inside.

"Oh my God," Betty whimpers. "There's a body."

Another hiss. Another niche. Another body. And then another one.

"I think I'm gonna hurl," Bob moans. But he backs up against the wall and stuffs it down.

The bodies have decomposed into mummified shrivels. The mouths hang open in silent screams, the fingers are curled into fists, the wrists and forearms bent awkwardly against the chest as if to fend off imminent threat.

"They just left 'em here. Just walked away," Ulysses moans. "Used 'em up and left 'em like trash."

Miki watches as her sister puts a gentle hand on the old man's shoulder, both comforting him and urging him away from the torment at the same time. She takes his place and resumes her work. The care Jennifer is taking as she circles these corpses taking pictures suddenly mitigates the shock of the moment. This is the Jennifer Miki remembers. Silent. Absorbed. Unaware of anything except the subject in front of her. Moving constantly, camera aimed, lens focusing, looking for the precise frame to capture. As she used to paraphrase Diane Arbus, "I don't press the shutter, the image does. When it's ready."

"Time's a wastin'," Ulysses finally warns after a few minutes, and the four of them dutifully follow him back into the colonnade for the return trip.

"Isn't he coming with us?" Miki asks as they hurry out of the tavern to cross the street. Night has fallen and drone beams in the distance are already sweeping the QZ. Ulysses is in the door of the tavern watching them go.

"He prefers to be alone, darling," Betty says.

"Says it's safer for everyone if he sticks to himself," Bob adds.

Miki watches the poor soul drift back into the gloom of the tavern and close the door. She can't help thinking about what he said as they left the building.

"Be careful. I might be standing right behind you."

She thought he was talking about when they got back to the street. Now, she wonders if he meant something else.

Back at the squat, Jennifer immediately busies herself uploading the photos she's taken into a digital file she created on one of the computer's hard drives. Miki watches as her sister adjusts exposure and color, not for artistic purposes, but to focus one's attention. *"Jennifer Preston isn't showing you the truth,"* the *Times* review said of her work. *"She's forcing you to search for it."* The file contains other photos of the QZ, its empty buildings, of the Club Nightshade wreckage, of the HazMats and heavily armed security on patrol, sometimes rousting other squats, arresting miserable tribes of refuseniks, some carried out in body bags, and now these new moments in that mysterious, deserted medical facility with its macabre stains on the walls and those grotesque corpses in their abandoned sarcophagi. Jennifer positions these recent photos next to ones she copied on Miki's flash drive, the ones with those spectral figures in the backgrounds.

"What were they doing down there?" Miki asks. "To those bodies, to Ulysses?"

"We can't be certain. There are no records we could find. Ulysses says he volunteered just after he enlisted in the Army in the early '60s. He was only eighteen. He's kinda vague about it all, but I'm pretty sure they were fucking with people's minds."

Her certainty about this last part chills Miki's blood. She wants to know if "fucking with people's minds" was something they did to her before she "escaped."

"You still haven't told me what happened to you, Jenn. When you went missing."

Jennifer continues working the images on the monitor screen, perhaps hoping she can change the subject, but Miki's stare finally forces her to lean back.

"Jonas thought I was being hysterical about my photos," she says. "About the images I was seeing in them. We'd been having some pretty intense fights about it. One morning I was so pissed, I threw hot coffee in his face. He walked out. All my fault. I couldn't reach him for days. Turns out I'd gotten under his skin. He discovered on his own that there were still people in here even though he'd been assured there were not. Ever since the Catastrophe, he'd been making public statements on behalf of the government that the QZ was completely evacuated. He'd been lied to. So he decided to investigate. I found out later he'd bribed someone to get him into the QZ."

"Willy G."

Jennifer nods. "Willy felt guilty about it and told me afterwards. So I made him take me back to the place where he left Jonas, and I went looking. I was terrified. Didn't know what I'd find. I thought the QZ was still contaminated. Had a gas mask and everything. Even a gun Mathis had given me before he got arrested. I had no idea where to look. It was such a stupid idea, but I was frantic."

"You weren't afraid of getting caught?" Miki says, "by the HazMats, the security teams?"

"Turns out there were worse things to be afraid of."

And Miki understands immediately. She's heard this before. "The Paramentals."

"I saw one," Jennifer confirms. "Right in front of me. This oily, vibrating thing. I almost took a shot at it."

"What would have happened if you had?"

"Never got a chance to find out. A little girl had been following me. She stopped me."

"Charlotte."

"Yeah, she warned me it would only bring the drones. She told me to take off my mask, there was no contamination. And when I did, that thing was gone. I thought maybe I'd hallucinated it, but now I'm sure it was really there. Anyway, she took me to her squat where she and others had hidden after the Catastrophe. Jonas was there. He'd been shot."

"Shot? By who?"

"The mercs. He thought he'd stumbled on to a refusenik squat. Instead he was walking right into a raid. He tried to explain that he was the spokesman for the Public Affairs Office, but they went crazy. Started shooting up the place, including each other."

"They shot each other?"

"Jonas said it was like some madness virus. Started with one of them, then spread. He says he saw Paramentals hovering around them. He got hit with a ricochet. Charlotte found him staggering in the streets. Brought him to her friends who kept him alive. I tried to convince them all to come out with me, through the QZ barriers so the press, the public could see how fucked this whole thing is. But the mercs caught up to us. We ran, and they shot several of us. In the back! The rest of us made it to the barriers and came out into a perimeter checkpoint. They couldn't shoot us all, not in front of the crowds there. So they immediately arrested us and took us away."

"But there was no news about this. No one told us you'd been arrested."

"They scrubbed the media. Confiscated all video. Called us looters, scavengers. They've even got Jonas saying it now." Jennifer's eyes are welling up, but she wills the tears not to fall.

"Where did they take you, Jenn? What did they do to you?"

"Some clinic out in Oyster Bay. They interrogated me, threatened me," Jennifer responds, but her unfocused stare leaves no doubt the procedure was more damaging than that.

"What are they, Jenn? Those things, the Paramentals. Do they come from that lab Ulysses showed us? Ghosts of the people they experimented on? Mutants, demons? What?"

It takes a moment for her sister to answer. And when she does, it's barely a whisper. "I think it may be worse than that."

35

Red had not wanted to come back down here. It was Shivers's idea.

"There's gotta be more," he's been saying ever since they found those important-looking documents with all the fancy writing, the ones Willy said the cop, Mathis, was excited about. "Wind probably blew those papers all over the place, right? So let's go see." Red has kept putting Shivers off. "Don't wanna press our luck," is how he's put it. But Willy G had been mighty impressed with their "initiative," and even though Shivers isn't sure what that word means, he's always ready to *press his luck* for Willy's approval. So Red has given in, if only to make his little partner stop bugging him.

Trouble is, they've been roaming these tunnels for the better part of an hour and still haven't found any more of those documents.

"Why are they so important anyway?" Red complains. "Just a buncha crap that doesn't even sound like English. *'Party of this agrees to convey to party of that.' 'Quit claim, this. Covenants of that.'* The kind of stuff adults always use to confuse you. Makes everything sound big and important and complicated so you feel small and ignorant and worthless. That's why school is such a waste of time. What the hell does algebra or who the President was a hundred years ago have to do with finding your next meal? How is any of it gonna help us get over on the street?"

Shivers ignores the complaints. They're important to Willy, and Willy is Shivers's hero. Besides, the wind is whistling in a crack in the wall no wider than a skateboard, and something is fluttering in there. "Hey, check it out!" Before Red can object, Shivers squeezes himself into the crevice and feels around. Something scampers across his forearm. He jerks back but he doesn't cry out. He's felt rats scurry across him before. Ain't no biggie. But his hand brushes across the thing that was fluttering. Yep. A piece of paper. Trapped between a pipe and the brick. Shivers tugs it free without tearing it. A legal-size sheet with more of that verbal diarrhea. But this one has a signature: *Angela Rossi.* He knows that name is important.

"Told ya," he calls out to Red. "Gimme a hand. Think I got myself stuck."

A sound deeper in the tunnel stops him dead.

"You hear that?" Shivers whispers as he cocks his head in several directions. A kind of shuffling. Yeah, he heard it, all right. No doubt about it. It's drifting toward him from the darkness. "Red. Pssst, Red!"

The ambience down here is confusing. Sounds don't have definitive origins. If he doesn't know which way that sound is coming from, which way does he go to get away from it? The shuffling is getting closer. *What if it's one of those things,* Shivers thinks, *those things Willy always warns them about? Paramentals. Why isn't Red answering him? Did it get him?* A figure pauses right by the crack where he's hiding. Shivers holds his breath and freezes against the wall. Maybe it'll just pass by.

Instead, long fingers push into the seam.

"C'mere, kid. I'm not gonna hurt ya." Those fingers reach in further, extended like a friendly handshake. "Let me help you outta there."

Probably just one of those bums who skulk around down here, Shivers thinks. *Some drunk he can probably knock over with a whistle if he tries anything funny.* He takes the hand and allows himself to be pulled out. A few scrapes and scratches, but he's not complaining. He got what he came for. Willy's going to be totally blown away.

"This how you get from one end of this city to the other without ever coming up for air, huh?"

And Shivers looks up into the menacing stare of Fat Freddie Pierce.

"What you got there?"

Mathis is waiting at his favorite noodle bar when Willy arrives. The kid sounded panicked when he called.

"They got Shivers," Willy yelled into the phone. "Down in the tunnels. Red saw it."

"Whoa, slow down, Willy. Who got who?"

"Shivers. My boy. That prick detective's got him. Your pal, Pierce."

Mathis's stomach lurched violently. "How do you know?"

"Red. He saw it. They were down there tryin' to find more of those papers from the Rossi woman. Was Shivers's idea. He wanted to show off. Pierce must've followed 'em. How did he know to do that!?"

"I told Freddie I got those documents from a CI," Mathis admitted. He couldn't lie to Willy. "He must have gone looking."

"You asshole. No wonder Pierce was down in that tunnel. He sees my boys with Benedict and he puts it together."

So baiting Freddie has backfired in a way Mathis never considered. And now he's got a testosterone bomb coming at him full force.

"This is your fault, Mathis!" Willy yells before he even sits down. "They never woulda been down there in the first place, if I hadn't agreed to help you."

"Where'd he take Shivers?"

"Red lost 'em on the streets. Pierce put him in a car and took off. I'm gonna get that dirty shit, Mathis. You know I don't go for violence, but I'm tellin' you he's gonna show me where Shivers is. And then I'm gonna end him."

"Willy, Willy, stop!" Mathis pleads. "Pierce is not a guy you want to mess with."

"Oh yeah? So what, I'm supposed to do nothing!? That what you're sayin'? You think he's just treating little Shivers to milkshakes and cookies!? You know what's gonna happen. If ... if it ..." Willy chokes on his emotions. It's all he can do to maintain his "manhood" and keep from crying. "... if it hasn't already." He's shaking now, and Mathis knows it's rage reaching its flash point. If he can't talk Willy down, this kid is going to storm into Pierce's precinct and end up dead.

"I knew I shouldn't have gone along with this," Willy says. "I try to be careful with my crew. No unnecessary chances. And here you come, pushing me for information. Why'd I ever agree to this!?"

Mathis knows Willy is thinking about his little brother. The one he couldn't save, the one who ran away from the abusive foster home in which they'd been placed. Mathis was part of a missing children's task force back then. That's how he met Willy. But they never found Willy's little brother, and Mathis has felt guilty ever since. So now, history is repeating itself.

"This is my mess, Willy. My fault. Let me handle Freddie. You got the rest of your crew to look after. What are they gonna do if something happens to you? If Shivers gives it up about him and you ..."

"He won't!"

Mathis is suddenly seized by the urge to smack the bravado out of Willy. The kid has no idea what Fat Freddie is capable of, but telling him so would only dare him, not deter him. "Freddie is no fool, Willy. If he finds out you put Shivers in with Benedict's crew, he's going to come after you and your boys. Unless ..."

"Unless what?"

"We let Freddie think that Shivers is my informant, and hope the kid holds up until I can get to him. He's tough, right?"

"He's ten, Mathis."

"Look, gimme a day. Lie low. Let me handle it. I'll get Shivers back. And then I'll take care of Freddie. I mean it." But another stomach lurch is telling Mathis it may already be too late.

For the first time since he got here, Willy has nothing to say. *Thinking it over,* Mathis hopes. The reality of going up against a cop like Pierce, the danger to the rest of his crew, the weight of the world crashing down on this sixteen-year-old who thinks he's a man but knows he's still a boy, maybe it's enough to give him pause. It's a solid bet Freddie's gotten what he wants from Shivers by now, and maybe Willy knows it deep down in his heart, too. To Pierce, kids like him and Shivers are disposable. Mathis can only hope he'll find evidence that will bring Freddie down before he can come after Willy and the others. No one likes a child abuser. Add that to being a cop in prison and Freddie could be singing soprano before his first week is out.

"I'm gonna be back here tomorrow," Willy growls. "Right here. And if you ain't sittin' there buying Shivers as much ramen as he wants, I'm going after Pierce. No matter what." He gets up from his stool and walks off. Then he stops and turns back. "Whatever happens, Mathis, you and me, we're done."

And Mathis is surprised at how bad that makes him feel.

36

When Miki wakes up, she's alone. It takes a few seconds for her eyes to focus and her mind to dispel the dream images of bodies on columbarium slabs, seeping gray mist from mummified pores that coalesces into menacing phantom shapes, jerking with a palsy resembling digital static. At first, she thinks the figure across the room might be one of them. Something she's conjured from her nightmare, driven from the realm of agitated neurotransmitters into the real world.

"How 'bout some coffee?" it says.

Betty. Lifting a sauce pan of boiling water from its perch above Sterno cans. "Got a couple of stale energy bars, if you're hungry." Her laugh is raspy, probably the result of too many cigarettes, Miki thinks.

It's dark again out the window. Miki must have been sleeping the whole day. "Where is everybody?" she asks when she realizes no one else is here.

"Should be back pretty soon," Betty says, pouring coffee into Styrofoam cups.

When they got back to the squat just before dawn, Miki remembers, she was left alone to watch Jennifer huddling with some new refuseniks who arrived over the next hour. Three men and one woman. Harder, edgier. Wound tight, on the verge of violence. She tried not to meet their suspicious frowns when they noticed her. The woman in particular scared the shit out of Miki. She was tiny and androgynous, and her stare was cold and merciless. She vibrated menace. They all carried themselves like cops or military, and they had weapons. Tactical small arms. Pistols, and a couple of compact semiautomatic rifles. "Liberated from those Merc bastards," Miki heard the androgyne tell Bob who was admiring her guns. The conversation was hushed, but Miki could make out a name among the intense whispers. Jonas! And something about a news conference.

"They're from another squat," Jennifer told her sister after the confab finally broke up. "They're going to help me."

"Help you what?"

Miki can't remember what her sister told her after that. She was so exhausted she fell asleep where she sat.

"Why do you stay, Betty? What good can it do?"

"It's our home, dear. Me and Bob, we've never lived more than a few blocks from here. I grew up in these neighborhoods." And Miki remembers what Mrs. Deluca used to say. Hopefully, Betty won't end up taking a dive out a twelfth-floor window, although something worse might actually befall her instead.

"Aren't you afraid?" Miki asks.

"Of the mercs? Sure. But it's not really their fault. They're just working for wages. It's the guys pulling the strings I want to get at. They're the ones that made this mess."

"Actually, I was thinking about a different kind of danger," Miki says, and she can see Betty stiffen noticeably.

"Have an energy bar," Betty smiles, changing the subject.

An hour later, Jennifer returns with those refuseniks from last night. All of them out of breath, wide-eyed, and adrenaline-pumped.

"Drones almost got us over on Second Avenue," Jennifer

explains almost too casually as they strip off backpacks and weapons and collapse against the walls with exhausted stares. They look like pirates just back from a marauding expedition. Betty hurries from one to the other passing out bottles of water and stale energy bars from a Whole Foods grocery bag. Miki waits patiently while they eat in silence and catch their breath. When Jennifer finally feels her sister's stare, she gets to her feet. "I need some air," she says.

Miki follows her out a door into a narrow, dark alley between buildings and crouches in a corner to light a half-used cigarette. She keeps the butt cupped in the palm of her hand to hide its burning tip as she gulps long choking drags.

"When did you start that?" Miki asks with a disappointed frown.

"Keeps me from smelling myself," Jennifer shrugs. "Been so long since I've had a proper bath, I'm getting pretty rank." But Miki can't help noticing how Jennifer's hands quiver slightly as she takes repeated drags one after the other. *Her nerves are shot,* Miki thinks.

"Is it safe out here?" Miki asks, scanning the starless sky.

"We'll hear 'em coming." Jennifer crushes the cigarette into the street, careful to make sure there are no sparks or embers left burning. "Listen, I need you to do something for me. For us."

"What?"

"I need you to leave the QZ." Miki stiffens. "Wait, before you start to fight me, you've got to understand why."

"B ... b ... better be good," Miki says, steeling herself for another confrontation.

"I've found out that there's going to be a press conference at the QZ perimeter day after tomorrow. They're going to explain why the quarantine has to continue. They're going to use Jonas to back them up. It's the opportunity we've been waiting for."

"Opportunity? To do what?"

"To show everyone they're lying." Jennifer holds up a flash drive. "This is proof of what's really been going on in here," she says. "That's what I've been doing. Documenting all the lies we've been told. There never was any exposed weapons dump. There never was any contamination. We're proof of that. And they're hunting us down because of it. What they're really doing is trying to cover up what was being done in those labs buried under Ground Zero. We need people to know, Mick." She grabs Miki's hand and presses the flash drive into it. "I need you to go to Mathis. I need you to give this to him."

"Why Mathis?" Miki asks.

"Because he'll know what to do with it. And because he deserves to know why his daughter was killed." Jennifer squeezes the flash drive tight into her sister's hand. "He'll listen to you. He'll believe you when you tell him where this comes from. He may be a damaged soul, but he's a decent guy. And he cares about you, Miki."

"How do you know?" Miki asks, but Jennifer's big-sister smile is all the answer she needs. "You've been spying on us."

"Just keeping tabs on my little sis, that's all."

"What about you? Why d ... d ... don't you do it?"

"There's one last piece of evidence I need to get. Then I'll meet up with you and we'll start to bring this whole fucking conspiracy down."

Miki leans back against the wall. She's no fool. There's more to this than being a courier for her sister. Jennifer's planning something. And whatever it is must be risky in the extreme. Otherwise, she'd come out with the flash drive herself after she gets that last piece of evidence. Miki is the *just-in-case*.

"I c ... c ... can't leave you h ... h ... here."

"I'll be right behind you. A day or two, a week at most. I promise. Trust me, Mick. Please. You're the only one I can count on. You have to do this for me."

The two of them just stare at each other. No more big sister, little sister. Just equals. Miki could defy Jennifer, argue with her, try to convince her to go with her, but once her sister has made up her mind she's harder to turn around than a supertanker in the ocean. What began as an odyssey to find Jennifer has morphed into a mandate to expose the Catastrophe that's haunted this city since New Year's Eve. Somewhere deep in her heart, Miki knows she can't refuse her sister's request. And then, the decision is made for her.

The door to the building opens behind them and Betty is there pointing to her watch. That androgenous virago with a semiauto is with her. Something passes between her and Jennifer, which Miki understands even if it is unspoken.

"I don't have any choice, do I?" she asks her sister.

And the silence that follows is answer enough. There's only one thing left to do. Miki gets off the wall and pulls Jennifer into her arms.

The trek across the QZ wilderness seems aimless. Miki, Betty, and the androgyne with her gun who knows this urban landscape like the Iroquois knew the forests of Pennsylvania. Every time they hear a drone getting within a few blocks of their location, she quickly leads them into a dark doorway and a detour sprint through empty lobbies and abandoned shops, only to emerge several blocks away from their original route, huddling a few minutes in the shadows to listen for the engine grind of mercenary vehicles patrolling nearby. None of them speak until they reach the intersection where Miki first emerged into the QZ the other night.

"Follow the tunnel at the bottom of those steps. Don't make any turns. When you come to the train yard, take the third tunnel to your right. It's a subway line that isn't used anymore. You'll come to a station that's been closed since the Catastrophe. You'll know you're in the right place by the graffiti on the wall. The stairs lead to the street about a block away from the QZ perimeter. They're gated off, but you'll see where it's been breached. On the floor, bottom right. You can slip through."

"Be careful, Betty," Miki says because she can't think of anything else.

The older woman smiles maternally and pulls a flashlight from her backpack. "Take this," she says as she pulls Miki into a hug. "You're a brave girl."

Miki never feels the envelope that Betty slips into the back pocket of her pants.

The flashlight helps, but it's so dark down here that Miki can only see what's caught directly in the beam. Peripheral vision is just a mess of endless gray. Miki is so intent on looking ahead, she misses the last step of that circular staircase and tumbles headlong into the dirt. Her shirt tears and an icy pain stabs her left ankle. But what's worse is the moan floating down the tunnel toward her.

"The wind," Miki mutters, trying to reassure herself "Just the wind." She limps off in the same direction she came the other night. She soon arrives back at that circular underground "yard" where rail sidings venture off into the black holes of other tunnels.

"Third tunnel to my right," she says, repeating Betty's instructions. There's a familiar scent in the air. Like cordite residue or burning electrical wires. Another thin, distant wail paralyzes her. That was not the wind. She sweeps the yard with her flashlight and almost doesn't see it at first, but when she whips the beam back, there it is. A Paramental. A tall indistinct shadow hovering in the inky mist of a tunnel next to the one she's supposed to enter. It doesn't move except to tilt forward slightly.

"I've got a gun," Miki lies, sliding her hand into her jacket pocket, but the figure ignores her. It just stares. At least that's what Miki thinks it's doing. She can't see any face. She moves slowly toward the third tunnel to her right, keeping the beam pinned on the Paramental all the while. She read somewhere that if you stare down a predator it will eventually back off, the theory being that if you posture aggressively you will confuse it. You'll make it worry that you won't be an easy meal, that you'll hurt it even if you lose. It may decide to hunt elsewhere for more timid prey. Miki always thought this was bullshit. Why would a tiger back off a villager simply because he screamed and yelled? Why would a rapist back off a girl simply because he thought she might fight back? Wouldn't that make him enjoy it even more? On the other hand, what else is she going to do? Stand here and let the thing have its way with her?

It's shimmering now with cold-blue incandescence, oscillating like a high-pitched wave form. For a brief instant, Miki imagines she's in some sleazoid reality show, on the run from a sinister special effects villain bent on maiming or killing her for sport while people watch live-streaming feeds from the safety of their homes or offices. Who knows, maybe some sick Hollywood fuck has already sold a pitch like that to one of the networks and she's accidentally stumbled into the pilot episode.

She's almost at the third tunnel to her right. If she gets there, maybe she can outrun it to the street. But that's when it starts to whisper. A freakish unintelligible hiss, penetrating deep into Miki's brain. Maddeningly hypnotic. Miki is entangled in its power, tugging at her from the inside out. A feeling of wickedness wells up deep within her, as if every vile and ugly feeling she's ever had, every malicious and hostile urge was reaching critical mass, like a seething volcano about to erupt. She wants to do something terrible. She wants to be mean, be hurtful. She wants to be violent!

"Fuck me!" she yells, dropping the flashlight, taking off full speed into the tunnel Betty directed her to. She covers her ears with her hands as if that could block out the awful contagion seeping into her mind. No luck. The sound is everywhere, in front of her, behind her, oozing out of the walls. But she doesn't stop. She ignores the screaming agony of her ankle and runs faster and faster. As Betty promised, she finally emerges into an empty subway station. One of the smaller ones. Trash and garbage scattered everywhere, and graffiti on the walls.

OMINOSITY KNOWS

Miki breaks for the stairs which are blockaded by heavy industrial fencing and barbed wire, except for a small breach near the floor. You'd miss it unless you knew where to look. Barely big enough for a small dog, or a big rat. Miki falls to the ground and slithers into the crack between fence and wall. For a frightening moment, she thinks she's stuck as the razor wire grabs at her pants, but she finally pulls free, dragging a long scratch down her torso which starts to bleed immediately. She can't help wondering when she had her last tetanus shot.

That hideous hissing wail follows her up the stairs and into the street, ringing in her ears like a feedback loop she can't shut off. She takes a moment to orient herself. There are only a few people out, but they don't give any indication they hear the noise that is tormenting her mind. Miki feels faint. Her ankle is throbbing viciously. All she wants to do is lay down, cover her head, pretend she's somewhere else, but she keeps going. Heading toward the light of buildings up ahead, away from the dead QZ behind her. But the siren call in her mind won't let go. It's coming now from the reflections in windows she passes, or car windshields. Or from the shadows looming in empty doorways. More of those things. Paramentals. Leering out at her. Is she hallucinating? Or going mad? One of these humanoid phantoms leans forward into the dim light of the street.

It has Miki's face!

She screams and leaps off the sidewalk, almost colliding with a garbage truck making its rounds. And reality snaps back. The hiss evaporates.

Behind her, the halogen glow of the QZ perimeter. Up ahead the buildings of Seventh Avenue.

Jennifer's apartment is that direction.

And Mathis.

She runs.

37

Mathis isn't sure what he'll do exactly once he gets to Freddie Pierce's cabin, but the choice was either confront his nemesis on the man's home turf, the precinct, where Freddie would be surrounded by colleagues still suspicious of Mathis, or look for evidence elsewhere first. Rumors of Freddie's cabin hideaway in the woods have circulated among the precinct boys for years, but no one has ever been invited there, and Freddie himself is always monosyllabic when asked about it. Certain well-known working girls have occasionally let slip a few tidbits about weekend marathons of lust, booze, and the occasional target practice on small animals from the porch of Freddie's upstate retreat, but when pressed for details, memories suddenly fail, or narratives quickly withdraw behind veils of dissemblance. *"Not what I said,"* or *"I was talking about someone else."* Fear of Fat Freddie has kept the truth in manageable check.

Still, it hasn't been difficult for Mathis to discover where the cabin is. He used to be a detective, after all. He was sure he was headed the right direction when he stopped at local Burger King a mile back and was given assurances that the *"fella from the city always stops by on the way to his cabin off Buckwheat Road."* Always ordering the same thing, no matter what time of day or night. Bacon Cheeseburger Deluxe. Side of onion rings. Yep. Sounds like Freddie.

Even on this moonless night, Mathis can see the small single-story building in the distance as he moves to the edge of a bluff overlooking it. No lights on. No one home. A nice quiet place to have a conversation. About Shivers. And lots of other things.

"Connect the dots," Mathis reminds himself as he leaves his car in the woods and heads down the hill on foot. Angela Rossi was being bribed by the Baron, Emeril Benedict, to collude in some kind of Quarantine Zone land-grab scheme. Dickie Prince, Benedict's bagman, was delivering said bribes to Rossi. The same Dickie Prince who was winking and nodding about his involvement in the nightclub explosion New Year's Eve that killed Mathis's daughter. The same Dickie that Mathis was accused of murdering and later arrested for by none other than Fat Freddie Pierce. The same Freddie Pierce who was seen recently visiting Benedict's restaurant right after Mathis showed him the documents Shivers discovered where Angela Rossi died. The Freddie who followed Shivers when he went back into the underground to look for more of Rossi's purloined papers. Angela Rossi, Emeril Benedict, Dickie Prince, Fat Freddie, Benedict again, Angela Rossi again. Full circle. So why does Mathis have this nagging suspicion there's still a piece missing? A grand design behind the bribes and profiteering. Was his daughter's life sacrificed for such dismal, mundane corruption? Or is there still something hiding behind the obvious? Maybe that hiding place is in Freddie's cabin.

Mathis isn't surprised by the security sensors he notices, and deliberately trips, on his approach. Motion-activated cameras, heat sensitive and infrared perimeter scanners, all wirelessly routed to Freddie's mobile phone, no doubt. But unless he's just down the street at Burger King, their alarms won't lure him here before Mathis has had a chance to look around and settle in.

He's sitting in Freddie's comfortably worn and cracked leather glider an hour later, feet propped up on a dented Army surplus footlocker, staring at the warm flames in the fireplace, when car headlights sweep this dark room, pushing animated shadows across the walls. Freddie surely knows he's in here. Mathis made no attempt to skulk his way across the property earlier, and Freddie's security setup must be sophisticated enough to zoom and enhance his image into indisputable clarity. The chimney smoke from the fire he built would simply confirm it. But apparently Freddie is in no hurry. Mathis glances out a window to see him still in his car, grooving to "Kinda Blue," waiting until Miles finally ends his restless "So What" solo and hands it off to Coltrane.

Soon enough, Freddie comes through the door finishing a BK Bacon Cheeseburger Deluxe.

"Jesus, Freddie, don't you ever stop eating?"

Freddie doesn't even flinch when he sees Mathis in his favorite chair. He pauses only to clock that Army footlocker under Mathis's feet then heads to the kitchen where he drops the food wrapper in the trash and opens the refrigerator for a beer.

"Haven't helped yourself yet?" he asks, pulling one out for Mathis, too. "Oh, I forgot. Still fighting the dragon, aren't ya." He eye-fucks Mathis while taking a long pull on the beer. Maybe he's hoping to see him drool.

"Nice place here, Freddie. Cozy. Quiet. Isolated. You got like, what, ten acres between you and anyone else?"

"Closest neighbor's a mile away."

"Nice folks?"

"No idea," Freddie shrugs. "Couldn't care less either."

"You can do pretty much anything you want out here, can't you? Who'd know? Who'd bother you? Wish I could afford a something like this."

"Maybe you could, if you weren't such a self-righteous prick."

"I'm just choosy about the company I keep. It's hard to wash off the slime of guys like Emeril Benedict."

Freddie's mouth smiles. His eyes don't. He takes another pull on his beer.

"Where's the boy?"

"Wanna jump right in, huh?"

"I put him up to it, Freddie. He's just a kid. No reason to hurt him."

"A little late for that," Freddie chuckles as he picks at his teeth and washes it down with more beer.

Mathis does his best to maintain a blank expression, but his guts are roiling with worst fears. "It's getting to be a habit with you, isn't it, Freddie?"

"What's that?"

"Hurting kids." He takes his feet off that footlocker and shoves it across the hardwood floor. "Found that in the crawlspace under the house. Not the most inventive hiding place I've ever seen."

"We don't get too many nosey fucks up here. People respect the privacy of others."

"Quite a collection in there. I counted three Sig MCXs, not to mention the Glocks and S&Ws. You've even got a forty-four magnum in there."

"I like to hunt," Freddie smirks.

"So I've heard. But what about those TNT tubes and the det cord? You looking to shoot animals or blow 'em up?"

"I'm clearing granite out back. Gonna build a pool."

"You got enough in there to clear a city block, Freddie. Bring down a bunch of buildings. Maybe even a nightclub full of kids." Mathis reaches down beside him and pulls up a small black box. Looks like a cigarette case. Except this one has thin wires sticking out of it. "Haven't seen one of these since Syria. Those fuckers used to build IEDs in the basements of their kids' schools. Pretty crude, these little triggers, but very reliable. This what you got Dickie Prince to use on New Year's Eve?" He starts twirling the trigger device by its wires.

Freddie decides it's finally time to assert the balance of power.

He reaches into his jacket, pulls out his service revolver and lays it on the counter in front of him.

"So it's gonna go down like that?" Mathis asks with a disappointed sigh.

"It's dark," Freddie says. "I'm surprised by an intruder. Breaking and entering. Seems plausible, doesn't it? An honest mistake on my part. Besides, you don't exactly have the best reputation these days. Who knows? Maybe my lawyer will claim you intended to do harm. Bit of revenge for the way you were treated when I arrested you for Dickie's murder."

"Or you could just bury me under the pool you're building and forget about it."

Freddie considers this. Maybe not a bad idea. One of the logs in the fireplace snaps loudly. "Thanks for building the fire," he says. "Saved me the trouble,"

"I love the smell," Mathis says as he gazes into the flames.

"You know, Mathis, I could never figure you out. You seem like a smart guy. You've been around. You know how the world works. You don't really believe there's a moral to the story, do you?"

"What story?"

"The story of us. Of people."

"I like happy endings."

"Nature doesn't. That's why I like it out here. It's not judgmental. It's indifferent. Doesn't give a fuck."

"Just predators and prey, right, Freddie?"

"Tell me something. What's the difference between here and that giant litter box in the Middle East where you got the bum leg? C'mon man, think about it. We're just a power outage away from savagery, right? History proves it. Time and again. Our demons are everywhere, Mathis. Always ready to show up. Always have been."

"And so you've chosen sides," Mathis says.

"I'm curious. What'd you expect coming here? You really didn't think you'd find the boy, did you?"

"No."

"Then what? This some kind of death wish, some sick way of atoning for all your sins?"

"I want to know why my daughter died. I want to be sure it wasn't just a simpleminded mook like Dickie Prince acting alone. I want to know why you helped him blow up that nightclub. I want to hear it from you. Why, Freddie?"

Freddie stifles a laugh. He's slightly surprised by the question. Isn't it obvious?

"It paid well." What other motive does one need?

Mathis visibly deflates. The hot power of his rage has been suddenly swept away by the utter banality of Freddie's reasoning.

"So now you know," Freddie says, turning his back to get another beer. "Here's your chance, Mathis."

But Mathis doesn't move. Something else does. In the shadows across the room. For a moment Mathis thinks it's smoke seeping out of the fireplace. But it's not. It's something animate, elastic, swaying back and forth as if it were sentient. In front of a large stain on the wall. A stain like all the others. Why didn't he notice it before? Was it even there before? Or has it just appeared, a manifestation of that thing now coagulating in front of it?

When Freddie turns back with his beer, he sees the gun still on the counter where he put it.

"Christ, Mathis," he says, sounding like he's disappointed in a child. "You want me to hand the damn thing to you?"

He never notices that thing behind him. Stitching itself together. Congealing into a sinewy mass of murk.

"You know how this ends, Mathis," Freddie says, picking up the gun.

But Mathis isn't looking at Freddie. He's staring at that thing behind him. He's not really surprised that one of these so-called Paramentals would show up here in this toxic atmosphere, feeding on the pervasive tension, the hostility, the vicious malevolence of Fat Freddie Pierce.

"Actually, I'm not sure I do," Mathis says, keeping his eyes on that slithery phantom behind Freddie. And unlike in the movies where the bad guy says to the hero, *"you can't fool me with that old trick, pardner,"* Freddie's instincts tell him to turn and see what Mathis is looking at. Who knows? Maybe the asshole brought along an accomplice who's about to join the party. But the sight of the nascent Paramental catches him completely off guard. And that's all the time Mathis needs.

He jerks out of Freddie's glider and hurls the small triggering device at him, clipping Freddie just behind the left ear. Freddie reflexively pulls the trigger. Dishes shatter on the shelf by the refrigerator. Mathis jams Freddie's face into the counter and grabs the gun hand, only to get a couple of severe elbows to the solar plexus in return. The two of them stumble back, tripping over that Army surplus locker, careening across the glider and into the fireplace. Sparks and burning logs fly as the two men scream and jump out of the flames. They struggle to the floor with Freddie ending up on top, struggling to bring the gun around toward Mathis's face. Mathis grabs the fallen beer bottle and smashes Freddie in the back of his neck. The shock to Freddie's brainstem causes him to drop the gun, and Mathis kicks it away. The two of them tumble away from the fire that's spreading from the burning glider and the flaring logs that have been kicked into the middle of the room. They stagger to their feet and start slugging it out. The fight quickly deteriorates into a sloppy brawl as each resorts to grabbing pieces of furniture and the objects on them to use as projectiles. They look like the fighters in Goya's famous painting, *The Duel:* two men thigh-deep in mud pummeling each other senseless with clubs.

The fire continues to spread.

A hideous shriek interrupts the fracas. It's the Paramental. Throbbing in the flames sweeping up a burning wall, feeding on them, drawing the flames to and around it like some infernal cloak. It's just enough distraction for Freddie to dive for the gun on the floor, kicking burning embers toward the Army surplus locker as he goes. Mathis dives away as Freddie fires at him. Bullets whiz over his head and penetrate through the unperturbed Paramental, smashing into the wall with loud *thuds*.

A strange hiss erupts. The det cord! It has ignited!

Mathis and Freddie see it in the same instant. Mathis breaks for the door. Freddie is still shooting at him when the dynamite explodes, throwing Mathis fifty feet through the air.

Random thoughts cascade with his fading consciousness as he falls.

The promise he made to Willy G about Shivers.

The evidence about the Club Nightshade explosion in Freddie's cabin he hopes his colleagues will find.

The last time he heard his daughter's voice New Year's Eve.

Miki.

And then he lets go. The last thing he sees is the cabin being consumed by fire. No sign of Freddie. Only the Paramental, in the doorway, shrieking triumphantly among the flames.

38

Technicians have been at work since dawn, and everyone's been warned. There is no room for error. The small array of microphones has to be working properly. Feeds to all the networks must be checked and rechecked. A press corral has been constructed just inside the checkpoint fence, its only access via a heavily guarded gate followed by a single file march along a narrow corridor of concrete barriers. The setup is clearly designed to convey an image of the press as troublemakers that need to be constrained. Early bird media arrivals are already complaining about being herded like animals to slaughter. A very nervous Public Affairs Officer, obviously chosen for his unexceptional appearance and accommodating manner, stumbles up to the mics every so often to mutter bland assurances that the news conference will begin soon, such assurances failing nevertheless to quell the cacophony of angry questions shouted from the press corral or the verbal abuse hurled by the gathering public kept at bay outside the QZ fence.

"The poor man looks like he's starring in his own nightmare," Stewart Whitfield chuckles from the safety of a VIP tent where he's watching at a bank of network monitors. Next to him, Hollings Keller manages a weak smile. Whitfield may find all this amusing, but Keller is impatient for the show to begin. If the plan works, he will have bought some valuable credit with the lads, as Whitfield calls them. On the other hand, there are many things that could go wrong. Success in conflict depends on deception, Sun Tsu says. It's just a question of who deceives who first.

"I presume our star attraction has been properly prepped," Whitfield says, turning to see Dr. Lewis Cameron talking quietly with Jonas Flack, former Communications Director of the Public Affairs Office, and Jennifer Preston's lover. Jonas is nodding pliantly to every prompt Cameron offers.

"I'm sure he'll accomplish what we need him to," Keller responds, being purposefully oblique.

***

A few moments later, Dr. Cameron escorts Jonas out of the VIP tent toward the microphone stage. The Public Affairs Officer has begun the press conference by rattling off meaningless statistics about the biomonitoring of the Quarantine Zone. But as soon as the press see Jonas they ignore him and begin firing questions.

"Ladies, gentlemen, please," the Public Affairs Officer shouts over the mob. "Mr. Flack is going to make a brief statement after which you can ask your questions. In an orderly fashion, please."

Jonas mounts the risers, nodding and smiling mechanically at the crowd assembled in front of him, some of whom he knew personally in his former, professional life. Whitfield has emerged from the VIP tent with several Bio HazMat professionals to watch from a discreet perch to the microphone's right, while Keller separates himself from them and casually strolls the perimeter. Just another official functionary. No apparent interest in the proceedings. In fact, he is concentrating on the buildings inside the QZ. Most of them shrouded in that thick plastic sheeting meant to signify contamination containment. Lifeless, empty. But Keller knows better.

She's out there, he thinks. *No doubt about it. She's watching.*

"As many of you know," Jonas begins, momentarily startled by the volume of his own voice in the PA speakers, "I was exposed to a serious dose of contamination when I unwisely ventured into the Quarantine Zone several weeks ago. My mistaken intention was to confirm rumors that survivors of the New Year's Eve Catastrophe were still alive and hiding there." His voice has the monotone apathy of someone on drugs.

Shouts erupt from the crowd outside the perimeter fence. *"They're still in there ... we saw them ... they're being killed ... we've seen the bodies!"* Jonas blinks rapidly as if his mind were going into reset mode, then gamely presses on.

"Unfortunately, I was unable to substantiate any of the rumors and speculation. The evacuation had been, it appeared to me, thorough and complete, and instead, I was taken into custody by security teams who mistook me for one of those misguided souls who have recently and illegally sneaked back into the QZ ..." Pausing for emphasis, he continued, "To loot, to vandalize, and as we saw the other night, to sabotage!" He sounds like he's regurgitating a memorized script.

The crowd erupts in a torrent of screams and boos. Shouts of *"liar"* and *"propaganda"* compete with *"tell the truth"* and *"Ominosity knows ..."* Security mercenaries rush to the fence, beating on it with their batons and gun butts to drive the crowd back.

"I came here today," Jonas continues as Dr. Cameron coaches him quietly from behind," because I want to reach out to those of you who have participated in or are contemplating more such actions. I urge you to reconsider what you're doing. You're hindering the very efforts of our Public Safety officials who are trying to restore the area, who are working tirelessly to make sure it's safe for everyone to return." His voice cracks, his words tremble as if his mind is doing battle with his mouth. "It is not safe for you in there. Believe me. I'm lucky to be alive. My recovery from contamination has not been easy." He glances over at Cameron with a look that could be interpreted as pure malevolence, and the doctor stiffens involuntarily, glancing around to see if anyone else notices this. But the veil of passivity sweeps down over Jonas's expression again as he turns back to the microphone. "I want you to know that the more damage you do, the longer you will prolong the very thing you want to end." He turns to make a dramatic gesture toward the vast lifelessness behind him. "The quarantine!"

He's not prepared for what happens next.

The explosion!

A blazing eruption that bursts out the upper floors of an empty apartment building just the other side of the QZ barrier. Violent enough to send flaming shreds of plastic sheeting swirling down into the checkpoint no-man's-land. At first everyone is paralyzed with shock. But when Molotov cocktails start raining down like rocks hurled from some medieval catapult, people start screaming and running. The Molotovs smash on the pavement and erupt with billowing smoke instead of fire. The security mercs are confused. No one knows which way to turn. Weapons sweep the area, but no one knows who to shoot at. And soon the smoke billowing from the smoke bombs makes it impossible to find targets anyway.

Jonas and Cameron are yanked from the stage and dragged through the thickening smoke to the VIP tent. Whitfield races to his car and dives into the back seat screaming orders at his driver to get him the hell out of there.

Inside the VIP tent, the security team that hauled Jonas and Dr. Cameron away from the microphones suddenly find themselves staring down the barrels of semiautos aimed at their heads.

"Put your weapons on the ground," Jennifer barks.

No one moves.

"Do what she says," Keller calls out, and Jennifer steps aside to reveal him. He's being pushed forward by that androgynous female who escorted Miki out of the QZ. His hands are bound with zip ties, and there's a trickle of blood coming from his lips.

The mercs do as they're told and are quickly shoved to the ground by the other refuseniks from Jennifer's group. She hurries over to Jonas and wraps her arms around him.

"What's going on?" he asks feebly.

"A rescue," she says.

Outside, screams and shouts are approaching. Jennifer nods to one of her men who quickly steps out of the tent into the smoke, fires off a barrage into the air, then ducks back inside. The yelling outside scatters as panicked mercs desperately try to orient themselves in the impenetrable fog.

"Okay, back the way we came," Jennifer shouts. She pulls Jonas with her to the seam at the back of the tent. Others grab Keller and yank him along. Dr. Cameron is left standing there, staring into the emotionally vacant eyes of the androgyne.

"Jennifer, please," he screams at Jennifer, who pauses only to glare back at him with disgusted contempt before vanishing into the smoke.

"Your lucky day," the androgyne says and raises her weapon. Cameron loses control of his bowels and she clocks him with the rifle butt. He drops like a stringless marionette.

Jennifer leads her little raiding party through the choking murk. A couple of flares left earlier guide the way. All around them, she can hear the chaos and pandemonium of security teams staggering about in confusion. And she can see their shapes moving in the smoke. But there are other figures, too, drifting in the blur. Evanescent silhouettes, never fully there, dissipating almost as fast as they are formed. These are more frightening than the mercs who are desperately searching for them. *Those things,* she thinks. *Paramentals. Conjured by the pandemonium, feeding on the confusion.*

Someone deep in the fog lets go a burst from a semiauto. Someone else returns the fire.

"They're turning on themselves," Jonas cries out, horrified.

"Keep moving, don't stop," Jennifer shouts to the men behind her.

They finally come to one of those biocontainment tunnels that lead in and out of the no-man's-land to the QZ. Klaxons are wailing. Emergency lights are pulsing, turning the smoke red and blue. Jonas trips over a disabled and zip-tied HazMat, but Jennifer keeps him upright. Behind her, Keller is gagging on the fumes. The doors of the "clean in/clean out" space have been shattered off their hinges and are swinging wildly back and forth. Jennifer shoves them aside and her team vanishes through the mists of disinfectant sprays that have been triggered automatically and are now spewing aimlessly in all directions.

Outside the checkpoint fence, Miki has taken shelter from the mob stampeding into side streets and boulevards, cowering between dumpsters in an alley several blocks away to watch the fire in the QZ spread to other buildings.

She's been looking for Mathis ever since coming out of the QZ the other night, but he hasn't been at McCoy's Tavern. He hasn't shown up for meetings at St. Eustace. All her calls to his precinct have been rebuffed with curt, dismissive offers only to leave a message for him. She's been hoping he'll show up at Jennifer's apartment, maybe in the middle of the night. But this morning when she awakened on the bed where she'd passed out waiting, still dressed and with no sign of him, she decided to make her way to the QZ perimeter to see the press conference Jennifer said was going to happen. Unlike everyone else, she was not surprised when the explosion went off. She knew her sister was planning something dramatic.

As the smoke bomb haze finally starts drifting away from the QZ into the rest of the city, taking with it those phantom figures she saw oscillating within the chaos, Miki is terrified.

What has Jennifer done?

In the QZ, the sky is blackened by flocks of those hideous drones veering wildly back and forth toward any sign of movement. Even the mere drift of trash in a breeze can cause a sudden descent by these mechanical vampires to investigate. The eerie silence that usually permeates the area is now polluted by the diesel growl of security vehicles desperately searching for Jennifer's improvised band of rebels. Fortunately, their small diversionary explosions going off in different neighborhoods are drawing drones and mercs away from their planned route to safe harbor.

Ulysses is waiting with the door open as they sprint the last twenty yards of vulnerable open space to the refuge of Poet's Corner Tavern. He bolts the door after they tumble inside, and they all momentarily lose sight of each other in the dark until he lights a small kerosene lamp and leads them behind the bar to that small door and the wooden ladder plunging into the dank stone cellar where he lives. Jennifer pulls Keller away from his escort and shoves him forward.

"You first," she orders. With his hands still bound, Keller's descent is awkward and slow.

"Careful," Ulysses says with a sneer. "Don't want you breaking your neck. Yet."

Jennifer turns to Jonas. "You want to see this?" After he nods tentatively, she sends him ahead of her, then closes the door behind them leaving the others at the bar to keep watch from the dark.

Ulysses has already shoved Keller into a chair at the far end of his hovel when Jennifer comes down the final rungs of the ladder. He's fussing with the kerosene lamp, positioning it on a rickety wine crate, making sure the wick is turned up, isolating Keller in a pool of illumination resembling interrogation scenes from old gangster movies. Jennifer pulls up a rusted cafeteria chair with a torn vinyl seat. Keller can hardly see her or the others in the chiaroscuro of this basement, but he can make out the figure of Jonas slinking into the shadows of a corner. *Play for time*, Keller reminds himself. *Keep the drama going until the* deus *ex machina*.

"I figured you might want to see what Jonas was going to say at that press conference," he says to the silhouette straddling the chair in front of him. "I just didn't think you'd be so damned dramatic about it."

"Had to get people's attention," she responds.

"Not sure it did your cause any good."

"Oh, but we're just getting started."

She is fiddling with something in her jacket pocket, but he can't see what it is. "They'll be doing a building-by-building search by now, Jennifer."

"This won't take long," Jennifer answers from the darkness.

And now he can see what she's toying with.

A syringe.

The effect of the drugs, whatever they are, is immediate. Keller's thoughts are drifting aimlessly on a serene lake of passivity. No pain. No anxiety. Just pleasant indifference to the world around him.

"Good stuff, huh?" A smile is recognizable in Jennifer's tone even if her expression is difficult to make out. "The pharmacy down the street has a lot of good shit. And since the quarantine, it's open twenty-four-seven. I'm told it's great for suppressing inhibitions."

"Making my throat dry," Keller croaks.

Jennifer nods to Ulysses who brings over a bottle of water and puts Keller in a headlock while he pours it into the man's nose and throat, making him cough and gag.

"Don't drown him, Ulysses," Jennifer admonishes.

"Why not?" the gaunt man chuckles. "Waterboarding works. Take it from me."

"What good is this going to do?" Keller chokes, spitting phlegm.

"We know about the lab, Keller. The one buried under Club Nightshade. Ulysses was a guinea pig down there back in the day. He showed us the way."

"Good for him," Keller says, looking up at the living testament to the horrors of Project Morpheus looming over him with that bottle of water, just itching for an excuse to use it. *What we might have learned from him,* Keller can't help thinking.

"So now you're going to tell us what was going on down there," Jennifer says. "You're going to tell us what those experiments were for, and why you had to cover them up."

Keller leans back and calculates. How much time does he have? How crazy are these people? How long can he stall them? Might as well tell her. Maybe if she sees the possibilities, he could seduce her to his side. A long shot, but what the hell. And it might delay more waterboarding. Besides, he's enjoying the drugs. Might as well ride the wave. He just needs to keep them interested long enough.

"Have you ever heard of the Greek god, Morpheus?" he asks.

"God of dreams," Jennifer says.

"Of the *subconscious,*" Keller corrects. "Came from a very

illustrious family. His father was Hypnos, god of sleep. His mother, Pasithea, was the goddess of hallucinations."

"Thanks for the history lesson," Ulysses growls.

"In the late '60s, there was a top secret Defense Department program called the Morpheus Project. Similar to Russian NKVD psychotronic experiments, or the CIA's MK Ultra programs."

"Nice company," Jennifer mutters sarcastically.

"Volunteers," Keller continues with a nod toward Ulysses, "were subjected to various psychotropic drugs, cerebral stimulation, psychological stress, and other techniques to excite 'electromagnetic emissions' of the mind."

"Or to put it more prosaically," Jennifer adds, "you wanted to fuck with their subconscious."

"With their *core consciousness*, Jennifer. Their primary consciousness. That essential biological phenomenon that exists in all of us, even in prenatal embryonic life. The neural network image of 'self.' Synapses creating neural systems, creating awareness! Morpheus scientists theorized that if they could drill deep enough, down to the core, and stimulate these neural systems and their electromagnetic emissions, they could influence them. And if they could influence them, they could manipulate them. But ..." He pauses with a sigh. "Like a lot of '60s bullshit, the experiments were a waste of time."

"Waste of time?" Ulysses snarls and grabs Keller's head again ready for another go with the bottle.

"Or so they thought!" Keller sputters in protest.

Ulysses pauses and glances over to Jennifer who shakes her head. When he reluctantly steps back, Keller rights himself in his chair.

"A few months ago, we started to observe a rash of disturbing violence occurring in the vicinity of one of the forgotten Morpheus labs. Inexplicable suicides, murder clusters, spontaneous nervous breakdowns. But even more troubling, they were accompanied by vague rumors of malicious paranormal entities that might be provoking these incidents."

"More '60s bullshit?"

"Sounded like new agey residue, at first. But hell, people still think the CIA did JFK."

"So you decided to bury it with the New Year's Eve explosion."

"Yeah, bad idea. Won't take credit for that one."

"And the contamination, the reason for the quarantine?"

"We planted evidence of biotoxins in the area so no one would go snooping around. Just enough to suggest the old weapons depot where the lab had been located might have been breached. Did the trick. Bought us time."

"Time for what?"

"Maybe those flakes from the '60s were on to something. Maybe they had inadvertently stirred up some kind of dark, psychic energy. My colleagues were frightened by the prospect. The Morpheus experiments were unethical, to say the least, certainly illegal in today's world. If something had leaked from those labs which could be causing the phenomenon, the blowback would be severe."

"But you were intrigued?"

"Imagine the possibilities! I initiated a secret plan to start up the project again. To see if we could do what the original team couldn't. After all, fifty years on, better technology, better psyche procedures, they might lead to something."

Jennifer is surprised by the level of detail he's willing to share. He's not only willing to talk about resurrecting Project Morpheus, he seems proud of it. No sense of irony. No doubt about the righteousness of his mission. *Those drugs must be better than I thought,* she thinks.

"So you've been experimenting on people you've taken from the QZ," she pushes. "People who were left behind."

"Stayed behind. Their choice," Keller insists.

"People who aren't supposed to exist."

"It's been convenient, I'll admit."

His nonchalance is getting to Jennifer. He seems completely

unconcerned with the amorality of his reasoning, or the dire situation he's in at the moment.

"So now you know," he shrugs.

"I'm going to expose you, Keller," Jennifer says. "I'm going to make sure the blowback starts with you!"

"And who's going to believe you? You're a girl who escaped from a psychiatric hospital, Jennifer. Your mind has been rotted by contamination. You're nothing but a walking conspiracy theory."

The worm of rage is burrowing deeper into Jennifer's mind, poisoning her reason, exhausting her self-control. "But now I have Jonas," she says. "He knows the truth."

"And just look at him." Keller's eyes swerve lazily toward Jonas's shadow in the corner. "He's more fried than you are." He leans forward, shedding his arrogance, adopting instead an intimate, almost seductive tone. "I had great hopes for you, Jennifer. You were different from the others. You didn't fight it like they did. You embraced what we were doing to you. That was your defense. You let it happen."

"I was trying to survive," she says, but her voice is losing its edge.

"Yes! That was the key, I think. You wouldn't let the madness swallow you. You swallowed *it*. You made it you!"

His voice is starting to sound far away. She can see his lips move but the words are out of sync, as if coming at her down a long, echoey tunnel. Is she having some kind of flashback? Some kind of sense-memory reversion to those terrible nights in his lab? The worm digs deeper. A parasite birthing something awful in her consciousness, something inexorably consuming her. She can feel the fury building inside her. Keller's wrong! It's not becoming her, she's becoming it.

"What did you do to me?" she whispers.

"I wanted you to help us, Jennifer," Keller drones on. "I wanted you to help me understand the phenomenon. You were strong enough. I could tell from the moment Dr. Cameron showed you to me. With you, I hoped to unravel the secrets of Project Morpheus. Think about it. You could have shown us the way into rooms of the core consciousness that have been locked away. You still could, Jennifer."

Jennifer is starting to feel faint. *"I can't let him get away with this,"* she screams inside of herself. *"I have to make him pay. He deserves to pay. For all the damage that's been done. To those dead souls in that lab. To Ulysses. To me. To this whole city!"*

There's gunfire upstairs! Glass is shattering. People are yelling.

"About time," Keller sighs, leaning away from Jennifer.

"How did they get here so quickly?" Ulysses shouts at her.

"Tracking device," Keller says calmly. "Implanted in Jonas."

"No!" Jonas screams as he starts scratching at his arms, his torso, his neck, in a vain attempt to find the bug.

"Should have gotten here sooner, though," Keller adds. "Walls down here must have interfered with the signal."

The worm inside Jennifer's mind finally explodes. She leaps from her chair and grabs the jug of water from Ulysses. "Hold him!" she yells.

Ulysses grabs Keller and pulls down his jaw. Jennifer upends the jug and floods his face.

"Jennifer, stop!" Jonas cries out, horrified by her homicidal fury. But she doesn't stop. Her mouth pulls back in a sinister grimace. Her eyes bulge with delirium. Dark, throbbing veins crisscross her skin, etching her face with a web of mania. Keller is gagging and vomiting, gasping for air that isn't there, inhaling water instead. His body is convulsing, but Ulysses holds him tight. And Jennifer keeps pouring. Evanescent wisps of smoke begin seeping out of her clothes, converging around her like a toxic shadow.

The door above that ladder suddenly opens. A small but insistent voice calls out.

"JENNIFER!" It's Charlotte, the young girl who was stalking Miki. Jennifer's messenger. "They've found us!" Upstairs the gunfire escalates. "We're out of time," she yells, climbing down the ladder.

Jennifer drops the water jug. The veins on her skin retreat. The blur forming around her evaporates. Her eyes blink repeatedly as if she were coming out of a dream. She hurries over to the old beer tap and the hole in the wall behind it that Ulysses used to lead them to the Morpheus labs. Charlotte meets her there.

"Did you get it?" Jennifer asks.

Charlotte holds up a tiny Data Memory Card. "Every word."

"You know what to do," Jennifer tells her, and the girl nods before throwing her arms around Jennifer's waist. "Go on now," Jennifer says, shoving her forward.

Charlotte scampers into the hole, and Jennifer pushes the beer tap back to hide it. Then she turns to Keller who is slumped in his chair, comatose. The gunfire is inside the tavern now. Footsteps are pounding across the plank flooring overhead. A moment later, a battering ram shatters the door above the ladder. A second after that a flash grenade falls and explodes. Tear gas follows.

Jennifer's eyes burn. Her lungs constrict in agony. Her hearing has been wiped out by the flash grenade, but she can see Ulysses staggering to his feet with his shotgun, aiming it at the top of the ladder.

"ULYSSES ... DON'T!" she screams, but she can't hear her own words. It's too late anyway. She can see the flare from his shotgun barrels and then the tracer-flare of return fire coming from above. A nonstop barrage. Ulysses is shredded. But the deluge of automatic weapons fire continues. The last thing Jennifer sees before she's hit is Jonas on the floor near that hole in the wall behind the beer tap.

Can't tell if he's alive or dead.

And now she'll never know.

40

At the Quarantine Zone checkpoint, the media is crushing against the fence shouting impotent questions at mercenaries and HazMats who ignore them. Ever since Jennifer's raid the perimeter has been in lockdown mode and movement there is tense and trigger-happy. There are sounds of intermittent explosions inside the QZ and clouds of smoke are rising over buildings in the distance. TV stand-ups are already speculating on camera that some sort of conflagration has commenced between the so-called rebels that attacked this checkpoint earlier and mercenary forces who are trying to track them down. No one in authority is offering any details.

Joseph Carlucci from *thedig.com* is stalking the crowd, looking for information, trying to get a sense of what's going on beyond the fence, but like everyone else he's left to imagine. He had been chatting up a pretty young source in City Hall, plying her with double Balvenie Caribbean Cask fourteen-year-old whiskeys, both of them getting nicely drunk, when the shit hit the fan. He abandoned his quest for inside dope on questionable real estate speculation in the Quarantine Zone and hurried here. But so far all he's had to show for the disappointing dissolution of his altered state has been rumor and exaggeration. Depending on who you talk to the raid here was either a well-orchestrated terrorist attack by heavily armed and professionally trained QZ resistance fighters, or some haphazard vandalism by disorganized scavengers who'd gotten themselves chased out of the QZ. As to hostages, no one seems to agree on the facts either. Some eyewitnesses insist they saw the invaders frog-marching a couple of suits into the "clean in/clean out" tubes snaking into the QZ. Others maintain that those were just looters being chased back the way they came.

What catches Carlucci's attention, though, and keeps him here instead of retreating back to his rudely forsaken City Hall source are the almost embarrassed whispers by seemingly credible witnesses who admit to seeing strange phantom specters hovering among the combatants. These ephemeral apparitions appeared to be encouraging the violence, goading the panic, feeding on the confusion. *Maybe he'd better stick around,* Carlucci thinks. *Maybe he'll be able to confirm the presence of the Special Crimes Task Force that authorities continue to insist doesn't exist.* An exposé of this mythical unit would do wonders for his career. Might even graduate his reputation from City Desk bottom-feeder to respectable investigative journalist.

Instead, he's handed something much better. Something that will surely enhance his prestige and, though he won't know it at first, imperil his life.

A small hand takes his and pulls him away from the commotion at the perimeter fence. It's a girl. Disheveled and haggard, with paranoid eyes.

"Make sure everyone sees this. Every word of it is true," she says and slips out of his grasp. He thinks about following her, but he's distracted by the thing she left in his palm. A SanDisk 80GB data card. When he looks up, she's already lost in the crowd.

Miki wasn't sure she'd seen the encounter between Charlotte and some man who looked like he was slightly drunk. The crush of people was too thick. She'd only caught sight of the girl out the corner of her eye, and by the time it registered who she could be, she'd been swallowed up in the mob and was nowhere to be seen. Miki shoved and pushed to get at the man who Charlotte, if it was Charlotte, was talking to, but he had vanished as well.

A phalanx of police is now wading into the mob, trying to disperse it or at least shove it into side streets and distant intersections. Threats of arrest are being shouted through bullhorns, and after what she's seen going on inside the perimeter no-man's-land, Miki wouldn't be surprised if tear gas and rubber bullets were the next forms of encouragement. She never saw Jennifer among the chaos inside the perimeter fence, but she has no doubt her sister was part of this mess in some way. All she can do now is hope Jennifer keeps her promise to meet up in a couple of days. Meanwhile, Miki has to find Mathis.

She turns and heads back up Seventh Avenue towards Jennifer's apartment. Maybe he has shown up there. After everything that's happened this morning, he'd want to check up on her. He'd want to know if she was all right. Wouldn't he?

Willy G is sitting on the floor in the hallway just outside the door to Jennifer's apartment when Miki returns. He has nodded off and never hears her approach until she's almost on top of him.

"Willy," she says softly, and he's so startled he leaps to his feet in a fight-or-flight stance until he recognizes who she is.

"Sorry," he mutters. "Haven't been sleeping well."

"Who has?" she asks putting a key in the door. "What are you doing here?"

He puts a hand on hers to stop her from going inside. She can tell from his expression this isn't going to be good.

"It's Mathis."

41

I t's the smell in the corridor that conjures terrible memories. That clinical smell. The commingling of bleach, body odors, disinfectants, and the "air fresheners" meant to cover them up. Even the basement fMRI labs where Miki was forced to lay motionless, sometimes for hours, listening to the metronomic banging of the machine's gradient coils, had that smell. It's the scent of illness, of damage. Of weakness. It's the smell Miki associates with her Tourette's and her father's obsession with getting to the bottom of her deficiency. A perfectly normal fixation for a scientist like him, of course, except that it reduced his daughter to a mere object of study. A study without conclusions as it turned out.

But this is where they've brought Mathis, so Miki suppresses the urge to flee and marches quietly behind Willy G, ignoring the moans coming from other patient rooms and the clinical dispassion of nurses or doctors emerging from them.

"He's been asking for you," Willy tells her as they approach the uniformed cop at the door to Mathis's room. "Ever since he regained consciousness."

"How did you know where to find him?"

"If the word's on the street, I know about it," Willy answers as if stating the obvious. He has told her everything he knows about what went down out at Fat Freddie's, what the cops have been willing to share with him, at least, but Willy knows more about what Mathis was doing there than they do anyway.

"This her?" the cop asks, then steps aside when Willy nods. "He goes in and out, so don't expect much."

"The docs say that's his brain protecting itself," Willy tries to reassure Miki. "Hiding from too much stimuli until it's ready."

Miki takes a deep breath as he pushes open the door.

"Mathis," Willy whispers, approaching the bed. "Mathis, it's Miki. She's here."

No response.

"Mathis," Miki says, leaning in close. "Levi, it's me." The sight of him, helpless on this hospital bed, tethered to a battery of monitoring devices with their repetitive, unnerving beeps and clicks, shocks her more than she expected. She takes his hand and holds it to her cheek, rubbing it gently, careful to avoid the intravenous line secured to the top of it. "It's Miki. Can you hear me?"

Fingers twitch, the chest rises and falls in a prolonged sigh, and finally Mathis's eyelids flutter, trying to blink away the stickiness of narcotized oblivion. His head slowly drifts to her, and he manages a weak smile.

"Mick." His voice is reedy, and he drools. She grabs a tissue from the table by the bed and dabs at his mouth.

"I need a drink," he whispers.

There's a lidded cup of juice next to the tissues. She picks it up and gently presses the straw between his lips.

"I meant a drink!" he coughs.

"Use your imagination," Miki answers and kisses his hand.

"I told her what happened," Willy says, moving up behind her.

"Good. You can tell me if I ever get out of here."

"Pierce is dead," Willy says. "Whole cabin went up in a blaze of glory. You with it, almost."

"Shivers?" Mathis asks.

It takes a moment for Willy to answer, and when he does his voice cracks. "I don't think we'll ever find him now."

"I'm sorry, Willy. I'm so … sorr …" Mathis turns his head away.

"Cap'n Bartok was here last night. Overheard him telling the Commissioner that crime scene guys recovered dynamite at the cabin, and they're sure it's the same shit Dickie Prince used to blow up Club Nightshade. Bartok thinks it's enough evidence to put Freddie into the frame on New Year's Eve. Once they dig into those Angela Rossi papers we got, there's gonna be a lot of nervous conversations goin' down at City Hall."

"And now we have this," Miki says, showing him the flash drive Jennifer gave her.

Over the next hour, she tells Mathis what happened to her in the QZ, about finding Jennifer, about Ulysses, about the awful Project Morpheus laboratory where sinister experiments had been carried out. It's all documented on the flash drive. The lab, the bodies, buried under the rubble of Club Nightshade.

Where his daughter was killed on New Year's Eve.

"It won't bring her back, Levi, but at least you know now why she died. The people responsible can be held accountable."

Mathis frowns as if he's not entirely certain of that.

"It's all comin' down like a bad hurricane," Willy insists. "Justice is gonna be swift and painful!"

Miki isn't sure how much Mathis is processing, but the moisture leaking out the corners of his eyes suggests he comprehends enough. She takes his hand again and pulls it to her lips. Then she lays her head on his chest. The rhythm of his heart is steady and strong. It's reassuring and hypnotic. Within moments they're both deep asleep.

She hasn't moved even hours later when Willy gently nudges her awake.

"You gotta see this," he whispers.

She looks up to see the TV on the wall and the banner of *Breaking News* scrolling across a grainy video of Hollings Keller in the basement of Poet's Corner.

"... top secret Defense Department program called the Morpheus Project," he's saying. *"Similar to Russian NKVD psychotronic experiments, or the CIA's MK Ultra programs."*

"Nice company," a woman's voice off-screen voice mutters sarcastically. Miki stiffens. She knows instantly who it is.

"Jennifer," she whispers to herself.

"Volunteers," Keller continues, *"were subjected to various psychotropic drugs, cerebral stimulation, psychological stress, and other techniques to excite 'electromagnetic emissions' of the mind."*

"Holy shit," Willy says, mouth agape.

Miki moves within inches of the TV screen. A terrible premonition is sweeping through her.

"... we planted evidence of biotoxins in the area so no one would go snooping around. Just enough to suggest the old weapons depot where the lab had been located might have been breached. Did the trick. Bought us time."

"Time for what?" the off-camera woman asks.

"Maybe those flakes from the '60s were on to something. Maybe they had inadvertently stirred up some kind of dark, psychic energy ..."

"She's dead," Miki says.

On the TV, Keller's confession retreats to an insert box in the lower corner of the screen and his audio is abruptly muted as the feed shifts back to the newsroom where a couple of startled presenters are fumbling with notes, teleprompter miscues, and off-camera directions signaled to them by floor managers.

Sitting with them is Joseph Carlucci, the reporter. Looking mighty self-satisfied at the moment.

"Pretty inflammatory stuff, Joe," the female presenter says. "How did you get hold of this video?"

"I'm afraid I can't disclose that. Confidential source. I'm sure you can understand."

"Well, yes, but how can we confirm the authenticity of ..."

"... uh ... we can confirm," the male presenter interrupts, trying to decipher the competitive chatter going on in his earbud, "that this is indeed one of the hostages taken yesterday morning during the raid on a Quarantine Zone checkpoint ... uh ... we ... uh ... are trying to confirm his identity ... but ... uh ..." His eyes dart off-camera as someone tries to get his attention.

The female presenter takes over. "We're now being told that, yes, this was a government official named Hollings Keller who was killed in the rescue effort inside the QZ several hours ago ... inside an abandoned tavern where the hostage takers were cornered ..."

The male presenter interrupts. "According to sources, all the hostage takers have also been killed in the ensuing firefight ..."

Willy moves forward to put an arm around Miki, but she doesn't even feel him.

On TV, the female presenter is handed a note by a tech. "We want to reiterate that we cannot confirm the authenticity of what the hostage is claiming about secret experiments and fabricated contamination ..."

"My source assures me every word is true," Carlucci interjects to protect his interests.

"He was obviously under duress, Joe," the male presenter challenges. "Maybe he was forced to make this confession ..."

The female presenter again. "We are trying to get official reaction ..."

"Turn it off," Miki finally says, and Willy releases her from his embrace to aim the remote and silence the TV. He retreats to a chair in the corner and buries his face in his hands, but Miki doesn't move. She remains there, a statue, staring at her reflection in the glass of the darkened screen.

So this is how it ends. This crazy odyssey she embarked upon all those weeks ago. This desperate search to find her sister, the only true friend she ever had. This is its epitaph. A brief confused news report about some sinister hostage takers, motives as yet unknown but surely beyond the sympathy of normal people who would never resort to such a thing, gunned down, probably on purpose, to maintain the nefarious fiction justifying the Catastrophe, the QZ, and the violence spreading as a result. A cursory recap of the failed attempt to rescue the hostage who may or may not have been forced to admit to some perverted conspiracy that the powers-that-be will surely use all of their resources to discredit.

And now, this awful tableau. The three of them, Miki, Willy G, Mathis, in the dreadful loneliness of this sterile room, listening to the mechanical beeps of indifferent machines, nothing left to do but suffer their losses and their guilt for not having prevented them.

"Miki." It's Mathis, gently calling to her.

He's sitting up now, holding out a hand to her. She manages a brave smile as she sinks to the bed next to him, but it doesn't last. He pulls her into his arms and holds her tight.

It will be a long time before she cries herself out.

Subscribe

Newsletter    

OPINION

IS IT REALLY OVER?

By Joseph Carlucci
Columnist/Editorial Board Member

Investigations into the New Year's Eve explosion at Club Nightshade have now expanded beyond the cover-up of a discredited 60-year-old Cold War program of psychological torture known as Project Morpheus, first revealed six weeks ago in the video confession of former intelligence operative, Hollings Keller. Newly acquired documents suggest that the cancer of this conspiracy extends beyond rogue government officials and into the dark hideouts of organized crime whose bosses have sought to profit from the New Year's Eve catastrophe and the subsequent quarantine in the center of our city. More disturbing, however, is the clear implication these documents provide that the explosion at Club Nightshade was a deliberate and coordinated attempt by colluding government and criminal actors to force the quarantine.

It appears that a quid pro quo existed between Keller's rogue intelligence unit that was trying to revive Project Morpheus protocols and the well-known underworld boss, Emeril Benedict, also known as The Baron. In return for orchestrating the devastation on New Year's Eve in order to cover up disturbing evidence of Morpheus experiments in a former lab underneath Club Nightshade, Benedict, with Keller's knowledge and active support, was able to bribe deceased City Official, Angela Rossi, into illegally transferring ownership of major properties in the Quarantine Zone to entities controlled by Benedict himself. Rossi was found dead in a city subway tunnel several months ago. That case, originally deemed a suicide, has now been reopened as a potential homicide investigation.

Although Hollings Keller was killed in a failed rescue attempt after he was taken hostage by a group of Quarantine Zone evacuation hold-outs, officials are dismissing the contention that his admission was coerced and should therefore be disregarded.

The Special Board of Inquiry recently empowered to investigate this conspiracy now consider his statements to be credible.

Independent special investigators have been sent into the Quarantine Zone to confirm his admission that a clandestine Project Morpheus laboratory existed several stories below Club Nightshade. Their report will also include detailed analysis of the extent, or lack of contamination that may or may not have resulted from its exposure.

The Board of Inquiry promises a swift and detailed report. Until then, we must ask…

Is it really over?

42

The scar in the middle of the city remains. The quarantine persists. The QZ has become a giant crime scene now.

Stewart Whitfield is exhausted. Four hours in front of that goddamn Special Board of Inquiry, groveling, eating shit, making promises about future transparency and cooperation they all know he'll break eventually but allowing them all to walk out of the room convinced they'd accomplished something. In the case of his inquisitors, a self-righteous certitude they got to the bottom of this Project Morpheus mess. For Whitfield, a dodge of the proverbial bullet. He and the brethren are barely scathed. Hollings Keller takes the fall.

These past six weeks have been a down-to-the-wire race to avert disaster. The lads in their cowardly self-interest had all retreated to the safety of preexisting home-front obligations, too-long-delayed vacations, or other evasive excuses to absent themselves, leaving Whitfield to do damage control solo. Fortunately, his negotiating skills and a deliberately glacial release of classified documents have provided enough distractions to give him time to secure any incriminating evidence left lying about and scrub clean the relationship with Keller.

Only one problem remains. Paramentals. Is the genie out of

the bottle? Is there even a genie? How long can he wait before he picks up where Keller left off?

Well, one crisis at a time. For now, it's to the club and a double Bombay. To start.

There's a posse of press lingering in the street outside Lewis Cameron's brownstone. Has been ever since the news broke about his involvement with the rogue intelligence operative, Hollings Keller, and those creepy experiments in mind control they were carrying out in secret at an Oyster Bay psychiatric hospital. License revoked, reputation and career in tatters, the good doctor spends most of his time these days in lawyers' offices strategizing ways to avoid imprisonment. Whenever he returns home, even in the middle of the night, the media jackals are waiting to swarm his car, shouting questions, flashing lights, corralling him so tightly as he runs the gauntlet from street to front door that he often fears for his safety.

He should be more afraid of the dark phantom hovering every night in the shadows down the street. The homeless-looking guy in the long coat and sweat-stained baseball cap. The one with the anemic complexion and pouchy eyes. The one with the lunatic expression.

Jennifer Preston's former lover. Jonas Flack.

Emeril Benedict, aka the Baron, is being perp-walked out the front door of his beloved Black Orchid restaurant, in full embarrassing view of his regular customers and various lookie-loos, to a waiting convoy of police vehicles parked at the curb. He is trying to maintain a dignified, if defiant, posture, but the walk is designed to degrade, and the humiliation of police pushing his head down with faux protective care as they shove him into the wire-meshed back of a police cruiser confirms the fall of the mighty.

As news cameras chase after Benedict's final ride away from the Black Orchid, no one takes any notice of his hostile eye contact with a plainclothes police officer remaining on the sidewalk, standing apart from his colleagues, smiling the smile of a cat that ate the canary.

Mathis. Triumphant. But still too emotionally sabotaged to gloat.

<hr>

An hour later, Mathis is at McBride's. His usual spot at the mahogany bar, watching the TV fastened to the wall, and the news video of Benedict's arrest.

"A local mob boss was arrested this evening for conspiracy and murder after police found evidence linking him to materials used in the tragic New Year's Eve explosion at Club Nightshade. Tammy Morrison was on the scene. Tammy…"

On the TV, the camera pans away from Benedict's convoy to a cute twentysomething with a go-getter stare, clearly excited to be doing this follow-up for the folks at home.

"Yes, Marsha, police are alleging that Emeril Benedict, also known as the Baron, along with recently deceased Detective Frederick Pierce and several others, was engaged in a massive land-grab scheme to fraudulently acquire properties inside the Quarantine Zone…"

"Why don't you just drink it this time, Mathis?" the taciturn bartender mumbles as he delivers the customary double Laphroaig sixteen-year-old, neat, with its accompanying glass of club soda on ice. "You should be celebrating, right?"

"Oh, I am, Sammy. I am." He picks up the Scotch, swirls it in the glass, raises it to the TV, then puts it back down without taking a sip. He lays a twenty on the bar and heads for the door.

A few minutes later, he's about to go down the steps to the basement of St. Eustace when footsteps move up behind him.

"Still doing the meetings, huh?"

Willy G.

"It's habit," Mathis says. What he doesn't say is that it's also become a private promise he keeps to the memory of his daughter, Louise.

"Saw the news about Benedict," Willy says. "Just wanted to say thank you."

"I think it's me who should be thanking you."

"Okay, let's stop before we get sappy."

"You doing all right, Willy?"

"Getting by. Me and the boys."

"Anyone hassles you, let me know."

"Oh, you can count on that. I still got your get-outta-jail-free card in my pocket."

A somber pause settles between them. The memory of their collaboration, the success of it, and the sacrifice it required will never again be far from either one's thoughts.

"Have you heard from her?" Willy asks, his voice almost childlike in its hope.

"No."

Willy nods. Disappointed but resigned. Miki was pretty insistent that she had to go home and be alone. Deal with the parents, sort out what was left of her sister's life.

"Add one of my prayers to yours down there, will ya?" Willy says as Mathis turns to the stairs.

"You bet."

Willy backs away into the night.

"Hey Willy," Mathis calls after him. "Take care of yourself."

"Always," comes the voice from the darkness.

43

The first few weeks back home have been a purgatory of inertia. The shock of Jennifer's death, her real death, not the one Miki called her parents about after her meeting at City Hall, but the one after her sister had been resurrected, the one in the news, the one that's left Jennifer either vilified as an anarchist or saluted as the catalyst of Project Morpheus revelations, *that* death has descended on the Preston household like a dismal fog. Her loss has subverted even the most mundane conversations and contaminated the simplest of activities. Miki can't even wash the supper plates without being reminded, usually by her mother, of how her sister never bothered with such tedious household chores because, unlike Miki, she was always too focused on important things, like her work. Even Miki's significantly diminished stuttering is only acknowledged by her father as a bittersweet irony of her sister's death. Grief in the Preston household has taken the form of stunned, uncomfortable silences interrupted only by her parents' manic pursuit of diversion. Miki's father retreating to the obscurity of his neuroscience research, suddenly and, Miki thinks, perversely fascinated with the continuing disclosures about Project Morpheus experiments. And her mother, ever the legalist harridan, embarking on a relentless campaign to join any and all investigating commissions looking into the New Year's Eve Catastrophe and the QZ land-grab schemes, her way of memorializing her deceased daughter, she insists. Miki, on the other hand, spends most of her time in her room. To her parents' dismay, she has neither mourned nor "got on with it." In their opinion, she is paralyzed by indecision. Which puts her back where she was in the family hierarchy before she went looking for Jennifer: the last consideration.

But Miki's inertia is not without purpose. It's given her time to consider the deeper significance of Jennifer's death and decide what to do about it. She's been musing over that heartfelt note Jennifer had the refusenik, Betty, slip into her pocket before she left the QZ. She didn't find it until days later, and it took a few days after that before she worked up the courage to read it. She can still hear Jennifer's voice in the words. Did she know she might never see Miki again?

> *... when you think of me, Mick, think about my*
> *photos. The ones I left in case something*
> *happens to me. Think about those anguished*
> *faces that prompted my journey into the city's*
> *dark heart in the first place. Each one had a*
> *story, Mick. Each one had a life, friends they*
> *once loved, families they once cared for. Until,*
> *that is, those dark phantoms began to hover in*
> *the background. Those agents of chaos that*
> *caused such awful, inexplicable violence. By*
> *preying and feeding on anxiety. By*
> *exacerbating fear and malevolence.*
> *You asked me what they were. I'm not sure*
> *I know. Will anyone ever believe they exist?*
> *Not if we give up! Because you can be sure*
> *whatever those wing-nuts who tried to*
> *resurrect Project Morpheus were doing will be*
> *routinely dismissed and discredited anywhere*
> *and everywhere. By authorities and so-called*

*professionals. Expert opinion will be mobilized
to rationalize the irrational.
So ask yourself, Mick. What's the
difference between those affected by
Paramentals and the rest of us? Is there any?
Given the right time, the right place, the right
circumstances, couldn't any one of us be
vulnerable?
How many of us are out there? How many
of ... them?*

Miki folds the letter carefully and slips it into the last pages of her journal which she shoves deep into her dresser under a pile of clothes. She's finished with it. She has other writing to do now.

She gets up and moves over to her desk and the purpose her sister has bequeathed her. It only takes a few seconds to boot up the computer and theominosity.com default page. Miki starts writing.

She never notices the small rust-colored stain on the wall behind the chair where she was sitting a moment ago.

There are monsters among us.
There have always been monsters among us.

We've invented myths and fairy tales to explain them.
Legends and fables are created to understand them.
Religions coopt them to describe angels and demons.

Science and enlightenment have stripped us of the ability to 'see' them.

But fantasy is no longer sufficient to conceal the truth.
And absence of evidence is not evidence of absence.

There are monsters among us.
There have always been monsters among us.

And the most dangerous monster of all...

May be the one inside of us.

THE OMINOSITY STILL LIVES

John Harrison is a writer, director, and author with a storied career in film and television. He has written and directed multiple TV episodes for a variety of networks including the classic TV series *Tales From the Darkside*, *Tales from the Crypt*, and *Creepshow*, as well as TV movies and miniseries. His miniseries adaptations of Frank Herbert's *Dune* and *Children of Dune* were Emmy Award winners. His film, *Tales From the Darkside: The Movie*, won him the Grand Priz du Festival at Avoriaz, France. He co-wrote the Disney animated feature *Dinosaur* and wrote and directed the movie adaptation of Clive Barker's *Book of Blood*. His novel, *Passing Through Veils*, was published by WordFire Press in August of 2023.

www.officialjohnharrison.com

Passing Through Veils

Our list of other WordFire Press authors and titles is always growing. To find out more and shop our selection of titles, visit us at:
wordfirepress.com